Volume 1

Daniel: Absolutes in a Gray World

Daniel's Life Through Age Forty-nine

*A fast-paced historical fiction where
the tough issues faced by Daniel
are addressed head-on, not dodged*

by
Jay Edwards

xulon
PRESS

Disclaimers

The author intentionally inserted slightly modified Biblical text into the dialogs. The purpose is to create a natural flow of logic and events. The three versions above were all used, and sometimes the phrases were mixed and matched within the same passages, along with the author's own inserts. The versions were used extensively, but not extensively word for word, so they are not footnoted.

Historical Observations are also mixed and matched from a wide variety of sources. Some are directly quoted and are foot-noted, but many are condensed from various sources. The author does not intend for the *Historical Observations* to justify a position or to provide study material for the reader, but rather, to show where the ideas come from or how they were generated. The author does not vouch for or attempt to defend any statements made in the historical observations. Each reader is encouraged to research items of interest independently.

This is a historical fiction, and should be read as such.

www.xulonpress.com

Dedication

This book is dedicated to my loving wife, Kirsten, and to my family. It has provided many hours of research and discussion. 'Daniel' has truly been a family project.

A special thanks to:

Hope Owsley,
the primary manuscript editor who dedicated many hours to the improvement of the original text,
and to
Brenda Pitts,
our copy editor.

INTRODUCTION

WHO WAS DANIEL?

Daniel was an orphan and was taken to a foreign country as an adolescent, or teenager. He received a full-ride scholarship at the top university in the land and graduated at the top of his class with a double major: political science and religion. He probably received a government position immediately following college, but soon he was sidelined because of his religious convictions. Later, through a strange set of events, he was reinstated into the government at a federal level. Eventually he served under three world rulers, holding the position of prime minister under the first and the third. He was known for his winsome personality, sharp administrative skills, unparalleled negotiating abilities, and incredible unchanging consistency. He was best known, however, for adhering to his absolutes in the very gray world in which he lived.

Volume 1: Daniel
Absolutes in a Gray World
   How did **Daniel** establish his **absolutes in a gray world** as he dealt with education, ambition and loyalty?

Note from the author . . .

About this book:
- It is historical fiction written under the assumption that the Bible and historians of antiquity provide for us true information.
- It is a book that considers real time and typical human behavior.
- It is a book that speculates on the situations surrounding the phenomenal character of Daniel, who served under three world rulers and held the position of prime minister under the first and the third, all while in Babylon, the cradle of perversity. At the end of his life, this same man was addressed by an angel as "you who are highly esteemed." He lived in favor with both God and man. How did he do it in *this* setting?
- It is a book that illustrates Daniel as a personage pleasing to both God and man in a setting in which these two are usually mutually exclusive.
- It is a book that shows how Daniel, Shadrach, Meshach, and Abednego might have handled the tough decisions they faced.

This book is not:
- A book that will give canned answers to difficult questions.
- A book that provides answers to our issues today. The reader must personally draw all parallels to modern-day issues.
- A book that deals with Daniel's latter-day prophecies.

This book will have special appeal to:

- Those who have done business cross-culturally and faced the maze of gray areas inherent to this endeavor.
- Those who are high enough in the business, political, or military world to face multiple catch 22 decisions.
- Those who face difficult moral issues.
- Those who enjoy a good historically based work of fiction.

Historical Observations
  I have included the historical observations for the reader's general information. Historical data does not always agree. What I have printed here is not necessarily my defense of a position, but rather the position on which I have chosen to base this story.

Historical Observations

*N*ineveh, the Assyrian capital, fell with the assault of the combined forces of Babylon and Media in 612 BC. Under the leadership of Ashur-uballit, the Assyrian military fled westward to Haran, from which they ruled the remainder of Assyria. Nabopollassar, the king of Babylon, marched in 611 BC against these Assyrian forces in Haran. In 610 BC, Assyria withdrew from Haran westward beyond the Euphrates River, leaving it to the Babylonians.

In 609 BC, the Assyrians sought the help of Egypt, and Pharaoh Neco II led an army from Egypt to join Assyria. Josiah, the king of Judah, hoping to incur favor with the Babylonians and knowing that the prophet Jeremiah had prophesied that the Babylonians would be victorious, sought to prevent the Egyptians from joining Assyria. Josiah's army was defeated, and he was killed at Megiddo in this attempt (2 Kings 23:28–30; 2 Chronicles 35:24).

Pharaoh Neco II proceeded to join the Assyrians, and together they assaulted the Babylonian coalition at Haran but were unsuccessful, presumably because of Nebuchadnezzar's occupation of the higher grounds and also because of his military prowess. Assyria retreated to Carchemish, and a four-year war ensued.

In 605 BC, Nebuchadnezzar led Babylon against Egypt and Assyria in the final battle of Carchemish. Egypt was defeated, and Carchemish was destroyed by the Babylonians in May–June of that year. Nebuchadnezzar purportedly pursued the Egyptian soldiers southward for two weeks until nearly all of them had been slain. While pursuing the defeated Egyptians, Nebuchadnezzar *expanded his territorial conquests southward into Syria and toward Palestine.*

Learning of the death of his father, Nabopolassar, Nebuchadnezzar returned from Riblah to Babylon in August 605 BC to receive the crown. Then he returned to Palestine and attacked Jerusalem in September 605 BC. After a short siege, Jerusalem opened its gates; King Jehoiakim remained in power! It was on this occasion that Daniel and his companions were taken to Babylon as captives. In this book, we will be working from the hypothesis that Daniel was fourteen when taken captive in 605 BC.

Nebuchadnezzar returned to Judah a second time in 597 BC in response to Jehoiachin's rebellion. In this incursion, Jerusalem was again brought under subjection to Babylon, and an additional ten thousand captives were taken to Babylon, among whom was the prophet Ezekiel (Ezekiel 1:1–3; 2 Kings 24:8–20; 2 Chronicles 36:6–10).

http://books.google.com.br/books?id=pGb-TUM5AgQC&pg=PA1 326&lpg
www.padfield.com/2008/carchemish.html
The Bible Knowledge Commentary: Old Testament By Walter L Baker, John F. Walvoord

Was Daniel a eunuch?
We do not know.

There are those who believe he was not:
- The main reasoning for those who hold this belief is that if he had been a eunuch, Scripture would have recorded it. This is not a particularly strong argument. Daniel wrote only of what God did. We know very little about his personal life.

There are those who believe he was:
- There is no mention of his offspring in the Scriptures. Of course, this argument is no stronger than the one above, which chooses to believe that he had a family.
- It was common practice in those days for the very top ranks of government to be occupied by eunuchs. It was presumed that eunuchs could better serve the king because they would have no family distractions.
- Nebuchadnezzar made many young men into eunuchs. Therefore, some believe that the young teenage boys who were of royal bloodlines (Daniel, Hananiah, Mishael, and Azariah, among many others) would have been emasculated at the time they left Jerusalem or perhaps when they entered the king's service. They were slaves and would have had no choice in this decision.

Therefore, the author does not take a position. No families are ascribed to the four, nor are they declared to be eunuchs.

CONTENTS

CHAPTER 1

At Home in Jerusalem

As Daniel walked home from the temple, his thirteen-year-old mind was filled with many contradictory thoughts. With so much information coming at him at once, it was difficult to sift through the myriad of incompatible facts; these were truly troubled times in Jerusalem. It seemed to Daniel that King Jehoiakim, most of the priests, and a few of the scribes, especially the younger ones, were on one side. These were espousing a modern, post-Josiah, progressive, pro-Egyptian mentality. As the young man considered Israel's state of affairs, he saw that Jeremiah, a handful of aged priests, and the older scribes strictly adhered to the Hebrew Scriptures. These men, quite to the contrary of the first group, spoke of the need for repentance, holiness, and self-sacrifice. Although the two positions were not mutually exclusive, it seemed their proponents were always falling into opposing camps. Daniel found it quite difficult to distinguish right from wrong on some of the issues.

Daniel's favorite time of the day was the period he spent at the temple. He liked everything about it, especially now that he was spending most of his time with the older scribes. In earlier years, his teachers had largely been priests. They were decent men, but most of them did not seem to have the zeal for God in their hearts as did the older scribes. The priests held their positions because they had been born into the tribe of Levi; the scribes were such by choice. This difference in commitment was truer of certain individuals than of others, but in many cases, at least to Daniel, the difference was notable. Now that he was older and was engaged in learning the finer points of Hebrew calligraphy, he and some of the more interested students were spending most of their time with the men who copied and counted the Scriptures.

Although some considered the scribes as less than productive citizens, Daniel had been raised to regard them as heroes of the faith. The verification process of a copy of the Holy Scriptures fascinated the young man. Daniel had even helped a scribe on one occasion to count the letters in a copy of Isaiah and find the middle letter. It worked! He had found the right one. He had watched the priest find the 777th word from the front and from the back, and that had turned out correctly also. Daniel had watched with fascination as the scribe copied down every seventh letter and compared the letters to the key, supposedly made off the original copy. The scribe had pointed out some hidden words in the key and had applied meanings to them for the young man, explaining that some thought this was mere coincidence, but he believed it was divine planning.

Daniel greatly respected these scribes, even to the point of thinking he might like to become one someday. He could now read the Scriptures on his own—on those rare occasions when he was allowed to hold the sacred parchments. Daniel had developed a special pride in his Jewish heritage. He longed to know and understand Yahweh, the most high God, creator of heaven and earth. The Scriptures thus enthralled him because they were his link to this knowledge and to the deep desire of his heart.

Especially of interest to Daniel were the prophecies. Yahweh knew the future! All through the Hebrew Scriptures, their God had foretold events that had come to pass. Abraham, Isaac, Jacob, and Joseph clearly demonstrated God's promise fulfilled. Samuel and Elijah were two other favorites, for obvious reasons. A true prophet of God never missed a prediction! In his adolescent logic, Daniel concluded, "You can never contradict God, because how could *He* be wrong? Our God is omniscient."

Ironically, it was just this belief that was causing him so much trouble in view of the current plight of Jerusalem, God's holy city. Forty-two-year-old Jeremiah, who to Daniel seemed like a very old man, was forever preaching that the Babylonians would besiege Jerusalem if God's people did not turn from their wicked ways, repent of their sins, and follow Him. The king and many of his political cohorts disliked Jeremiah. To say the least, he was

----

Historical Observations

[1]*Babylon's conflict with Assyria lasted approximately four years. The crown prince, Nebuchadnezzar, went against the Assyrians in an attempt to capture all of Asia Minor. Pharaoh Neco of Egypt marched his army north to help the Assyrians. These battles, culminating in the battle of Carchemish, proved to be some of the bloodiest in the history of mankind.*

King Josiah, knowing that Jeremiah had prophesied that Babylon would win, perhaps attempted to stop Pharaoh Neco, the Assyrian ally, by not allowing him passage through Israel. Josiah was killed by Pharaoh Neco, who replaced him with Jehoiakim as his vassal king. There is controversy over this date, as detailed in the Kings' Calendar.

Jeremiah was considered a pro-Babylonian prophet because he predicted that Babylon would conquer Jerusalem. King Jehoiakim was, therefore, quite opposed to Jeremiah, as his loyalties belonged to Pharaoh Neco of Egypt.

King Jehoiakim had a form of godliness in that he offered sacrifices and performed other religious acts. The priests, the scribes, the politicians, and anyone else who wanted to be politically correct had to side with Jehoiakim and Egypt. According to Jeremiah, King Jehoiakim was a religious hypocrite who trusted in man (the Egyptians) rather than in God. Gleaned from Biblical references and from the Kings Calendar

----

quite controversial. Some simply declared that he was a lunatic. Most of the scribes believed that Jeremiah was a legitimate prophet of God. Some of the officers in the military accused him of being a Babylonian spy and insisted that Jeremiah should be killed, but anyone who watched the old man would not have thought him to be spy material.

As Daniel opened the door to his house, he looked past the well-furnished room to see his father and uncle standing in the breezeway to the patio. They were obviously engaged in serious conversation. Daniel, somewhat hesitantly, moved across the room to listen to the intriguing dialogue. It was not until Daniel's father raised his hand and beckoned him to come that Daniel felt at liberty to join the men. It didn't take long for Daniel to understand why they were so serious.

"Rumor has it that the Babylonians have decisively won the battle at Carchemish, that Pharaoh Neco is on a fast retreat, and that the Babylonians are headed for Jerusalem," stated Daniel's father.

Immediately Daniel spoke up. "Isn't that what Jeremiah has been saying would happen all along?"

"Yes," answered his father, "but he began saying *that* decades ago—even back when I was a little older than you and the only conceivable threat to Jerusalem was Assyria. Even then, Jeremiah was insisting that it was Babylon who would conquer our nation."

Daniel's father, a successful merchant, was of royal blood and had a vote in the Jewish governing body. Many times before, Daniel had asked his father what he thought of Jeremiah, but the elder's words had always come back carefully measured and noncommittal. Daniel knew that his father upheld Jewish tradition as well as the Scriptures and had a great reverence for God. His lack of commitment to Jeremiah seemed to be caused by a very deep desire that his prophecies would not come to pass. His father also harbored a tiny bit of doubt as to whether Jeremiah was, in fact, delivering *God's* message. Although not opposed to Jeremiah, he had never been outwardly supportive of him either.

Even though Daniel was only an adolescent, he was well aware of the major events. He knew that King Josiah had been a man of reform and had caused the people to follow God. He remembered when the king had been killed four years earlier in the valley of Megiddo. He knew that Israel, having been soundly defeated, was *forced* to take a pro-Egyptian position, and he understood that Pharaoh Neco had placed Jehoiakim on the throne as his vassal king.

For the last three and a half years, Daniel, as well as all of Israel, had been observing the wars between the Egyptian-Assyrian coalition and the Babylonian-Median forces. The Babylonians, under the audacious leadership of Prince Nebuchadnezzar, had routed the Assyrians from their primary capital of Nineveh, then from their secondary capital in Haran. After bloody battles in Haran, the Assyrians had retreated to the city of Carchemish, setting up their third and final capital in this smaller but well-fortified stronghold. The war seemed to have lingered into a bloody stalemate.

The Babylonian surprise attack at Carchemish, near the upper Euphrates, was a bold and unexpected move. Nebuchadnezzar's depleted forces had been considered by many to be no match for the Egyptian-Assyrian coalition hunkered down within the fortifications of Carchemish. Many had expected a siege, although some were not sure the Babylonians could afford such an expensive option. All of Asia Minor held its breath, wondering which of the superpowers would emerge victorious.

King Jehoiakim and most of his court were pro-Egyptian, for the obvious reason that he was simply a vassal king for Egypt, but those who believed Jeremiah's prophecies felt sure that Babylon would eventually win. It was politically dangerous and economically disastrous to speak out against Egypt, although those who believed Jeremiah was a prophet of God were decidedly pro-Babylonian.

The two men resumed their conversation, seeming to ignore the presence of young Daniel. Knowing that he shouldn't interrupt and ask for explanations, Daniel was forced to glean what information he could from this weighty adult discourse.

His uncle spoke, "How long? About four . . . maybe six weeks?"

"This changes everything!" Daniel's father emphatically declared.

"How many caravans are out?"

"Will the three make it in? Do you remember which route they were to take?"

"Options? What options? The desert is out. Our greatest security is right here."

"Near term, you're right. I'm looking way down the road."

"You're looking at a siege, right?" questioned his uncle.

"That's how Jeremiah calls it. But besides that, I think it's the most likely option."

"I think we could outlast a siege. It would be extremely expensive for Babylon to maintain the army for as long as we would be able to hold out. They can't cut off our water, I doubt that they can get over the walls, and we probably have enough food to last for a very long time."

"King Jehoiakim has always counted heavily on Egypt."

"He's just a puppet for Pharaoh Neco." His father spoke in a disgusted tone.

"I know." agreed Daniel's uncle.

"You know, I have a gut feeling that we are beginning to see a prophecy fulfilled. If so, one way or the other, Jerusalem *will* fall to Babylon."

"You can't think like that! That's like giving up before you start!"

Daniel's father had the last word. "No, it's not a surrender. It's more like a relinquishment of our plans and a recognition that our only hope is to return to God, repent of our sins, and beg for mercy from the Lord our God!"

After his uncle left, Daniel continually watched for a moment when he could ask his father all the questions zooming around in his head. He watched his father talk to his mother, two older brothers, and two or three servants. When they finally sat on their pillows to eat, his father was up and down, not able to keep his mind on the meal. Daniel thought he would be able to speak with him after supper, but just then three fellow members of the king's advisory board arrived and his father stepped out to talk to them. Soon Daniel's mother told him to go to bed, and all opportunity was lost.

The next morning as Daniel headed for the temple, he decided to go a little out of his way to the location where Jeremiah sometimes preached. King Jehoiakim had relentlessly persecuted Jeremiah, who had consequently spent much time during the last few years in and out of jail. Daniel knew, however, that Jeremiah had been out for the last few weeks. At this time of the morning, there were usually not more than five or six somewhat disinterested listeners, but today the plaza was packed! Although he could not see the prophet, he could certainly hear him. It was the same message he always preached, but this time there was extra fervor in his words, especially in his admonition to repent.

As Daniel hurried on to the temple, he felt nearly overjoyed with the realization that he was seeing a prophecy come true. Jeremiah's prediction might actually be happening. Now, if it was to be like some of the stories in the Scriptures, the people would repent, the king would put on sackcloth and ashes, there would be a great revival, and God might even perform some miraculous sign against the enemy! Would He strike them blind? Would He cover them with darkness? Would He send down plagues on them? Would He drown them? Would He rain down hailstones on them? Would He strike them with leprosy?

With grandiose thoughts of salvation still dancing in his head, Daniel entered the outer courts of the temple and took his customary place. He perceived at once that the scribes did not share his enthusiastic ideas of salvation for the nation of Israel. The day's lessons were quite spontaneously set aside as everyone's thoughts were on the still unconfirmed rumor that the Babylonian army was headed for Jerusalem. After quite a bit of discussion, one of the older scribes summed up their collective opinion about the fate of Jerusalem at this point in history. "Even though none of us want to believe it, the most probable interpretation of the Scriptures may be that we will be carried into captivity; then, after the time is complete, God will bring our nation home once again to this land."

The old scribe spoke redundantly, gaining ever more zeal as he rambled on. "Let me make one thing clear: *our Lord is never wrong.* We do not always know how to interpret His words, but *He has never been wrong.* If you have a clear word from God, stand on it. If anyone contradicts God, you can be sure that this person will be proven wrong. *God is never wrong.* Even when all the evidence is stacked against God's Word, stand on it anyway. *Our God is never wrong.* If during your lifetimes there are times when you find yourselves among those who do not respect our God, do not be deceived into thinking they may be right. Our God has said He will triumph in the end, and He always will! *Our God is never wrong!*" It was a speech that Daniel would not forget.

Deep in thought, Daniel was suddenly jolted back to reality when a fellow student next to him asked, "Are we all going to die?"

The same old scribe who had given the previous speech continued with the answer. "We see in Scripture that although God's judgment of sin is certain, He seems to be willing to postpone His wrath to another generation if the current one repents." All at once, Daniel's original excitement flooded his mind once again. So there *was* hope! All that the people had to do was repent. Maybe this wouldn't be as difficult as it had seemed only a few moments earlier.

In the weeks that followed, before the Babylonians' arrival, Jerusalem was abuzz with activity. Even though Jeremiah consistently had an audience and even though there were now a few others helping him preach the same message, the people did not seem to catch the idea of repentance. Everyone was considerably more interested in stockpiling food than they were in repenting of their sins.

Some moved out of Jerusalem, while others thought it was safest to stay inside the city walls. Everyone was stowing away edibles of all kinds. Even though there was more food around than Daniel could ever remember seeing, no one was eating much of it. Families would buy a whole cow or several lambs, cut them up in tiny pieces, and then salt the meat and place it in the sun to dry.

Just before the Babylonians encamped around the city, the last of his father's caravans arrived. Much to Daniel's surprise, his father did not sell any of the goods, but rather he stashed them away. Two days later, the gates of the city were closed for good; the Babylonian army had surrounded Jerusalem.

Although the siege had begun, it wasn't anything like Daniel had expected it would be. Many of the Babylonian soldiers were so far away he could hardly see them. The mood of the people inside the city was that of confidence. Israeli soldiers systematically marched around the top of the wall in seeming defiance of the Babylonian multitude. Patriotism abounded.

The marketplace was still bustling, as those who felt they had more than enough endeavored to sell their surplus to those few who still had money and were afraid that their stockpiles might be less than sufficient. Jeremiah continued preaching the same message, although now his delivery seemed to be resolutely monotone. The scribes returned to teaching the boys, but unlike Jeremiah, they had a sense of urgency in their teaching. They *must* impart knowledge. It appeared to have become their entire mission in life. Since Daniel enjoyed learning, he was quite captivated by the increased attention and devotion demonstrated to him by his mentors.

It was not until the second week of the siege that Daniel was finally able to sit down with his father and talk. Unlike other times, his dad was no longer busy. There was almost no commerce, no caravans to look after, no one wanting to sell anything, and not even many meetings with important people; everything had ground to a halt.

As they talked, Daniel began to realize the grave seriousness of their situation. His father talked as if life as they knew it was now over. He did not seem particularly depressed, but there was a pervasive sadness in his eyes and voice. Almost indignantly Daniel spoke out. "Don't you believe that God can deliver us?"

After a long pause came an answer that stayed fixed in Daniel's thoughts. "I believe that God can deliver us, but I don't know that He will." After a period of silence, his father continued, "The king has spoken to the council several times, and I hear nothing but pride in his voice. It doesn't look like there is going to be repentance on his part, and generally, the people follow the king."

Daniel countered, "The people follow the king, but you believe Jeremiah, don't you?"

His father answered, "Yes, I do, Daniel. It's not so much that I believe Jeremiah, but it's that I believe God, and I am now convinced that God is speaking and has spoken through Jeremiah."

Daniel, feeling that he understood his father's thoughts, asked, "Well, father, why don't you just tell the king what you think?"

The patriarch explained, "It's not that simple, Daniel. The king is very upset with Jeremiah and is accusing him of being part of the problem—possibly even the *reason* the Babylonians are here.

Anyone who sides with Jeremiah is at risk of being considered a traitor. At this point, King Jehoiakim still thinks that Pharaoh Neco will come to our rescue. He talks of God, but he looks toward Egypt."

Daniel appealed, "But, Father, the king's own brother Zedekiah often listens to Jeremiah and even seems to agree with him."

Father laughed and said, "Zedekiah? Zedekiah is politically motivated. He's just playing both ends against the middle."

Daniel questioned, "What do you mean?"

"Zedekiah wants his brother, the king, to think he is spying on Jeremiah for him. If things go badly and Jerusalem falls to Babylon, he knows it would be best to appear to be on Jeremiah's side, because the Babylonians would consider that as disloyalty to King Jehoiakim. It wouldn't even surprise me if Zedekiah already has a contact or two among the Babylonian ranks. He is the type of self-serving politician that Israel could do without."

Deep in thought, Daniel questioned, "Getting back to Jeremiah, you said you believe his message. What are you going to do?"

"I don't know yet, Daniel. I do know one thing, though. I'm going to do more than I have done in the past. My prestige, my business, and my prominence in the city have been very important to me. I think now that they have been too important. Getting back to your question, I intend to exert as much influence for God as I am able while still maintaining my position."

Daniel was confused. "But I thought you just now said position wasn't important to you anymore."

Father continued, "It's not important to me personally, at least not as much as it was. I see my position as a tool to be used for God. I intend to support Jeremiah, but I plan to do it in a fashion that will not get me killed or imprisoned, because if I allow *that* to happen, I'll obviously lose any influence I may have otherwise had. I will do my best to honor God and will weigh every decision accordingly."

Encouraged, Daniel reasoned, "If you do that, don't you think God will save us?"

"Daniel, our Lord is able to save us from the Babylonians, but even if He does not, we will still serve Him."

For the first time ever, Daniel did not see his father as an important politician, a fun-loving father, or even a progressive merchant. He more closely resembled one of the scribes or maybe even Jeremiah. Daniel realized that his father had perhaps not changed all that much, but rather that the circumstances they now encountered were shedding light on the underlying commitment that had possibly always been there. Daniel had always respected his father, but for the first time, he was seeing in him some of the qualities by which he had earned the respect of others.

Four weeks after the gates had closed, the mood in the city was still outwardly positive, but no longer as optimistic. On a personal basis, however, Daniel was *quite* optimistic. He was immensely enjoying his time with the scribes at the temple, he was able to spend hours talking to his father, and he had celebrated his fourteenth birthday. Daniel had a lot of good friends, especially Hananiah, Mishael, and Azariah from his tribe, the tribe of Judah. The only notably negative aspects of Daniel's life were the meager daily rations of food and the ever-nagging realization that neither the king nor the people were repenting.

Many times near dusk, Daniel and his friends would sit on the wall to stare at the Babylonian army. They would make comments like, "I'd give anything to leave this city for a while and roam those hills like we used to," or "They will never get us in here," or "If they ever get into the city, I've got a hiding place where they will never find me." The comments seemed so shallow to Daniel. Why wasn't anyone talking about true repentance and begging for God's mercy like Jeremiah said they should? In general, it seemed to Daniel that no one drew any particular correlations between a material problem and the probable spiritual cause.

It wasn't that *no one* drew these correlations, for some did. In fact, an ever-growing division at every level of Jewish society was developing. Folks either believed Jeremiah or didn't. As the weeks rolled on, it seemed that everyone was taking sides, either voluntarily or because they were forced to do so through outward circumstances.

Not only was everyone taking a position, but they were also feeling the need to defend it against those who disagreed. This was partly the influence of the king, considering his never-ending dispute with Jeremiah, and partly a natural outcome of the need to blame *someone* for the dire situation in which they were submerged. If the king was right, Jeremiah was to blame. If Jeremiah was right, the king was to blame because he had not led the people in repentance toward God.

Even the religious community was divided. In spite of the fact that Jeremiah came from the tribe of Levi and was the son of a priest, most of the priests were against him, siding with the king. On the other hand, most of the scribes were in Jeremiah's favor.

King Jehoiakim may well have had Jeremiah killed but for the fear that this might possibly cause a civil war right there inside the city limits. Another reason he allowed Jeremiah to live was that it was looking more probable that Pharaoh Neco was *not* coming to Israel's rescue and that he might have to strike a deal with the Babylonians. King Jehoiakim could only assume Nebuchadnezzar knew that Jeremiah spoke in his favor. King Jehoiakim could *not*, therefore, risk incurring Nebuchadnezzar's wrath in order to satisfy a personal vengeance against the "pro-Babylonian" prophet.

Although by no means a majority, the followers of Jeremiah were now large enough in number to cause the king to handle Jeremiah very carefully. The dynamics of ruling a city under siege were becoming increasingly volatile. To say the situation was potentially disastrous was quite an understatement.

Nearly three months had passed since the Babylonians had formed a human wall around Jerusalem; people were frightened and becoming paranoid. Rumors of all kinds abounded, and food was getting more scarce. Actually, it was not yet in short supply, but the fear of a continued siege made everyone hoard it as if supplies were inadequate. Many wanted to surrender, but the king would not yet entertain the thought, as this might mean death or torture for him personally. King Jehoiakim had lost most of the public support he had enjoyed during the first few weeks of the siege. Although he denied it, common rumor from fairly reliable sources had it that he was trying to negotiate a personal arrangement with Nebuchadnezzar, a settlement that would allow him to stay on the throne.

On the one hundredth day of the siege, the king addressed the people once again with a positive, upbeat speech. He spoke of how the Babylonians were weakening, how there was still plenty of food in the city, and how they were working on some secret plans to break through the Babylonian camp if need be. He also alluded to possibilities of rescue from an unidentified neighboring country, which, of course, everyone understood to be Egypt.

The king aspired to convey confidence and control. He talked of prayer and acknowledged his dependence on God. He assured everyone that God would deliver them, just as He had in the days of old. He spoke of how unbelief and negativism thwarted the movement of God's Spirit, carefully leaving out any direct reference to Jeremiah but making it clear that he laid the blame at the prophet's feet.

Daniel listened carefully to the speech, but with a new level of understanding. The last hundred days had taught him much. In spite of his father being blacklisted by the king and despite the scarcity of food, Daniel had benefited from his trials. He was becoming a student of human character. When faced with possible starvation, many people's convictions followed their stomachs; they were willing to do almost anything for food. What had formerly been considered wrong suddenly became acceptable. Lying, cheating, stealing, deceiving—the need for food seemed to justify all these.

Daniel had learned to watch people's gestures, their eyes, and their body language. These mannerisms provided more evidence of what was really going on in their minds than did their words. Sadly, Daniel had discovered that he could trust very few people. Assessing the situation, Daniel realized that most of the scribes were largely unchanged; their hearts were pure. However, most of the priests were no different than was the general population. Many of his friends would do whatever was expedient to meet their needs. Daniel suspected that some of them would kill for food, if it came to that someday.

Daniel had also observed his father over the last three months. An ever-growing commitment to God had caused him to publicly defend Jeremiah's message on several occasions. He had seen his father come dangerously close to losing his life twice, both times without flinching in his commitment to Yahweh.

Daniel had observed that those who were completely sold out to God in their hearts were usually the ones who could be trusted. A great truth had rooted itself deeply in Daniel's heart: when spiritual values rule one's life, physical needs don't determine one's actions.

In Jerusalem things were going from bad to worse; it simply could not continue in this fashion for much longer. Now, at fourteen years of age and after this imposed crash course in human behavior, Daniel did not listen to the king's speech with academic interest, but rather with deep analytical thoughts, observing the king's tone, his choice of words, his demeanor, and his probable motivation behind each line. In Daniel's mind, it had become clear that the nation of Israel was deeply engaged in a spiritual battle and that the wrong side was winning.

[1]*[http://www.kingscalendar.com/kc_free_files_no_frames/CHAPTER_02.htm]*

[http://www.padfield.com/acrobat/booth/OT-Extra-Quarter.pdf l]

CHAPTER 2

Captivity Begins

Disaster happened fast. Late in the year 605 BC, in the fourth month of the siege, King Jehoiakim's arrangement with the Babylonians became apparent. The sad saga of events began one morning while Daniel was at the temple studying with the scribes. A self-appointed messenger came bursting in, announcing that the Babylonian army was marching toward Jerusalem and that King Jehoiakim and all of his court were standing by the gate waiting for them! What's more, he claimed that the Israeli soldiers were not on the wall!

The scribes began to pray, and a few began to wail and cry as the boys left class and ran to the city walls. Daniel climbed atop the wall just as a lone contingent of Babylonian officers neared the gates of Jerusalem. The gates swung open before them, and about a hundred Babylonian officials surrounded King Jehoiakim and his court.

The Babylonians were rough, although it was apparent they were carrying out a predetermined plan as they placed people in groups, checked writings and notes, and placed bronze shackles on King Jehoiakim. Although the boys could not really comprehend what they were seeing, no one asked a question or said a word.

About ten minutes into these preliminaries, a signal was given and the entire Babylonian army began approaching the walls of Jerusalem. Daniel's heart sank right into his stomach as he watched the human encirclement closing its noose. When his gaze returned inside the walls, he realized how many people were watching this event. In the distance, he noticed his father standing on a market-square platform with many other men in order to get a better view of the king and his court in chains. Immediately Daniel's thoughts shifted to his family.

Quickly climbing down from the wall, he made way to his father as quickly as he could. When he arrived at his side, Daniel's father asked what the Babylonians were doing with the king. When Daniel finished the brief explanation, his father slowly nodded, took Daniel by the arm, and said, "Let's go home."

On the way home, he explained to Daniel his understanding of the situation. King Jehoiakim had reached an agreement with the Babylonians to stay on the throne and had turned the city over to them. He had probably given them a list of political enemies who needed to be eliminated if he was to rule uninhibited as a vassal for Nebuchadnezzar. Father ended by saying, "If he did give them such a list, Daniel, you can be sure that my name is on it."

Daniel protested, "But, Father, I saw them put shackles on King Jehoiakim."

"Son, I could be wrong, but I see those shackles as a political move." Daniel's father, both discouraged and confident, continued, "It is best for both King Jehoiakim and for the Babylonians that he appear helpless before his captors. If he is handcuffed, the horrible things the soldiers are about to do are less likely to be blamed on him. From Nebuchadnezzar's viewpoint, this shows all the people that Jehoiakim is a mere puppet. If it were not as I am saying, King Jehoiakim never would have peacefully opened the gates of the city."

Daniel could hardly swallow. What was going to happen? How could his father talk about it in such a matter-of-fact fashion? This was worse than the worst nightmare he had ever imagined. Where were some weapons? They had to fight! Where was their Israeli army? Where was God? How could He be letting this happen?

Daniel felt goose bumps on his legs and arms. His eyes were watering, but he was too scared to cry. He wanted to trust God, but he couldn't. He remembered that some of the scribes had been praying and wailing when he and the others had hurried off to the wall. He realized that they probably knew or at least suspected what his father had just explained to him. Were they all going to die? Were they going to become slaves?

As they stepped into their home, suddenly Daniel's mind was flooded with a host of good ideas, which he expressed to his father in rapid succession. "Let's get out of the city!" . . . "Maybe we could slip through the crowds unseen." . . . "I know a secret place behind the sheep gate where we could hide." . . . "Maybe you could pay them; soldiers always like money!"

It was during these moments that Daniel's mother and some younger brothers and sisters entered the room. Staring at each other, his parents seemed to be temporarily paralyzed until his mother burst into tears, falling limply into her husband's arms. Ignoring the bewilderment of the younger children, his father, whose eyes were also now full of tears, looked at Daniel and said, "When the gates of this city were opened, our own soldiers systematically cut off all the other exits from the inside. Jehoiakim literally sold us out to Babylon. Some of us might be killed, others will be enslaved by the Babylonians, and some will be left here to pay taxes to our new conquerors."

Daniel objected, "But you were on Jeremiah's side, and the Babylonians know that Jeremiah's prophecies have been in their favor, so they should respect you for that!"

"It may seem like that, Daniel, but I'm afraid it probably will not be so. Nebuchadnezzar is likely to save Jeremiah because he is a prophet of God. He is likely to spare Jehoiakim's life because he has apparently agreed to do so, and it is also politically advantageous. In order to gain some points with his new vassal king, Nebuchadnezzar is likely to put to death at least some of Jehoiakim's enemies, if not all of them."

Just then Daniel's two older brothers came bursting into the room. "Our own soldiers have surrounded the house! They were not even going to let us in until we told them who our father was and convinced them that we lived here!"

Father stood up and embraced the two. "I would to God that you had not told them anything and that they had not let you come in. I fear telling them that I am your father has sealed your fate." He went on to explain to them much of what he had just explained to Daniel.

Knowing that the end was probably near, the patriarch of the family wanted to make every moment count. He was not crying anymore, nor did he convey the same sadness Daniel had seen in him recently. He was determined, almost invigorated, as he began addressing the family.

"I do not know what is going to happen next. We may all die; some of us may be taken as slaves to Babylon, and it is even possible that some of the younger ones will be set free. But one thing is for certain: we will never again be together as a family like this here on earth.

"King Solomon wrote that the rain falls on the just and on the unjust. Good King Josiah was killed by evil Pharaoh Neco. Evil happens to good people as well as to bad. In the end, we know that justice, goodness . . . well . . . our God will triumph in the end.

"We are not at the end of this story; we are in the sad middle. Our nation is being punished for its disobedience to God. Even though *we* did not disobey, we are being punished along with everyone else. God *will* punish Jehoiakim and all the other traitors in due time.

"Those of us who have committed our hearts to God are on the winning side. Even though it seems like we're losing now, we will be triumphant in the end. If our hearts remain true to God, even though we are split apart now, we will be together in the end. Whether you live or die, the most important thing in life is to always, always stay true to God."

Those words were barely out of his mouth when Babylonian soldiers surged through the front door. Daniel stared at them in disbelief. Those who had drawn swords now rested on them or put them away as they perceived that Daniel's family was not prepared to fight. The leader was looking for something. Momentarily he unrolled a small parchment and announced Daniel's father's name. Father stood up.

Then, to Daniel's utter amazement, the guard said, "Which one is Daniel?" Daniel looked at his father, but Father did not look his way. Instead, he continued looking straight ahead and remained as stiff as a statue. There was an awkward moment of silence, and then Daniel stood up. The guard motioned for him to be removed.

One of the soldiers came up to Daniel and grabbed him by the arm. When Daniel resisted, the soldier hit him so hard in the face that he nearly lost consciousness. As he looked back over his shoulder, he could see the other soldiers moving in with drawn swords toward his family. He heard screams, and he tried to break free. Another blow to Daniel's head kept him from seeing the horrendous scene that ushered his family into eternity.

When Daniel returned to semiconsciousness, he found himself chained to a post near his house. His head throbbed. One eye was swollen shut, and there was blood on his chest, which he soon determined was coming from his nose. Although he realized what had happened to his family, he was in too much of a state of shock to cry over the matter. He wished he had been killed with them. He had no desire to live. Why did they save *him*, anyway? He had never been politically active in any way, for either side. He was sure the king didn't even know who he was!

Historical Observations

We know that King Nebuchadnezzar was very interested in education. He took time to interview graduates from the "University of Babylon" and took a personal interest in the best of them. He (Nebuchadnezzar) found them (Daniel and company) ten times wiser than the others. Nebuchadnezzar consistently called for his wise men, advisors, astrologers, diviners, counselors, etc. It is therefore probable that Nebuchadnezzar intentionally selected the brighter students from conquered countries to be indoctrinated in Babylonian culture and religion. These students, once indoctrinated, could help govern their original homelands more effectively than could native Babylonians.

Nebuchadnezzar was interested in religion. He took articles from the temple in Jerusalem and placed them in the temple of his gods in Babylon, possibly as a type of good-luck charm. It should be noted that he did not use them for himself, which leads us to believe that he knew better than to do that. (His successor is later severely judged for using these utensils in his drunken feast.) Nebuchadnezzar also gave Daniel and the others Babylonian names that had as their roots the names and/or qualities of Babylonian gods/demons.

Depending on the exact route taken (how far north they went and how much backtracking was done while collecting spoils of war), the march to Babylon was probably between eight hundred and eleven hundred miles and could have taken from six to eighteen months to complete.

It is unlikely that one could march in crude shackles for a year without having all sorts of physical problems, especially infections. It should also be observed that thousands of slaves were needed to carry home the spoils of war. Since education was important to Nebuchadnezzar, it is probable that slave classification took place soon after each conquest. Otherwise, a valuable educated slave might be given to a soldier, traded for food, or "wasted" in some other way.
[Selected]

Soon Daniel began to be more aware of his general surroundings. From where he sat, he could see four or five dead bodies and at least twice that many people chained to something or someone. When he saw soldiers, they were not rushing madly through the streets as he had imagined they would. They were systematically executing a plan, and their helpers were the *Hebrew* soldiers. How could someone stoop so low as to turn over his own countrymen to an invading army? It was nearly incomprehensible! And to think that Jehoiakim had arranged the whole thing so that he could stay in power! Daniel remembered the verse "The heart is desperately wicked; who can know it?"

A guard roughly unlocked Daniel's chain from the post and yanked him up. He was led past his house toward a slave-chain unit with at least fifty other prisoners shackled in a line. He stumbled as slowly as possible past the front of his home. The emotion of knowing that his family lay murdered inside was almost more than he could bear. The pain in his heart far outstripped the pain in his head. He had never in his life imagined that this sort of thing could happen: not to his family—not in Jerusalem—not to the people who served Yahweh! Where was justice? Where was God? He was chained into the line, and the guard left. Daniel sobbed uncontrollably.

The afternoon advanced at an incredibly slow pace. The sun seemed motionless in the sky. Daniel was thirsty and was hungry, but more than that, he wished he really knew if everyone in his family had been killed. What if some were only wounded? Maybe they had not killed his older brothers. They would have been good slaves! If they *were* dead, they should not have been killed. It was extremely wrong to kill an entire family just because the king didn't like something the father had or hadn't said, especially when the father was right and the king was wrong! What about his little sister? Perhaps she had been overlooked, or perhaps others had fallen on her and the soldiers had thought she was dead when she really wasn't!

Daniel's shackle was so tight that it almost seemed to cut off circulation to his hand, but as he thought of his family, he began working the iron back and forth so desperately that he rubbed his wrist raw and it began to bleed. He continued with this futile endeavor until he knew for sure that it was physically impossible to free himself. He made a mental note to himself that in the future when he thought back on these events, he would never have to wonder if he could have somehow gotten free and returned to help those he loved. He resolved not to feel guilty. He had done all he could do—which was absolutely nothing. Daniel wept again.

The line of captives stood and began to move slowly. It was close to sundown. Daniel was so thirsty he could barely swallow. One of the prisoners near the front of the line was being released! As he approached the man, he realized why: the prisoner was dead. Evidently he had bled to death from a wound in his abdomen.

Now they were stopped again, a few feet away from where they had been. The Babylonians were barking out orders in Chaldean, which he could not really understand. Although he had studied this language, it seemed different to hear it spoken. Daniel did, however, catch one word that he understood: *water*. He was sure that was what the guard had said, and he hoped that it meant he would soon get a drink.

Daniel recognized some of the people in line. He did not know them well, but he knew who most of them were. No one spoke. Daniel imagined that some had families who had suffered similar fates as his. He did notice that some families were still together. As he pondered this, it dawned on him that he was among the youngest. There were some boys a little younger than he, but he guessed that there was no one under twelve years of age. There were no older people. Daniel reasoned, therefore, that he was chained in a line that would march to Babylon.

Orders were given for the line to move forward. Guards poked the blunt ends of their spears at those who had not understood. After a fifteen-foot advance, the line halted again. In another thirty minutes or so, it would be dark. Daniel wondered what the night would bring. He was reminded once again of home, the home he would never again see. He thought of his bed, of his room, of his brothers and sister, of his mother fixing a meal. He was only a few short steps from this memory, yet he would never see it again. As he imagined the bodies of his family members there on the floor, he could sense an almost jealous feeling welling up inside of him. They were enjoying the afterlife, and he was chained in a slave line! Oh, how he wanted to be with them!

The line moved again; this time it advanced some two hundred feet before slowing to a halt. Now Daniel could see. It was true! They were giving people water! Not only that, but the prisoners were also receiving portions of food! As the food supply moved closer to him, he could see that one of the men helping was a scribe from the temple. No, not one, but four or five of those handing out food and water were older scribes. It thrilled Daniel to see the scribes almost as much as it did to know that he was going to get a drink.

As one of the scribes approached him, Daniel's heart leapt. He had been with this scribe only hours earlier in the temple, even though it seemed like forever. There were tears in the scribe's eyes as his met Daniel's. The pain of seeing his prize student in chains was almost more than he could bear.

The scribe handed Daniel a large clay cup filled with water, and Daniel drank deeply. When he lowered the cup, the scribe clinched Daniel's arm tightly and said, "Always, always stay true to Yahweh!"

Daniel's mouth dropped open, and the thought crossed his mind that this scribe must have rehearsed these words with his father so that they would both say the exact same thing. No, that would have been impossible. This morning no one even knew that the Babylonians would take over the city this very day.

Daniel, softly but quite earnestly, said, "Please find out about my family." The scribe nodded as the untimely presence of a guard loudly tapping his spear on the cobblestone road behind them made it impossible for the two to continue their conversation.

As the scribe released Daniel's arm, he stated, "Hananiah is farther up in this same line."

Hananiah! So they had captured him too! Daniel wondered what had become of Hananiah's family. He knew all of them so well; he hoped they had not suffered the same fate as his own.

A few minutes later, those carrying baskets of bread and dried meat came to Daniel. As he reached for a small loaf of bread and a piece of dried lamb, the server shook the basket toward Daniel as if to beckon him to take more. He looked at the lady's face in the fading light of dusk and saw that she was an old widow lady from the marketplace. She used to sit on the ground not far from his father's store and mend clothes for a meager living. Daniel had often stopped to talk with her. The woman tried to smile at Daniel but was unable to do so. She just hung her head and moved on to the next in line.

Before Daniel could finish eating, the line began to move again. This time it did not stop. Even though it was now dark, they moved along the road for nearly an hour. Daniel knew they were far beyond where the Babylonians had been encamped. He also knew they were heading north. The closest trade route to Babylon was toward the south first, then nearly straight east through Dumah. He wondered why they were moving north or possibly northeast.

As they topped a small hill, those in the chain gang could see their destination. There in the valley in front of them were hundreds of campfires and thousands of people. Other chain gangs ahead of them were descending toward the campfires. As they neared the valley, it seemed to have a bizarre life of its own. There were happy sounds of the singing and dancing of drunken soldiers, but these were mingled with sounds of screaming and crying.

Daniel had the distinct thought that this scene was not fitting or appropriate for humans; the closer they grew to the campfires, the more he felt like a mere animal. The guards treated them that way. Those who needed to wipe or wash could not do so. They reeked in their own filth. Daniel thought longingly of the clean clothes he had left behind in Jerusalem. If he could have packed for this miserable trip, it would have been much more pleasant. This was an inhumane nightmare beyond his wildest imagination.

He also felt like an animal because he knew his value was based almost entirely on the price he would bring on an auction block. He remembered the story of Joseph and how he had been sold into slavery. But Daniel felt like his plight was considerably worse than Joseph's. Joseph's family had lived, and they had eventually been reunited. Joseph's captors had paid money for him, so they probably valued him more than if he had just been a prize of war. And Joseph had been sold into a household where he was able to use the skills that God had given him. Daniel hoped he would have the same opportunity. But where would *he* end up?

His chain gang circled around a fire and sat down uncomfortably. He saw Hananiah across the fire and smiled weakly at him. Hananiah acknowledged him with a nod of his head. Since the prisoners remained chained together, they could converse only with those nearest them.

The soldiers left, and Daniel realized that they were going to spend the night right there in that position. The captives tried to get as comfortable as they could; some whispered to each other and exchanged stories. After an hour or so, a group of half-drunk soldiers stumbled onto their group. They unshackled several of the younger females in the group, who desperately tried to oppose them, but to no avail. The girls were led away, some of them crying and screaming and some simply despondent.

Daniel had been thinking about the open wounds on his wrist and lamenting the impulsive actions that had left him with the raw now partially scabbed skin. When the girls were dragged away, though, he realized that he had nothing to complain about. He prayed for them, but his prayers seemed useless. Where was God when you needed Him? If He *was* their great deliverer, then why didn't He *deliver?* What had Daniel done to deserve this? What had those girls done to deserve being raped by Babylonian soldiers? Nothing! Why? Why?

Daniel's mind drifted from thoughts of his family to the Hebrew girls to his personal discomfort. There were no answers, only questions. Where was the God of the Hebrews? Why had He allowed these things to happen? It was not fair. Nothing was fair!

Daniel could not sleep. Most of those around him could not sleep either. Daniel listened to the conversations. Two men were cursing God, King Jehoiakim, and the Babylonians. Two others were pondering whether Jeremiah was responsible for bringing this whole thing to a head and seemed particularly troubled by the fact that he was supposedly *not* one of the prisoners. Daniel could also hear at times a couple of women on the other side of the fire exchanging stories and sobbing through their recollections of the events of the day. Only one comforting thought came to Daniel's mind on his first night of captivity: he knew the scribe would indeed check on his family. No matter what had happened to them, if some were still alive, he knew that the scribe would take care of them as best he could. This was especially comforting as

----

Historical Observations

[2]*The Battle of Carchemish: Carchemish was the eastern capital of the ancient Hittite Empire. Under one ruler or another, it had been a highly strategic military and commercial center of northern Syria for many centuries. It lay on the Euphrates River, about sixty-five miles northeast of Aleppo.*

There were several important battles fought at Carchemish, the most decisive of which was the so-called Battle of Carchemish, in which the Babylonians under Nebuchadnezzar defeated the Assyrian-Egyptian coalition, led by Pharaoh Neco.

Assyria had first lost its capital of Nineveh to the Babylonians in 612 BC. The capital was then moved to Haran, but the Babylonians captured that city two years later, forcing the Assyrians to set up still

another headquarters in Carchemish, about thirty-seven miles east of Haran.

The Battle of Carchemish was the end of the Assyrian Empire. This same war reduced Egypt to a second-rate power. Babylon was master of the Middle East. Israel became important once again, but only because it was the gateway to Egypt.

The site of Carchemish was excavated from 1912 to 1914 by Sir Leonard Wooley and T. E. Lawrence (Lawrence of Arabia) for the British Museum. They found substantial remains of that powerful city, with forts, palaces, temples, marketplaces, and a great wall sculptured with a procession of warriors, along with the king and crown prince celebrating a great victory.

----

he thought of his little sister. Just before daybreak, Daniel drifted off to sleep.

It seemed that no sooner had Daniel gone to sleep than he was awakened again. Everyone was standing. The soldiers were barking out commands, which his mind was too fuzzy to understand; it was too early in the morning to understand Chaldean, especially "soldier Chaldean." Daniel could see that the others at the far end of the valley were already marching north. Now, in the daylight, Daniel recognized the surroundings. They were roughly headed toward Jericho. It was a familiar route to Daniel, as he had traveled it with his father and their caravans. He knew some people in Jericho, and he wondered what had happened to them.

Even though they got an early start and did not stop to eat all day, they did not make very good time. A few of the weaker ones passed out during the day. When this occurred, the soldiers killed the prisoners, unshackled them, and left them lying where they had dropped. These actions motivated everyone else to continue on. Daniel was thankful that he had no injuries to his legs or feet and that he had on his thicker-soled school sandals. His wrist was sore, and he hoped that it would not get infected.

The second night of captivity was largely like the first. Daniel wondered about the girls who had been taken from his group on that first night. He wondered where they were and how they were doing.

The next day brought about changes. Having passed through the southern tip of the Jericho municipality, they arrived at the Jordan River by early afternoon. For about an hour, the soldiers took turns bathing and playing in the water. After this they formed a human wall around the prisoners then systematically unshackled large groups of them. When it was Daniel's turn, he felt like he had been given new life. With the iron cuff off his wrist, he could move freely once again. Quickly descending into the water, he washed and splashed and dove under the water again and again. He thoroughly washed his wrist, even though it was painful to do so. Suspecting that opportunities to bathe would be few and far between, he kept washing himself, almost as if trying to store up cleanliness for the future days.

After a while, Daniel's group was ordered out of the water, and the next group descended. Hananiah spotted Daniel as he walked up the hill and came nearer. They made plans to be shackled together or at least in close proximity so that they could talk.

Much to their surprise, however, the guards were only reshack-ling the men, not the women or younger prisoners. When the guard approached them, he hesitated just a moment, as if trying to decide whether they were men or not, then moved on. Hananiah said, "I always wanted to look older than I am, but just now I tried to have that same silly look that my eight-year-old brother has!"

They both laughed then immediately caught themselves. Tears came to both boys almost instantly. Daniel questioned, "What happened to him? Do you know?"

Hananiah sobbed, "I don't know *anything!* My father came home and said the soldiers were going through the city killing people and taking slaves. He said that there would be no way to hide the entire family together and that King Jehoiakim would perhaps have him killed.

"My father said a short blessing over us three boys then told us to split up and hide, hoping that some of us would live. I was going to hide in the temple in the old-parchments room, but the guards were already there, and one of them caught me before I could hide.

"I wish I knew what happened to the rest of my family. I don't like King Jehoiakim, but I really don't think he would ask the Babylonians to kill my father, even though he sided with Jeremiah. My father has always been on the advisory council and is well respected—just like yours.

"I wish I had stayed with my parents. Last night I was really angry at them for telling me to hide, but I guess the main thing is that I just wish I knew what happened to my family."

Daniel almost spoke but then refrained. He wanted to say that he wished he didn't know what had happened to *his* family. However, he wasn't even sure that was true. As he thought, he quickly determined that he would rather know the truth than to be kept in the dark.

After somewhat regaining his composure, Daniel explained to Hananiah everything that had happened to him the previous day. He went on to draw the conclusion that Hananiah's father's order to split up and hide had possibly saved Hananiah's life and maybe the lives of his brothers. Daniel quite candidly declared to Hananiah that King Jehoiakim had indeed used this opportunity to rid himself of many political enemies; he was a traitor to his own people and had sold out Israel to Babylon in order to stay in power. Hananiah looked away from Daniel. Daniel sat next to him, and neither of them said a word, their hearts breaking in solemn silence.

For several minutes, they were oblivious to the world around them; then suddenly reality struck. Twenty men came dashing up from the river and tried to break through the soldiers' barricade. Swords flashed, spears flew, men yelled. One young man broke through the line, only to be struck down as three arrows thumped into his back almost simultaneously. A few of the soldiers continued to stab bodies that they deemed might still have some life left in them. Then, silence.

The ghastly silence was broken by hearty laughter as the soldiers began to gloat over their latest adventure. Their comrades on the other side of the river began shouting and waving their swords in approval. Both Daniel and Hananiah realized how futile it would be to try to escape at this point in time.

The soldiers did not allow more than three or four people to talk together at a time, nor were prisoners allowed to move very far from their spot. From where they sat, the two Hebrew boys could see an organized effort on the far side of the hill. It was not a rebellion, because the Babylonians seemed to be coordinating the event. Two hours later, a unit came to Daniel's side of the hill.

First came food—and lots of it: bread, fish, fruits, vegetables, and raisin cakes. Some of the raisin cakes had been formed in a mold that Daniel recognized to be from one of the larger bakeries in Jericho. He wondered if the place was still in business and what had become of the owners. After the food was distributed, others came through offering medical aid, which consisted mainly of two ointments and crude bandages. Daniel asked the man to put both the ointments on his arm, which he gladly did, after which he measured out some of the bandage cloth for Daniel to use as he saw fit. Daniel was grateful that at least the flies would now stay off his wrist wound.

Hananiah commented, "I don't know why they are being so nice to us."

Daniel slightly smiled and answered, "Didn't you take good care of *your* animals? We aren't worth anything dead, and we have a long way to go to Babylon. If we are not in good health, we will never make it. Just pretend like you're a helpless little sheep and they will feed you and water you and you'll be fine!" Both laughed, not particularly because of the humor, but because the laugh felt so good, almost as good as the food.

After the medical and food personnel had completed their tasks, along came a host of clerical staff. They were taking down information and seemed to be cross-referencing some of it. One of the preliminary clerks approached Hananiah and began asking questions. This clerk was a Hebrew!

Hananiah indignantly questioned, "What are you doing on their side?"

The young man sternly looked at Hananiah and said, "Theirs is the *only* side now. I volunteered for this job because this is the only side there is. Now tell me your name."

The boys answered all the questions: name, tribe, age, father's name, grandfather's name, years of education, and other miscellaneous questions. The volunteer left and after a long while returned with an official Babylonian clerk and a translator. The boys once again answered many of the same questions, but this time they did so very slowly, as the answers were translated and some of the information was written down by the soldier-clerk.

The tedium of the next day was almost unbearable. Neither Daniel nor Hananiah moved more than a hundred feet all day long, except for the two times they were allowed to go to the river. At least they could visit with each other, which proved to be a fruitful time of recollection and contemplation. The terrible events of three days ago seemed to be in the distant past. Jerusalem was barely out of sight, yet it seemed they could not even remember exactly what it had been like. Life was so different now.

Even though both boys desperately missed their families, they were now far enough removed from the situation to begin thinking of it from different angles. In the middle of the afternoon of the fourth day of captivity, Daniel began to make headway in his battle to understand some of the whys of their unfortunate circumstances.

"You know, Hananiah, many of the Israelites deserve this bad treatment. They worshiped idols, they worshiped money, and they worshiped themselves. Not many people in Jerusalem truly worshiped God; and just like the prophets of old, Jeremiah said that God would punish them, and He did."

Hananiah answered, "Yes, I know that. What I don't understand is why God punishes the innocent people along with them. Take us, for instance. We were trying to serve God, and we were studying His Word with the old scribes in the temple. We shouldn't be punished! And what about those girls taken from our group that first night? They didn't deserve that either! I would kill those soldiers, if I could."

"Hananiah, don't you remember that time when the old scribe talked about God's levels of judgment? How was it? One level was individual judgment, and another level was family-unit judgment— you know, that part about God visiting the sins of the fathers on the sons. And then it seems there was a tribal judgment, as in our case for the tribe of Judah; and after that there was a national judgment. I've been thinking about that, and I don't think we are being judged individually or for the sins of our families or even for our tribe. This is a national judgment, and we just happen to be alive at a point in history when God is judging our nation."

"It's still not fair for us or for lots of other people!"

"Of course it's not fair! There are a lot of proverbs and songs of David that talk about the wicked prospering. In the end, they will not fare well. But this is not the end; this is the sad middle. I've heard *that* somewhere before!"

"Where?"

"My father said it."

"Oh."

"If you look at it from God's viewpoint, it's easier to understand. God told our nation to serve and worship Him. We didn't do it. God told us He would punish us. We still didn't listen. If Jeremiah was right—and now we know he was—then God even told us *how* He was going to punish us: with the Babylonian army carrying us into captivity!

"We *still* did not listen. Even as the Babylonians encircled the city and Jeremiah continued to preach, everyone was more worried about stocking up on food than they were in asking for forgiveness for their sins. Even at that point, our nation did not repent! God had no choice but to keep His Word and to punish us!"

"Daniel, you are missing the whole point! God is punishing us— you and me, the good guys—along with all the bad guys. That's the whole point, and you are missing it!"

"No, I'm not. You are starting from the premise that good things should happen to good people and that bad things should happen to bad people. I do not believe that God is attempting to establish *that* type of justice here on earth. We lost that in the Garden of Eden! Here on earth, good things happen to bad people, and bad things sometimes happen to good people. It rains on the just and on the unjust. Isaac kept losing his wells. David ran from King Saul's unjust persecution. Joseph was sold into slavery. Moses was taken from his family and raised in Pharaoh's courts. Many of the prophets were killed. There are many other examples."

"I don't know . . . It seems different when it's us. Besides that, in most of those examples, something good came out of it. I don't see that happening to us or to those poor girls."

"I don't understand it all either, Hananiah, but I don't see any choice other than to trust Yahweh. Our God obviously knew the future and revealed it *exactly* through his servant Jeremiah and through many other prophets in the past. We cannot sit here and judge His ways. He is true, and He is truth. No matter what we think or feel, we *have* to line ourselves up with His words and command-ments. He is God, and He makes the rules—not us."

"I guess so. But it's just not right to punish innocent people as harshly as we are being punished."

"All right. If you insist on being stuck on that point, then look at it this way: God did *not* punish us. When He punished the nation, we could have died with our families—well, at least I could have died with mine. *God* saved me, and He saved you too. We were not punished; we were spared. Perhaps God wants to do something in and through us!"

"Daniel, you have one great big imagination!"

"If I do, I have no doubt that God gave it to me so I could talk some sense into you!" As Daniel said these words, he reached over and lightly bopped Hananiah on the back of the head. Both boys laughed, and the conversation drifted toward lighter matters.

That night both boys slept well. They were full, relatively clean, their hands were not shackled, and they had each other to rely on for support as they faced the uncertain future. The next day, as in the previous, they sat around until noon, when a Hebrew boy came up to them leading three "soldiers" with him. Right away Daniel and Hananiah realized that these soldiers were not Babylonian, although they did wear the same type of tunic. They also quickly noted that the soldiers had no weapons and that they spoke only Aramaic. The tallest one announced as importantly as he could that they had come to take Hananiah and Daniel to the taskmaster general.

Hananiah objected, "Why are *you* wearing that Babylonian tunic?"

The young soldier answered, "We are cadets in the Babylonian military."

"After all they did to us, how can you join them like that?"

"It's better than being sold into slavery! If we serve twenty years, we will be free men again!"

"You won't serve two years before you are *dead* men! Not only are you traitors, but you're also fools!"

The taller Hebrew-turned-Babylonian cadet lunged for Hananiah. His two friends held him back while Daniel grabbed Hananiah. The soldier's friends calmed him down while Daniel told Hananiah that if he didn't control himself, *he* would be the dead man.

The soldier cadets led Daniel and Hananiah toward the taskmaster's area. Along the way, the taller soldier threatened Hananiah. "I could have helped you, but you ruined your chances. I'm going to make your life so wretched you'll wish . . ." He quickly cut off his words as they approached the taskmaster's tent and the translator barked at him to leave the prisoners. The Hebrew soldiers quickly excused themselves as Daniel and Hananiah exchanged anxious looks.

[2]*[www.gracenotes.info/topics/carchemish.html]*

CHAPTER 3

The Road to Babylon

Historical Observations

By 605 BC, the most commonly spoken language was Aramaic. It was the trade language, the international default means of communication. Daniel wrote most of the first part of the book bearing his name in Aramaic and the second part, the prophecies, in Hebrew. Therefore, we can assume he had a good command of both languages. It is probable that he studied mostly in Chaldean and would have been exposed to both Greek and Egyptian as well. It is a fact that he spoke three languages. It is possible that he spoke five or more.

Daniel and Hananiah were among a crowd of about fifty waiting outside the taskmaster's quarters, all of whom looked bewildered. Occasionally soldiers or other important people would come, talk to the taskmaster, choose or be given a few prisoners, and then leave with them. From where Daniel and Hananiah stood, they could see a lot of activity around several makeshift tables in the center of a circle of tents. It was obvious that there was a concerted attempt to organize this great multitude into effective groups.

A middle-aged man of slight build held a scrap of parchment in his hands and stepped into the pool of confused people, stating loudly in Aramaic, "I want Daniel and Hananiah!" The boys looked at each other and simultaneously raised their hands. The man motioned for them to follow, which they did. He continued through the circle of tents, through a gorge on the other side, and straight toward the military headquarters of the Babylonian generals. As they walked, the boys wondered if they were going to be enlisted as soldiers, and if they were, what they should do or say.

Their leader, without paying very much attention to them, began chiding them with difficult, unrelated questions. "So, tell me, how far is the moon away from the earth?" . . . "Why is the ocean blue if water is clear?" . . . "Have you figured out yet why your God lost the war?" . . . "Hebrew education—now there's a contradiction in terms!" . . . "So how does it go: if you can't figure it out, you just believe it by faith?" . . . "Prophecies! Now I'll have to admit, you've got me on that one. We need to get a handle on those Jewish prediction techniques!"

After almost every question, Daniel and Hananiah looked at each other with puzzled looks. This man had spoken to them, although with an accent, in both of their native languages: Aramaic and Hebrew. He was clearly not Jewish; he was not a soldier, nor was he a slave master, because he brandished neither sword nor whip. He did not seem worried about them running off, because he never looked back. His mannerisms were nearly comical; yet the intensity of his voice, the speed of his gait, and his rapid-fire, off-the-wall questions kept them from laughing.

Arriving at the military headquarters, he paused only briefly, waiting for a signal from the guard to proceed. Daniel and Hananiah followed their leader, but not without slowing down to stare at their surroundings. Gold vases, fancy pottery, elaborate wall hangings, and many other valuable items were strewn everywhere. They were led onto a carpet, then into a beautiful tent made of purple, red, and pale yellow fabric. Once their eyes adjusted to the dimness, their leader, now quite serious, began delivering to them a speech that he had obviously given several times already,

----

Historical Observations
Babylon Overview

[3]*Babylon means "babilu" (gate of god). It is an ancient city in the plain of Shinar on the Euphrates River about fifty miles south of today's Baghdad. Babylon was founded by Nimrod, who also developed the world's first organized system of idol worship, which the biblical God of the Hebrews condemned in Genesis 11. It later became the capital of Babylonia and the Babylonian Empire. It was of overwhelming size and appearance.*

Babylonian cultural achievements left a major mark upon the entire ancient world. Even present-day civilization is indebted culturally to the Babylonian civilization for its system of telling time, which is derived from their base 60 numerical system. Babylonian influence is pervasive throughout the works of the Greek poets Homer and Hesiod, in the geometry of the Greek mathematician Euclid, and in ancient astronomy, astrology, communication and literature.

Nothing remains today of Babylon except a series of widely scattered mounds. It is amazing that such a powerful kingdom and such a culturally developed city should perish from the earth. Isaiah predicted this. Isaiah 13:19–20 says, "Babylon, the jewel of kingdoms, the glory of the Babylonians' pride, will be overthrown by God like Sodom and Gomorrah. She will never be inhabited or lived in through all generations; no Arab will pitch his tent there, no shepherd will rest his flocks there." This came true.

"Young men, your names were on the list as some of the finer students in the Jewish synagogue in Jerusalem. In due time, you will have a chance to prove how much you know and how quickly you can learn. At this point, we are assuming you value your traditions and your literature; therefore, you are being designated as scroll bearers. Needless to say, this is a high honor, but it is also one that you will lose quickly if you do not behave yourself in an expedient fashion.

"You will be expected to guard your assigned scrolls with your life. You will each be assigned a registered and sealed container of scrolls, the same of which will be required of you when we reach Babylon. Should you fail to deliver your scrolls in the same condition as you received them, you will either be put to death or sold at auction as a common slave. If you complete your task and deliver your scrolls unscathed, you may be given a chance to prove yourselves and continue your education—if, in fact, you could actually have started an 'education' in Israel!"

He pointed to the neatly piled stacks of scrolls and books that the tent harbored; then he turned and walked out, motioning them to follow. Once outside, his personality seemed to undergo a transformation. Jovially he explained to the boys that he was the curator for the University of Babylon and in actuality was a slave himself. In his opinion, it was better to be an educated slave than an uneducated free man in Babylon. He explained that Nebuchadnezzar was a self-made man, and although he was a prince, he had *earned* his own place on the battlefield as a military genius. Nebuchadnezzar valued ability, not birthright. Some of his generals were of noble birth, but most of them had earned their positions.

He went on to say that Babylon never should have won the war at Carchemish. Even though the Chaldeans had dealt heavy blows to the Assyrian armies, after Pharaoh Neco arrived from Egypt and joined Assyria, the Babylonians were greatly outnumbered. They were tactically and defensively positioned to hold their ground, but any and every advance demanded great human sacrifice. He also candidly admitted that morale was down because of these factors and because they were at the end of a tiring military campaign. Without either Daniel or Hananiah asking a single question, he went on to state that most of the military strategists, including himself, had suggested that Nebuchadnezzar retreat. Having made that statement, he smiled, chuckled, and stretched.

Daniel asked, "Why are you telling us this?"

The curator answered by asking, "Why are you listening?"

Without moving his head, Hananiah glanced toward Daniel, his eyes seeming to say, "Did I miss something?"

Daniel, showing little expression and ignoring the question, asked, "What should we call you?"

A one word answer came their way: "Professor." After contemplating his answer for a moment, the professor went on to add, "If you turn out to be considerably smarter than you look, I may be one of your teachers someday at the University of Babylon."

The professor suddenly turned serious and said, "Don't think of me as your friend, because I'm not. I will drop you like a rock if you do something wrong. If I do not perform my duties, my head will roll; and before that happens, I will make sure that yours do too."

The boys nodded respectfully and solemnly, having no doubt that the professor would probably do what he had said. The professor lightened up and said that he would show the boys to their quarters and admonished them to brush up on their Chaldean because he was getting tired of speaking to them in Aramaic and had already used all the Hebrew words he knew.

As they were walking toward a canvas shelter, Hananiah worked up the courage to ask a question that had been rolling over in his mind. "Sir, why did Nebuchadnezzar go against you and his other advisors in the battles at Carchemish?"

The professor thought for a long moment, contemplating whether to answer. "You boys, being Hebrews, will appreciate what I'm about to say. Unlike me, Nebuchadnezzar believes strongly in the gods. He knew that your prophet Jeremiah was predicting that Babylon would lay siege to Jerusalem, unless the people repented— whatever that means. It surprised him when King Josiah went to battle *against* Egypt, the only ally you could have possibly had to protect you from us.

"Furthermore, our intelligence told us that Jeremiah and Josiah were on the same side! Our wizards determined that your God must be playing tricks on you, as He apparently gave conflicting signals to your king and His prophet Jeremiah, who were, as I think I said, thought to be on the same side politically. Nebuchadnezzar reasoned that the gods were lining up in favor of the prophet Jeremiah, because the Israeli army delayed Pharaoh Neco just enough for us to get an upper hand on Assyria and gain the high ground we needed to control in order to withstand the Egyptian onslaught. When Josiah was killed in the battle with Egypt, Nebuchadnezzar became totally convinced that the gods were on Jeremiah's side.

"As the war dragged on, Nebuchadnezzar would ask for news from Jerusalem to learn what the prophet Jeremiah was saying. His message never changed, as you know, and Nebuchadnezzar, his advisors, soothsayers, astrologers, and even some of the generals used this omen to determine that the gods were still in their favor, as evidenced by Jeremiah's consistent pro-Babylonian position. That's really why they never gave up, and that is also why they didn't listen to the mathematicians and some of the other more objective advisors.

"Personally, I don't put much stock in what I have just told you. However, I will admit that it has sparked my interest in Jewish literature and especially in the prophecies. We have to learn those prediction techniques."

The professor directed them to stay close to the tent then left and went about his business. When they walked into the tent, shouts erupted. Before their eyes could adjust to the darker quarters, several boys jumped up to embrace them, or perhaps "affectionately tackle" would be a better description. Daniel and Hananiah were reunited with some of their temple-school friends.

In this tent, there were eight boys from the southern kingdom, all of whom had been studying at the temple in Jerusalem. Daniel knew at a glance that these were the smartest young men in Jerusalem. Altogether in the quarters there were about seventy young men who called themselves Hebrews. Except for the eight from the southern kingdom, the rest were from the northern kingdom, some from Samaria but most from the Assyrian repopulation projects farther north, including Haran. They would band together because of their similar heritage. Daniel and Hananiah were especially glad to see Mishael and Azariah, as they were also from the tribe of Judah.

After a supper of fish and dried figs, some of the boys shared their experiences of the last few days. Nobody talked much about the last day in Jerusalem, but it kept coming up in everyone's mind. After only an hour or so, no one felt like talking anymore.

Daniel found a fleece on which to lay his head, buried his face in it, and cried. He missed his family desperately. He missed his home and his former life. His grief multiplied with the knowledge that it would never be like that again. He would have been embarrassed, but he knew that many of the other boys were doing the same thing.

Nothing happened for almost a week, and boredom would have set in had Daniel, Hananiah, Azariah, and Mishael not found something to do with their time — but they did. Taking the professor seriously, they decided to work on the Chaldean language. Every time there was a native speaker available, they coerced him to speak with them. Because of the ready availability of native speakers and because the boys already had a basic knowledge of the language, they made great progress in just one week.

During this time, the Hebrews observed from a distance the logistical chaos involved in moving thousands of people at the same time. Everything had been organized in the headquarters close to where they were staying, so it had been easy to pick up information. They learned that they were only a small part of a large contingent of specialty slaves and prisoners. There were five or six kings of conquered lands, goldsmiths, coppersmiths, and artisans of all kinds. There were translators, scribes, parchment-preparation specialists, a few legal-document carriers from other countries, lawyers, priests, idol bearers, astrologers, wizards, and several other religious types.

On the first day of the following week, the professor and five or six helpers spent the morning assigning and registering scroll boxes to the Hebrew boys. Hananiah, Daniel, and Mishael were called, assigned scroll boxes, and officially registered as scroll bearers. The boys waited and waited, but Azariah was not summoned.

The professor's helpers began strapping wooden scroll boxes onto each scroll bearer's back. As they were fitted and adjusted, each of the three spoke to the helpers in their still somewhat broken Chaldean and asked them to include Azariah. The helpers completely ignored their pleas. Meanwhile, Azariah had been given orders to help take down tents and pack up all the other miscellaneous items that needed to be readied for the march.

As they moved out, the professor eventually ended up beside the Hebrew scroll bearers. Daniel began talking to him in Chaldean, and he was immediately impressed.

"If I had known you could speak Chaldean this well, I wouldn't have been speaking to you in Aramaic last week," said the professor.

Daniel calmly answered, "I don't speak it nearly as well as Azariah. You ought to hear him speak Chaldean!" Although Daniel was not sure that this statement was exactly true, he really did believe that Azariah's language skills were at least as good as his own. Without hesitation, the professor asked which one was Azariah, because he wanted to speak with him. Daniel lamented, "He was left behind to carry the tents, but believe me, he should be a scroll bearer!"

The professor smiled and said, "He's your friend, isn't he?"

Using the best Chaldean he could, Daniel answered, "Yes, he is, but what I am saying is true."

The professor was deep in thought, as though playing a game of wit in his own mind. He called a helper and told him to go back among the tent bearers and find Azariah, the Hebrew. As the helper was leaving, the professor gave these further instructions: "If he doesn't speak Chaldean, leave him back there."

After the helper left, the professor watched Daniel closely as they walked along. "What was your name again?"

"Daniel."

"You worked hard on your Chaldean this week, didn't you?"

"Yes, sir."

"Did Azariah do the same?"

"Yes, sir."

"Are you confident that Azariah will pass the language test?"

"Yes, sir."

"Did you study with him in the temple?"

"Yes, sir."

"Do you always stick up for your friends like this?"

"Yes, sir."

"If Azariah doesn't speak good Chaldean, I will never trust you again. Did you think about that before you set me up?"

"Yes, sir."

"I'm tired of your 'Yes, sir' answers. I want full sentences."

"Sir, I thought of all those things. I think Azariah's language skills are at least as good as mine, and I don't think he will have any trouble passing the test. He is a good friend of mine, and I wanted to help him out."

The professor stated sarcastically, "That's dangerous . . . . uh . . . what was your name again?"

"Daniel."

"Yes. Daniel, it is dangerous to stick up for friends. Sooner or later, they will let you down and place you in bad situations. If you want to survive in Babylon, obey the authorities, look out for your own interests, and watch your back."

The professor said no more, and Daniel prayed silently that Azariah would be able to pass the test. After about an hour, the helper returned with Azariah and presented him to the professor, who immediately began speaking to him in Chaldean. He spoke to Azariah with rapid but simple successions of words. Azariah, though not clearly understanding what was going on, answered all the questions appropriately and with only slight hesitation. The professor ended their short conversation by stating, "You should thank your lucky stars for your friend. You will be an alternate scroll bearer."

As the weeks dragged on, the scroll bearers became increasingly glad they were carrying ten- to twenty-pound scroll boxes and not sixty-pound tent supplies. The Israelite boys generally marched along with other scroll, cuneiform, and idol bearers; in this crowd, everyone seemed to think they had an edge on the truth. They exchanged ideas with other young people from several different cultures and walks of life. Daniel made many friends but quickly learned that there were very few indeed who could be trusted.

It was disconcerting that almost no one believed in their God; some had not even heard of Him. Mention of the "Hebrews' God" was more in terms of culture or rituals or fables of past miracles, such as the crossing of the Red Sea. This caused some of the Israelite youth to doubt their heritage, made some despise it, and drew others together in a close-knit bond to shelter and comfort one another in their hostile intellectual environment.

The march to Babylon settled into a routine, but it was never enjoyable. They were slaves, and this fact was constantly demonstrated. They ate the leftovers, and they washed last. If there was nowhere to get out of the rain or cold, they would stack their precious scrolls and other cargo in a tent and sleep out in the rain. Daniel estimated that about 15 percent of the slaves had died along the way, and they still had a month to go. Everyone looked forward to arriving in that faraway, glorified fortress on the Euphrates and to establishing any sort of daily schedule, no matter how humble it might be, where they would sleep inside on a mat and have their own bowl, cup, and candle.

[3]*[www.mazzaroth.com/ChapterThree/TowerOfBabel.htm]*

CHAPTER 4

Arriving in Babylon

B abylon was in sight! It was hard to believe. As they drew closer, the height of the walls and the dimensions of the city became more apparent; it was much larger than the newcomers had imagined it could be. They were sad about leaving Jerusalem almost a year ago, but they were certainly glad to have arrived at their destination.

The thousands of slaves were divided into large groups. There were guarded holding areas set up around the Euphrates, and this is where Daniel, his friends, and multitudes of others were placed.

Historical Observations

⁴Babylonian society was roughly divided into three classes: "awilu" (upper class), "musheknu" (free, but of little means), and "wardu" (slaves). All groups were protected by law and enjoyed a minimum of personal rights. All groups, including the slaves, could engage in business and borrow money. However, there were differences between all classes in all fields, and many of these differences were fixed in the laws. It was not necessarily a bad thing in this society to be a slave, if one also had a responsible position. Daniel, later to be prime minister, was a slave.

The slaves who had been bearing precious cargo were all in one area. The next day, soldiers and clerks came to retrieve the cargo. One by one, the packages were opened and the merchandise examined. One of the boys who had joined their group later had been carrying a specially packed gold-inlaid vase. When his bundle was opened, the vase was broken. The clerk nodded, and a second later the boy lay dead, a sword thrust through his heart. The others looked on in horror, wondering how their precious cargo would look when it was opened. As it turned out, all the scrolls from Jerusalem were safe and in good condition. They were glad, both for the sake of the ancient prophetic treasures and for their own sakes as well.

In the makeshift camp, food was scarce and rats were abundant. The days wore on. Had they been forgotten? What about the professor? He had implied they would have a chance to prove their education or at least their ability to learn.

Slaves stole food from one another when it was convenient. Often fights broke out, and sometimes slaves killed each other before the conflicts could be broken up. After three weeks, the Hebrews could tell that there were fewer slaves than before, especially over in the common slave-holding areas.

Most of the female slaves were now gone. The boys reasoned that the loot had to be divided up among the Babylonians and money had to start circulating before the king would begin putting slaves on the auction blocks. The females were worth less for hard labor, so they sold them first, hoping to save the heavy investors' capital for the strong, top-dollar slaves. They also noticed that the common slaves were being fattened for sale and now had plenty of bread to eat. The boys almost wished they were common slaves.

In the early morning, they awakened to the sounds of clerks, servants, and soldiers. They were setting up tables in Daniel's holding area, which now housed around five hundred young men from fifteen to twenty years of age. The young men watched in amusement; nothing this interesting had happened for a month. They saw the professor. They also observed several older gentlemen in rich robes and guessed them to be professors from the University of Babylon.

Parchments were being unrolled, and crudely bound books were being opened. They suspected that these were the same ones that had been written in on their first days out of Jerusalem. The professors began calling names. When called, the person went forward. Sometimes he stood there a long time, and sometimes he was quickly sent over to the common slave-holding pen. One out of every seven or eight young men was told to go stand along the wall to the left of the tables. This process lasted all day.

Around 5 p.m., Azariah was called. When he approached, the professor, who was seated at a different table, stood and said in Chaldean, "Where are your friends, the other three scroll bearers?"

"They are seated over there in the shade of the wall."

"What are their names again?"

As Azariah answered, the professor called out loudly, "Hananiah, Mishael, Daniel—come here!"

When they arrived at the tables, the professor turned and said to the scribe and those professors who had grown bored enough with their own activities to listen to the curator, "These young Hebrews have proven themselves during our trip back to Babylon. They are quick-witted and are both trustworthy and intelligent. Although they know of no religion but their own, I believe they have potential and should be given a chance." The professors nodded their assent, and the four took their place of prestige along the wall.

Soon after this, it was time to take down the tables. Unsure of their new status, Daniel and his friends began helping the servants to dismantle the tables. The servants quickly rebuked them.

The professors formed a tired line as they beckoned to the newly chosen students to follow them. The servants brought up the rear, bearing tables, benches, parchments, and other paraphernalia. There seemed to be a lot to carry for no more than had gone on that day. They had been used to traveling light. Now there were fifty servants carrying supplies for eight professors.

The youths gaped in awe as they walked the causeway over the Euphrates up to the gates of Babylon. Beautiful blue tiles of lions and other creatures adorned the walls and walkway. They entered through the gate and were led to another magnificent gate, larger than the first. The boys quickly recognized this as the famous Ishtar Gate.

As they entered the bustling city, darkness was approaching. Street lighters were lighting lamps along the main avenue. They had never even dreamed of public lighting before this moment. Slaves, animals, soldiers, servants, and merchants all made way for their procession. It was almost surreal.

As they arrived at a courtyard, the gates were opened and they continued in; the gates were shut behind them. One of the professors began to speak. "One hundred and fifty of you have been chosen to study. Not all of you will make the grade, and we will be reducing your number to around one hundred in the next few months. King Nebuchadnezzar is a great king with much foresight. He was named for his god, Nebu, the god of learning, or the god of books. He values education, and he will value you if you prove useful in his kingdom.

"You are being given a chance that few in the entire world have been given. You are slaves, but if you show yourselves capable, you will control the lives of free men. It is up to you to prove yourselves.

"Tonight you will have meat and bread, but tomorrow you will begin eating from the king's table. Small cabins line this courtyard. You will sleep four per room. There is soap and lotion in each room, as well as new clothes. You can bathe here at the well in the court-yard. Throw away your clothes—what there is left of them—in the trash box by the entrance gate. If there are those of you who did not understand what I said, get someone to translate, and learn the language. Be ready for further instructions at sunup."

The young men remained quiet as the professors and soldiers left, but as soon as the courtyard gate was closed, the cheering was likely heard all the way to the palace. Everyone hugged each other. Everyone talked loudly in his own language, not caring if anyone else understood. What a turn of events!

Servants were already setting up the food tables. The boys formed a line at the well to wash up with soap. It was a large, two-bucket, two-hoist well, and the young men kept the buckets busy for over two hours. They spread the lotions lavishly; never had they been so clean or smelled so good. They ate to their hearts content. This was the happiest day there had been for a long, long time.

That night Daniel, Hananiah, Mishael, and Azariah roomed together. Daniel led the conversation and kept reminding them how they *must* serve their God, the maker of heaven and earth, here in Babylon. He compared their plight to Joseph's. He repeated Jeremiah's words that someday they would return to Jerusalem. As they pondered their situation, the boys' thoughts kept them awake well into the night.

Before sunrise they could hear others stirring, and they quickly got up and got ready. At sunrise all one hundred and fifty young men were waiting in the courtyard. They ate breakfast, which consisted of leftover stale bread and tough dried meat from the night before. And they waited . . . and they waited.

Around 9 a.m., the professor showed up with several helpers and clerks and promptly strode to the shady side of the courtyard where there was a built-in ledge between two columns. He sat comfortably in the shade and had the young men sit in the morning sun in front of him. As the clerks were setting up their tables, he announced, "My name is Ashpenaz, master of the king's eunuchs. Some of you know me as the professor, because that is how I wished it to be known on the pilgrimage to Babylon. Now you may call me by name and title.

"The king gave me the task of . . . well . . . let me read it to you: 'Bring to me the seed of royalty and of the nobles; youths in whom is no blemish or defect, but well-favored, and skillful in all disciplines and in wisdom, and endued with knowledge, and understanding of sciences, and such as have the aptitude and ability to stand in the king's palace. Teach them the learning and the tongue of the Chaldeans.'

"Our first task is that of renaming you. We are not going to try to learn all of your hard-to-pronounce names. Besides that, you are the property of Babylon; you need Babylonian names."

The young men looked at each other, but no one objected; slaves do not object, especially when they are being treated well. The names had already been chosen by the prince of the eunuchs, so the renaming went fairly quickly. Each young man was asked to stand, hear, memorize his new name and its meaning, and then sit. They were to use this name from then on and insist that everyone else use it when addressing them.

The clerk called out, "Daniel." He arose. "From now on, you will be called Belteshazzar, in honor of the Babylonian chief god, meaning 'Marduk will protect.'" Daniel sat down. He had memorized his name all right, and he hated it—"Marduk will protect," or in the Hebrew translation, "Marduk, guard my gate." They were trying to take away his identity, his tie to his own God, the one true God, the maker of heaven and earth. He would not do it. He could not.

The others were called out and stood one by one. To Hananiah, the name Shadrach was given, meaning "inspired of the sun god;" Mishael became Meshach, meaning "one who belongs to the goddess Shock"; and Azariah received the name of Abednego, meaning "servant of the god Nebu."

After the renaming ceremony was complete, the students-to-be had about an hour before they were to be escorted to the king's banquet hall to eat their first meal from the king's table, although they didn't really know what the "king's table" meant.

All of their names had demon-god implications. Back in their rooms, Daniel said, "Don't you ever call me Belteshazzar."

"Others are going to call you that name."

"I can't help that, but I refuse to be called by my pagan name among my friends."

"Daniel, your name doesn't have to influence who you are on the inside."

"I know that. But this is an orchestrated effort to get us to forget our past and our God, and I am not going to allow that to happen. I'd rather die."

"If God has placed us here, He doesn't want us to give up and die because we've been renamed."

"I understand that. But I also see that we are going to have to draw the line somewhere. Israel was punished because she did not follow God's laws. If we have learned anything from the fall of

Israel, it should be that we must follow the Lord our God with all of our hearts, souls, and minds."

The others agreed, and Mishael led out in a prayer. Soon all joined in. They would indeed draw the line somewhere and would serve the Lord their God, the most high God, whatever the consequence.

Lunchtime! The bell rang at the courtyard gate, and the young men guessed what it was for. They followed the king's eunuch in a slightly organized mass, wondering all the while what lay ahead. To their surprise, they were actually very close to the outer palace wall. The gates opened, and they walked through toward the second pavilion on the right. Over a thousand people ate here every day: about three hundred at the king's tables, which sported delicacies of every kind; and about seven hundred at the servants' tables, which were called the water-and-vegetable tables.

As the students were seated, the servants began placing thick slices of pork on their plates. This was followed by meat and vegetables cooked in wine and animal blood. Golden roasted duck was served complete with entrails. Their plates were piled high, and many varieties of wine flowed freely. The servers would not stop coming.

Daniel stared at his plate and said to himself, "This is where I draw the line." He looked at his friends and declared, "Most of this food is not kosher; we can't eat it." They looked back at him, knowing that he was right, but the temptation was still nearly overwhelming. Daniel picked out some figs, some bread, and some fresh vegetables from serving bowls in the center of the table.

He could have drunk the wine by law but did not, because he didn't know for sure what else might be in it. He was also well aware of the Nazirite vow and reasoned that it would be better not to drink the wine. Daniel drank only water and ate fruits and vegetables; his three friends followed his example.

Ashpenaz, prince of the eunuchs, observed the young men gorging themselves and noticed Daniel and his friends with their plates full of uneaten food. He laughed, "What's the matter? Haven't you ever seen good food? Eat up! This is the same food that is served to the king!"

Daniel smiled but continued eating the vegetables. The eunuch came right up behind him and said, "What is your name again?"

"Daniel."

"No, your Babylonian name."

"Belteshazzar."

"Eat up, Belteshazzar."

"Today I prefer just water and vegetables, if you don't mind."

"All right, maybe tomorrow you can enjoy the good food."

"Sir, we appreciate all that you have done for us. This is really quite a feast! Thank you so much for looking after us."

"It's my job, but thanks for saying you like it."

From there the students were ushered onto the university grounds, which was a series of open-sided classrooms. Most of the classrooms had clay and styluses available, and the more advanced-level classrooms had an abundance of parchment, ink, and quills. The students were divided by age, so the four Hebrew boys stayed together all afternoon.

Many of the other boys did not feel well after the meal. Their stomachs were not accustomed to so much food at once, and the rich nature of the food was also more than some could take. Besides that, some were slightly drunk.

The afternoon consisted of each professor bragging about how learned he was, what importance he had in the king's advisory council, and what they could expect from his class. The four Hebrews did not like any of the professors very much but did enjoy being in an academic environment once again.

Altogether, there were twelve Hebrew boys who had made the cut for the university: Daniel, Hananiah, Mishael, and Azariah, from the tribe of Judah; three from the tribe of Benjamin, also from Jerusalem; and five from the other tribes. These five were not well versed in the Scriptures, since their parents had been deported by the Assyrians before they were born. They had heard of the temple in Jerusalem and had memorized the Ten Commandments and a few other passages, but Jewish teachings were not an integral part of their identities.

That night Daniel called all twelve of the Hebrew students together and recounted the events of the dinner table and his conversation with the prince of the eunuchs. Eight of the twelve had eaten all they could of everything and saw nothing wrong with it. Daniel and the others went back and forth on the issue.

One of the Hebrews from the ten northern tribes said, "Why do we have to keep Yahweh's laws if we are not in His land?"

Daniel answered, "That has nothing to do with it. The commandments are not conditional to geographic locations."

"Well, it is really going to seem ungrateful if we don't eat that wonderful food they provide."

"I thanked Him for the food today; I just didn't eat it."

Another boy joined in. "Oh, Daniel, come on. You know it is going to look bad if we don't eat their food. It's like we think we are better than they are."

Daniel answered, "I know, but I have a plan. I'm going to ask the professor tomorrow if he will simply let us eat from the servants' table. Most of it is kosher. The vegetable table would be just perfect, if they would allow us to eat over there."

A third Hebrew boy now spoke. "If we do that, all the other students are going to laugh at us."

Abednego quickly said, "So?"

The first Hebrew spoke again to Daniel. "I just think you, Hananiah, Mishael, and Azariah are taking things too far. I'll bet Joseph and Moses ate the king's foods."

Daniel looked a little disgusted. "Think! They didn't even have the laws of Moses yet! It's different for us! Didn't we learn anything from Jeremiah's preaching? We must obey the Lord our God with all our heart, soul, and mind. Eventually He will deliver us."

Another of the Hebrews from the ten northern tribes chuckled and said, "With meals like the one today, I don't know if I want to be delivered too quickly! Who is Jeremiah anyway?"

Another answered before Daniel could. "He's that pro-Babylonian prophet that caused Israel to lose the war."

Daniel interjected, "It is so easy to accept cheap explanations given by people with no spiritual insight. Do you think Israel fell because of Jeremiah or because of Babylon's power? No, it fell because the people would not acknowledge God and turn from their wicked ways. If you look back in history, this has happened over and over again."

No one said any more. The eight were too tired; their stomachs and heads ached, and they were tired of thinking.

The next day the students were expected to be at class shortly after sunrise, although they would soon learn that they would never know if the professors would show up. When the professors were late or absent, usually no explanation was given. They were far too important in their own minds to give any kind of explanation to mere students. If an explanation was given, it was generally in the form of bragging about how much time the king had required of them or how he had sought their counsel. The students soon learned that these ramblings were mostly lies.

Mealtime! The bell near the university well rang. Another feast! The students rushed to the dining hall and quickly sat around the king's table. Daniel, Hananiah, Mishael, and Azariah were last. Daniel went straight to Ashpenaz and said, "With your permission, sir, we'd like to eat bread and vegetables from the servants' table."

Ashpenaz laughed and said, "I like you Belteshazzar, but I have to deny your request. If you look weaker than the rest when the king comes to examine the students, he could have my head. Although I like you, I like my head better. Now sit down and eat the king's food. It will increase your intelligence and make you fatter."

Daniel and his friends sat at the king's table, but like the day before, they ate little of what was set before them. Daniel managed to put some of his food onto a friend's plate, and Hananiah, Mishael, and Azariah were also able to hide food, share some with friends, and dump some under the table. They managed to get through one more meal.

Historical Observations
Babylonian Math

[5]*The Babylonians had an advanced number system, in some ways more advanced than our present systems. It was a positional system with a base of 60 rather than the modern system of base 10.*

They divided the day into 24 hours, each hour into 60 minutes, and each minute into 60 seconds. This form of counting time is still used today. To write 5h 25' 30", or 5 hours, 25 minutes, 30 seconds, is to write the sexagesimal fraction 5, 25/60, 30/3600. We simply adopted the notation 5, 25, 30 for this sexagesimal number. A base 10 fraction sexagesimal number 5, 25, 30 is 5 4/10, 2/100, 5/1000, which is written 5.425 in decimal notation.

Perhaps the most amazing aspect of the Babylonians' calculating skills was their construction of tables to aid calculation. They used the formula $ab = [(a + b)2 - a2 - b2]/2$ to make multiplication easier. Even better was their formula $ab = [(a + b)2 - (a - b)2]/4$, which shows that a table of squares is all that is necessary to multiply numbers, calculating the difference of the two squares that were looked up in the table then finding a quarter of that value.

Division is a harder process in their fractional system. The Babylonians did not have an algorithm for long division. Instead, they based their method on the fact that $a/b = a(1/b)$, so all that was necessary was a table of reciprocals. Museums still harbor their reciprocal tables up to reciprocals of numbers to several billion!

The next day at noon, Daniel tried a different strategy: he called aside the steward, whom the prince of the eunuchs had appointed over the students, and said, "With your permission, sir, we'd like to eat the food from the servants' table. I believe we will be healthier and smarter if we do not eat the rich food from the king's table."

The steward liked Daniel's demeanor but said, "What makes you think you'll do better eating from the servants' table?"

Daniel looked him straight in the eye and said, "My God told me so. All I ask is that you let us try it for ten days. If we are not just as healthy or healthier than the others, then I will not bother you again. Just give us a chance to obey our God."

The steward thought a moment and said, "All right, but just ten days."

Daniel, Hananiah, Mishael, and Azariah went to the servants' table and helped themselves to bread, vegetables, fruits, and some meat they knew would be kosher. They were immediate celebrities with the servants; all of them wanted to talk to the four. Just as quickly, they became laughingstocks of the other students.

During the afternoon sessions, the comments were abundant: "Hey, your God lost the war; you don't have to obey Him anymore." . . . "Israel is so poor that they have never seen good food; that's why they're scared to eat it!" . . . "Hey, your God just told you not to eat the good food because He couldn't provide it for you." . . . "Lighten up! Don't take your religion so seriously! It's only food!" . . . "They know they will never make the final cut, so they want to get in with the servants." . . . "Yeah, if they won't *eat* the food, maybe they will be *serving* it to us someday!" . . . "Marduk defeated Jehovah and robbed His temple! Did you forget?"

Historical Observations
Babylonian Math

[6]*Babylonian mathematics went far beyond arithmetical calculations. Their geometrical ideas were quite advanced as well. They constructed tables for $n3 + n2$, and then with the aid of these tables, cubic equations could be solved.*

*The equation $ax3 + bx2 = c$ is a modern notation; nothing like an algebraic representation existed in Babylonian times. Nevertheless, they could handle numerical equations by using sets of rules. For example, in the above notation, multiply the equation by $a2$ and divide it by $b3$ to get $(ax/b)3 + (ax/b)2 = ca2/b3$. Putting $y = ax/b$ gives the equation $y3 + y2 = ca2/b3$, which could now be solved by looking up the $n3 + n2$ table for the value of n satisfying $n3 + n2 = ca2/b3$. When a solution was found for y, then x was found by $x = by/a$. All this was done **without** algebraic notation. This showed an incredible depth of understanding, mental concentration, and the ability to carry simultaneous abstract thoughts to several levels.*

It was not easy to endure, but Daniel, Hananiah, Mishael, and Azariah stood their ground. They knew they had to be healthy after ten days; they worked out, they ran, and they even wrestled one another at night. It was a challenge that they took very seriously.

At the end of ten days, right there in the dining hall, the steward ordered about thirty young men to stand up from the king's table and come to the center of the dining hall. He ordered Daniel and his friends to join them. The steward observed them closely. Most did not know what was happening, nor did they know of the ten-day test.

At length the steward announced for all to hear, "Well, your God was right. You do look better than the others. You have better color and you are stronger. You may continue at the servants' table as long as you like or as long as your God tells you to."

Daniel and his friends smiled and returned to their table. The others laughed at first, as they caught on to what had taken place. Soon, however, the laughter was followed by hateful statements: "They did this whole stunt to try to show us up." . . . "They are trying to get an upper hand on us and cut us out." . . . "They are undermining our chances. They have the servants on their side, and now they have the steward thinking they look better. Those four seemed like nice guys, but they are snakes in the grass!"

That night Daniel, Hananiah, Mishael, and Azariah talked of the day's events. The last thing they had wanted was to drive a wedge between them and the other students.

"Why do you think we looked better?" asked Mishael.

Hananiah quickly responded, "We are never drunk, we've not been sick, we don't miss classes because of hangovers, we don't have diarrhea all the time from the rich foods we're not used to, and we never overeat! How can we—on *vegetables!*" Everyone laughed.

"Our minds are sharper," continued Daniel. "There are reasons for the laws God gives. We are seeing some of these at work in this test."

After a period of small talk, Azariah spoke up. "It is going to be a long three years if we can't do something to bridge the gap between us and the other students. Besides that, we may work with them someday, and they will always be undercutting us if they can, because they are jealous." The four brainstormed about ways to be friends to their fellow students, prayed about the issues, and then fell asleep.

As time passed, Daniel, Hananiah, Mishael, and Azariah proved they were sharp. The professors and the students all knew it. The answer to their prayer about being friends with the other students came in the form of helping them with their studies at night. Almost every night, some or all of the four would help someone with his work. Soon, however, Daniel and his friends would face an entirely new problem, and it would be a serious one, causing them to even consider quitting college and opting for making bricks.

⁴*[http://looklex.com/e.o/babylonia.htm]*
⁵*[http://education.uncc.edu/droyster/courses/fall06/pdfs/appendixa. pdf]*
⁶*[http://hem.passagen.se/ceem/tartagli.htm]*

CHAPTER 5

The Dilemma

Daniel and his friends faced a serious issue. One night by candle-light, Shadrach voiced his concern. "They have us learning numerology, astrology, divination, cultic meditation, demonic medi-ation, and all sorts of other supernatural phenomena!"

"We can learn the subject without internalizing the belief," insisted Meshach.

"Maybe so, but our scribes back in Judah would never have let us learn these things — not even read or repeat these words!"

"Yes, but we are not under them now, nor are we in Judah. We know these things are wrong; we don't have to accept them."

"You know in Deuteronomy it says to kill all those who practice most of what we are learning about. Won't God judge us?"

Abednego joined in. "But our God has put us here. He must have a plan!"

"I don't doubt that, but are we negating His plan by not standing against these things? Are we bringing destruction on ourselves?" questioned Shadrach.

"I don't know for sure, but the worst part about learning these lies is the oppression and fear that seem to creep in."

Abednego exclaimed, "That is a sign we belong to God! The enemy is fighting us!"

Daniel broke into the conversation. "Perhaps *that* is the key. We belong to God. We can never do anything personally that compromises this. We cannot eat their food or bow to their statues, because we would be personally compromising what our God has forbidden. Our God did not say, 'Don't learn about Gentile religions.'"

Meshach challenged, "Maybe not specifically, but in principle He sure does! Remember all the orders to annihilate the nations who practice these things?"

"We are helpless on that point," Abednego noted. "We are not in control, and we can't kill them. We are under their authority!"

It was quiet for a long while; then Daniel softly prayed, "Somehow, Lord, honor our commitment to You!" The four stood in a huddle, arms on one another's shoulders, and echoed their prayers of commitment. They also promised to hold one another accountable if they began to waver in their dedication. The last facet of their prayers was to ask for wisdom like Solomon's, so that they would be able to answer their professors and fellow students with the right measure of tact and truthfulness. Things were not black and white anymore. Most of the issues seemed to come in shades of gray.

The following term, they learned about the cosmos. The professor related information in such a way as to leave no doubt as to the total authenticity of what he was saying. He described Marduk leading a rebellion of the gods against the goddess Tiamat, who had planned destruction for them. Marduk was originally a minor deity but later became a powerful ruler. He was considered a creator god.

After defeating Tiamat in single combat, he created the heavens and the earth, organized the year into months, and arranged the planets and stars. He created the Tigris and Euphrates rivers from her eyes and made mountains from her udders. He smashed the weapons of Tiamat's army and put images of them at the gates to the underworld. He set up his temple at Esharra and his seat in Babylon. That was why Marduk, the most powerful god, was the patron god of Babylon. After Marduk won the heavenly war, he was eulogized by the other gods in a comprehensive list of fifty names of gods, which can be traced back to all the gods of antiquity. Marduk became supreme because he gained the respect of *all* the gods.

Daniel listened patiently for a long time before he decided to ask a question. "Do you believe in the Hebrew God?"

"Yes. It is widely accepted that Yahweh parted the Red Sea and drowned the Egyptian army."

"Yahweh does not honor Marduk, and He would have to be in that list."

"The truth is, son, that Yahweh is an elusive God. He shows up when He wants, He is able to work miracles when the stars are lined up with His will, and He has quite accurately predicted the future. However, He makes a lot of claims He can't deliver."

"Such as . . ."

"Such as creation. Marduk created everything out of Tiamat's body. Yahweh tried to make these claims and it bothered Marduk, so he caused Yahweh to go into hiding. Now, where was I? Oh yes . . . The great statue of Marduk and its attendant regalia have been stolen by conquerors several times throughout history, and their return has always been connected with reincarnation and the resumption of Marduk's rule over the earth and, of course, his return to Babylon. Marduk, being our patron god, is honored by the three-hundred-foot-high ziggurat, which is his temple on earth."

With this, the professor pointed to the ever-looming ziggurat not all that far away. He went on to say that New Year's Day was the most important day of the Babylonian calendar and that during the ceremonies, the statues of Marduk and his son Nabul would be carried to a special shrine outside the city where Marduk would prophesy and Nabul would interpret his words.

But Daniel's mind was elsewhere. He came back to the present as the teacher was saying, "This epic is read aloud every New Year's Day in Babylon in front of the statue of Marduk."

Daniel raised his hand, and the professor acknowledged him. "Sir, how do we know these epics of the gods are true?"

Much to Daniel's surprise, the teacher said, "We don't. We take it by faith as it has been revealed to us through the prophets of the gods and handed down over the years."

Daniel continued the thought. "I take it that you are familiar with the holy Hebrew Scriptures."

The professor smiled and said, "Yes, son, I've read them, and I read them in Hebrew."

Daniel then asked, "Why would you say they are not true or that the Hebrew Scriptures cannot be taken by faith, just as you are taking the epics of the gods by faith?"

The professor, energized by the debate, expounded. "The Hebrew Scriptures are a masterpiece, a watertight philosophy that claims their God as supreme, His laws as irrevocable, and the future ultimately controlled by Him. Yes, they are a masterpiece; but if one believes it, one becomes narrow-minded. But of course that is how Yahweh wants His followers to be, so that is supposed to be acceptable. The Hebrew Scriptures ignore the other facts around us. They do not even recognize the other gods. They say that there are no other gods at all."

Daniel challenged, "But *what if* the Scriptures are correct?"

The professor chuckled. "Belteshazzar, if the Hebrew Scriptures are correct, I face damnation! If we are all a little more open-minded, we can glean the good from all religions. Class dismissed."

One of their courses featured a master sorcerer. He claimed to be in direct contact with some of the more dreadful gods and could strike death at will upon whomever he wished. Rumor had it that he had died in the temple of Moloch during a human sacrifice, had laid out there on the floor in front of the altar, and had been left for that day and part of the next because no one was willing to touch his body to carry him away. Then the following afternoon, he had sprung to life again.

Historical Observations

[7]*The temples were objects of special focus for Nebuchadnezzar. He devoted himself to the completion of Etemenanki/Tower of Babel/ Temple of Marduk. Construction of this ziggurat had begun in the time of Nebuchadnezzar I, six hundred years earlier. It stood as a ruin until the reign of Esarhaddon of Assyria, who resumed building about 680 BC but was unable to finish it. Nebuchadnezzar was able to complete the whole temple.*

The dimensions of Etemenanki are found in the Esagila tablet, which was found in the late nineteenth century. Its base measured about three hundred feet on each side, and it was three hundred feet in height! There were five terrace-like gradations, and the actual temple stood on top. This was about twice as high at the next highest temple in Babylon.

There is speculation that the lions' den or other prisonlike facilities were built under or into the base of this temple to Marduk, the patron god of Babylon. The gods were important to Nebuchadnezzar. He also built many smaller temples in Babylon and throughout the country.

Daniel and his friends simply did not know what to make of these things. The next day, they were to participate in a class with this sorcerer, and they dreaded it. Those in the class before theirs came away oohing and aahing. He had made a classmate float in midair! Daniel wondered if it could be a trick.

When the time came in their class, a volunteer was selected from the audience and laid down at the front of the class. The sorcerer invoked the gods, shouted, and spoke unintelligible words. Nothing happened for at least ten minutes. The sorcerer eyed the students. "Someone here is inhibiting the work of the gods. The gods are displeased! They won't honor you with this spectacle because someone does not believe or is invoking an enemy god! Damnation to you! A curse be on your heads! Away with you all!" Immediately the students bolted from their seats and rushed from the room.

That night there was elation in the room of the four Hebrews. "Our God *is* real!"

"Did you see that?"

"The class before ours saw the body float, but he couldn't do it in our class and it was because of our presence!"

"No, it was because of our God's presence—our God, the most high God!"

Back in the classroom the next day, the Hebrews were more courageous and also more curious as to how the professors might respond to some of their questions. At the right moment, Daniel brought up the following point: "Are there any other gods who are known for their prophecies?"

"Not exactly," responded the professor, "but many of them know the future."

"How do we know that?"

"Because in the epics, it is told."

"Are there any gods who had mere men write down what was going to happen in the future?"

"Okay, I know where you are going with this, and the answer is no."

Another pupil raised his hand. "How do we know that the Hebrew prophets didn't write the things down after they happened?"

The teacher answered, "There are some who believe that is what happened; however, most of us who have studied the scrolls will concur that they are, in fact, much older than the date of the occurrences that they predicted. In all due respect to the Hebrews, Yahweh is a god, and He should be recognized as such."

Daniel's hand was back up. "Sir, from what you are saying, Yahweh is the only God that we can really, physically prove to have known the future before it happened." The teacher reluctantly agreed.

Daniel continued, "Sir, are you aware of any prophecies that were incorrect?"

The teacher responded, "I am not. However, that remains to be seen, for there are many unfulfilled prophecies. Take, for instance, your release from captivity."

Everyone chuckled; Daniel cordially mused at the humor also but continued, saying, "I guess if I'm forced to consider believing in the epics by faith or believing by faith in the God who knows the future, it is not a hard choice for me."

The teacher surprised Daniel again by responding, "You've got a good mind, Belteshazzar. Keep it open."

It was supposed that Nebu, the god of wisdom, learning, and books, had taken a special role in the development of modern Babylon because he was the patron god of Nebuchadnezzar. There was a statue of the god Nebu there on campus. Although the Hebrew boys didn't believe in the gods, the statue reminded them that the day was coming when they would stand before the great king Nebuchadnezzar and be tested.

Much of their learning was both challenging and enjoyable. Math, biological sciences, agricultural sciences, architectural designs and calculations, mechanical drawings, literature from many other places, languages and language roots, and the relatively new field of Greek philosophies all offered a feast for their hungry minds. Nebuchadnezzar had conquered most of the kingdoms of the earth, and their wealth of literature and knowledge had been brought to Babylon.

The students and scholars had access to original copies of much of the learning available in their world, Jewish scrolls included. Not many were interested in the Hebrew Scriptures, so they were easily accessible to the four Hebrews during scheduled study hours.

As time passed, unbeknownst to Daniel, Hananiah, Mishael, and Azariah, they were often the topic of conversation among their teachers.

"Did you hear about the answer Meshach gave the other day to the pi-squared equation as it applied to leverage in the Egyptian example? I couldn't believe it."

"They have a special interest in everything that is difficult. The hanging gardens project is almost beyond human conceivability. Do you see how their eyes gleam whenever we let them help with the thought processes and calculations?"

"What about their constant challenging of the epics? They have good reasons behind their statements, even if they are wrong."

"For being some of the brightest students we've ever had, they are certainly humble and respectful."

"The other students don't like them very much."

"You're wrong. Everyone likes them. You can't help but like them. Some of the other students are jealous."

"They won't say the prayers to the gods."

"I made them say them in my class; I told them it was their term grade! They had every one of them memorized perfectly."

"Well, they won't say them out by the statues of the gods or by the altars."

"They know the information, but they don't believe it. They read their own Scriptures in the library."

"They cling to Yahweh."

"So what? Babylon has temples to fifty-six gods. Who cares who they worship?"

"There are plenty of people who care about that, and the God of the Hebrews is not a popular god. It will get them into trouble. You know how Babylonian politics work: first the king, then the prophets of Marduk. If you want to be anybody, you've got to keep on the good side of both!"

"Anyway, when the four stand before the king, he may consider raising our salaries. If Yahweh is a force to be reckoned with, His power is clearly working through them." Several of the professors nodded in agreement.

The day came to stand before the king. Of the one hundred and fifty beginning students, there were only forty-three who were now to have the privilege of standing before the king. The others who were deemed less worthy had received many other important types of clerical jobs, but they would not have the chance to serve directly in the king's court.

New clothes were issued to the select few. The professors gave last-minute advice. The young men were briefed on how to address the king, how to stand in his presence, how to step forward, how to step back, and so forth.

As for the king, this was a delightful day for him. He had set aside his busy schedule and dedicated the entire day to evaluating these graduates. It was his personal joy to learn. He prided himself on his vast array of knowledge. Nevertheless, he asked for summaries of all the subject matter to be prepared for him ahead of time so that he could systematically question the young men and verify the answers.

Historical Observations
Babylonian Math

[8]*In one example which was found, presumably for the purpose of teaching, a scribe wrote, "Two-thirds of two-thirds of a certain quantity of barley is taken, one hundred units of barley are added, and the original quantity recovered. Solve the problem."*

The solution given by the scribe is to compute 0; 40 times 0; 40 to get 0; 26, 40. Subtract this from 1; 00 to get 0; 33, 20. Look up the reciprocal of 0; 33, 20 in a table to get 1;48. Multiply 1;48 by 1,40 to get the answer 3,0.

It is difficult to understand the scribe's reasoning unless one translates it into modern algebra. We have to solve 2/3 2/3 x + 100 = x, which is, as the scribe knew, equivalent to solving (1 - 4/9)x = 100. This is why the scribe computed 2/3 of 2/3, subtracted the answer from 1 to get (1 - 4/9), then looked up 1/(1 - 4/9); and so x was found from 1/(1 - 4/9) multiplied by 100 giving 180 (this is 1; 48 times 1, 40 to get 3, 0 in sexagesimal). To solve a quadratic equation, the Babylonians used standard formulas. They considered two types of quadratic equations, namely x2 + bx = c and x2 - bx = c, where b, c were positive but not necessarily integers. The form that their solutions took was, respectively, x = √[(b/2)2 + c] - (b/2) and x = √[(b/2)2 + c] + (b/2). This was the basic math that Daniel and his friends studied!

The students filed into the brightly lit throne room. Sunlight streamed in through the arched windows and glistened off the golden urns and vases. Couches and tables were draped in bright silks. It was hard to concentrate on the task at hand. Daniel prayed for the outcome of this test to be as the Lord saw fit. He knew his friends were praying the same way. As he thought about it, he realized that every student there was praying to some god or another.

Nebuchadnezzar was cordial yet scary. Even with his perfect manners, pride seemed to remove all possibility of kindness. He was straight to the point and proud, yet he was pleasant. It was like a game to him. The professors were there too, off to one side; this was a big day for them as well. They could lose their jobs or their heads, or they could be acknowledged and commended.

Nebuchadnezzar started systematically calling the students by name from the list before him. He asked them each seven questions per round about different subjects and had the scribe take note of how many they got right. In the morning sessions, most answered many of the questions correctly, but Belteshazzar, Shadrach, Meshach, and Abednego were the only ones who didn't miss any. To Daniel's surprise, at lunchtime about half the students who had been interviewed by the king ate with them at the servants' table.

In the afternoon sessions, the king was in a jovial mood and was quite intent on reaching the outer limits of their knowledge. Two hours into the drills, his strategy changed. He read complex mathematical problems and asked the first person with the answer to raise his hand. Approximations were accepted, since this was an oral drill. Often one of the Hebrews was the first with his hand up. Each answer was correct, until Meshach stepped forward to answer a difficult mathematical question.

"Your Majesty, the answer is $1/(1 - 4/9)$."

"Wrong! The answer is $1/(1 + 4/9)$."

Meshach stepped back; he was shocked. As others thought about it more and more, so were they. The king began asking another question, but Meshach stepped forward.

The king stated, "You challenge me?"

"Yes, sir. The answer has to be $1/(1$ *minus* $4/9)$."

"Mathematicians, work the problem again."

They did, very carefully. Within moments they reported, "Oh king, forgive us for the mistake on your copy, but Meshach is correct." Everyone relaxed again, and the questioning continued. By the end of the afternoon, Nebuchadnezzar had narrowed his questioning to the four Hebrew scholars.

They answered question after question correctly on every possible subject. At times Nebuchadnezzar would ask questions pertaining to their personal beliefs. At these times, they respectfully stated their opinions, even though they knew their positions did not match Nebuchadnezzar's.

Then tensions rose as Nebuchadnezzar stated, "As you know, Marduk is the patron god of Babylon. We must pay homage to him. Belteshazzar, you are named after him. Pray to Marduk for me. Pray the consecration-and-blessings prayer."

The professors looked at one another in dismay. The day had gone so perfectly so far—but now this. Daniel eyed his comrades, then turned toward the king. With eyes wide open, and with an overly monotone voice, he repeated the prayer, word for word.

Nebuchadnezzar stared at Daniel and said, "Belteshazzar, you neither bowed down, nor did you close your eyes."

Anxiety grew, but Daniel answered, "I did not bow down, nor did I close my eyes because Marduk is not my god, oh king."

Nebuchadnezzar hesitated for a moment then laughed. "He's not my god either. My god is Nebu. At least you know the prayer if you ever need to use it!" Everyone breathed a sigh of relief. By the end of the exams, Nebuchadnezzar had found the four Hebrews ten times wiser than all the others and ordered them immediately instated into his royal service.

[7] *[http://www.britannica.com/bps/browse/alpha/e/59]*
[8] *[www-groups.dcs.st-and.ac.uk/~history/HistTopics/Babylonian_ mathematics.html]*

CHAPTER 6

Into the Real World

Most of the graduates received posts in the Babylonian administrative machine. Along with this came a small allowance—and much prestige. Daniel and his three friends received work assignments, but in addition, because of their excellent performance on the day of the exams, they were also appointed to the king's council of wise men, astrologers, magicians, enchanters, and sorcerers. This group of almost one hundred was mostly an elite collection of backbiting, egocentrical old men. They had high salaries, higher egos, and special access to the king. Daniel, Hananiah, Mishael, and Azariah were as out of place and about as secure as lambs in a den of lions.

The first few times the wise men were summoned, the four Hebrews were also called. They went to the council but were forced to stay near the back and were not permitted by the others to participate or even see what was going on. Soon the leaders of the king's council decided not to even call the four Hebrews. The councilmen were relieved when the king didn't miss them and even more relieved when, over time, the Hebrews didn't complain about being cut out.

Historical Observations

[9]*The Babylonians inherited much of their technology from the Sumerians, especially in the areas of irrigation and agriculture, which were the most important areas for the national economy. In order to manage agriculture, they had to be able to make maps, perform precise surveys, and do advanced mathematical calculations for irrigation.*

They used a well-developed though awkward mathematical system founded on a base 60 numerical system, as opposed to the base-10 system now in worldwide used. As mentioned earlier, it was the Babylonians who divided the day into twenty-four hours, the hour into sixty minutes, and the minute into sixty seconds. We still use this facet of their system today.

In order to be well prepared for different seasons, when there was a chance of flood or a chance of little water, they developed almanacs. These were used in great detail and were tied in with a good calendar system that had largely been developed by the Sumerians before them.

As for Daniel and his friends, they couldn't have cared less about becoming one of those stuffy old men. They wanted to work, to be profitable servants for those who were over them, and to honor their Lord. However, they were soon to discover that the gray areas they had faced in college were nothing compared to what they'd face in the working world.

Babylon's main source of income was agriculture. Over the centuries, ever since the Sumerians, irrigation and fertilization practices had been cultivated and honed to a fine science. There in the middle of the desert, the expansive flatlands around the Euphrates had become an oasis of blooming fields with produce of all kinds. Trade and commerce were also important but were secondary to agriculture.

Hananiah, Michael and Azariah soon became known by their Babylonian names, Shadrach, Meshach, and Abednego. Daniel was different; he hated being called Belteshazzar and would correct people, saying, "Just call me Daniel; it's shorter."

Shadrach was appointed as a servant paid by the king to assist the main procurator of fertilizers. Shadrach's boss was responsible for the fertilizers used on the royal gardens and fields that produced food directly used by the local Babylonian government. The man was glad at first and welcomed Shadrach's help. However, this positive relationship between manager and assistant did not last as long as Shadrach had hoped it would.

In Shadrach's very first week on the job, his boss explained to him the measuring system and also the accompanying accounting system, including the value placed on the different weights and types of fertilizers. Although it was a little complicated, Shadrach soon caught on.

The lighter fertilizers, such as dried manure and dried mulch, were brought in baskets and measured only in volume; no weight was recorded. Other heavier mineral fertilizers were measured out and leveled off in weight-count boxes. Each boxful was a precalculated weight, so the boxfuls were merely counted and multiplied. The heavier materials were loaded onto oxcarts, the lighter ones onto donkeys, and sent to their respective destinations. Small parchment receipts were signed and countersigned; then Shadrach would deliver them to the accounting wing of the palace for official recording at the end of each week. At the end of the month, the transactions were summarized and etched in clay.

Shadrach's boss commanded approximately a hundred slaves and a few freemen in his operation. Technically, he worked for the king, but he acted more like an independent contractor. As the fertilizer came in, he would measure or weigh most of it, but some he would remove without its being weighed or measured. At first Shadrach did not question this because he wasn't sure who owned the supplies or who received payment for them. However, Shadrach began to receive complaints from the vendors that the weights and measurements were not correct. After three weeks of careful observation, Shadrach realized what was happening and confronted his boss, citing numerous examples.

The boss was angry at first but then lightened up. "You've been a big help around here. You already know how to run the whole yard. I wasn't really sure if I wanted a partner, but now I must admit that I'm enjoying it." He walked into his private office and returned a moment later, dropping a small bag of coins in front of Shadrach, saying, "We all work for the king; we may as well enjoy it together."

As he turned to leave, Shadrach called after him, "You do not have a partner."

"Son, you signed false statements just like I did."

"Yes, but I did not know that I was signing false statements."

"Do you think they will believe that? Don't forget, stealing from the king is treason. Of course, part of our game is stealing *for* the king—we just don't give him all we take for him."

"I am not going to sign any more false statements, nor am I going to help you steal for the king or yourself."

"What is your problem, Shadrach? Are you so much better than everyone else? What are you going to do? Turn me in? I'll have you killed—you know I will."

Shadrach thought for a long moment then said, "I'm just not going to help you cheat anymore. I can't do it."

"Okay, then you are confined to this room. If I see you in the receiving yard, I'll arrange for you to have a fatal accident. Understand?"

Shadrach nodded. The boss turned to leave then looked back and sarcastically stated, "Oh, Shadrach, I've just had a change of heart. I am not going to steal from anyone forever and ever. Every receipt that comes in here for you to sign will be totally, 100 percent correct. Now you can sign the receipts with peace of mind."

There were many ways to steal in the fertilizer business. Both suppliers and receivers occasionally complained to Shadrach, but he would tell them there was nothing he could do, since he was not allowed out of the office. He suggested that they complain to the authorities, but as far as he knew, no one ever did. It was not worth the risk.

Each week when Shadrach turned in the receipts, he would drop hints like, "I am not allowed into the yard, but these are the receipts that have come to me," or "I am signing this receipt, but I could not personally verify the merchandise." Those receiving the receipts in the governmental accounting offices always seemed more intent on getting the signed parchment than they did on hearing Shadrach's excuses.

Meshach's stars all lined up—or at least that's what some of the other students said—because he was made an apprentice to the head architect for the hanging gardens project! Next to the dream of human flight, the challenges of the hanging gardens ran a close second. The head architect was a scientist through and through. Though lavished on all sides with money and goods, he appeared not to notice. His objective was to create a layered forest of lush green plants—350 feet in the air so as to be seen by all those approaching Babylon. It was to be an opulent, layered Eden-like paradise.

The year was now 600 BC. The foundations for the "gardens in the sky" had been laid three years earlier in 603 BC and had originally been projected to cheer up Nebuchadnezzar's home-sick wife. Amyitis, daughter of the king of the Medes, had married Nebuchadnezzar to create an alliance between the nations. The land she came from was green and mountainous, and she found the flat sunbaked terrain of Mesopotamia depressing. The king decided to re-create her homeland by building an artificial mountain with rooftop gardens, beautiful waterfalls, and small cool arbors.

Only a wild dreamer like Nebuchadnezzar could have thought up the idea. It was considered by many as a totally absurd dream and a feat that was just as impossible. Eventually, however, the same master architect who had designed the newer waterways under the walls and created flowing water through the middle of the city had taken on the challenge of the sky gardens. It had become his mission in life.

He and Meshach soon became fast friends. Meshach called him Bezalel one day in fun, and he had stopped cold.

"Why, thank you!"

"Do you know who Bezalel was?"

"Of course I do! He was the craftsman who made the temple ornaments for the Hebrew God after they came out of Egypt!"

"I'm surprised you know that!"

"Any true craftsman alive would know that. Bezalel, Bezalel! Call me that anytime." That became his name from then on, at least for those in the inner circle.

Bezalel seemed to have no personal life. He supposedly had a family, but Meshach saw no signs of one. He was totally consumed with his work and the hundreds of scientific experiments to be performed.

How much water would be consumed by a fifty-foot eucalyptus tree on a hot day in the desert? How much water would be consumed by a twenty-five-foot pine tree on a hot day in the desert?

How could he get an oak tree to flourish? How many cubic feet of root space would it need? What would be the lateral pressure on twelve-foot-thick sidewalls if the oak tree was forty feet high, weighed four tons above the ground, and was being pushed by a twenty-mile-per-hour wind? A thirty-mile-per-hour wind?

What type of soil would hold the tree up in these winds? If the tap roots were 75 percent of the tree height, then a fifty-foot tree would need almost forty feet of space straight down for the taproot. This would mean huge hollow pillars filled with dirt. It would also mean designing much of the hanging gardens around the large trees and their roots.

How could he keep the water-sensitive plants from becoming waterlogged? Would sideways osmosis take away the excess water for more than a furlong, or would he have to have drains more often?

How many pine trees could flourish in a certain section of space in the tier below the shade of the oaks? There would be shade from the afternoon desert sun on the east side, so that meant the pine trees must be planted there.

How many tons of green matter would eventually be growing? Around 150,000?

It would take a small stream river of water flowing from the top down to keep everything green there in the desert.

The biggest feat of all was how to propel enough water to the top to form a small stream. It could not be done—but it had to be done! There had to be a way. Slave labor carrying buckets was out of the question. One thousand slaves carrying water all day up four hundred steps could not provide half of the water needed. Would a 750-foot chain with buckets dipping into the Euphrates do the job? How about a water screw powered by the flow of the Euphrates? What about a series of dumping tanks with long leverage arms and with slaves dumping them from one to the other all the way to the top? What about a round clay channel with a chain with large leather washers on it and pulleys on both ends? The weight of the water in the tubing would be 3.7 tons, plus the friction of the washers. If there was 40 percent back-spillage in one minute, the chain would have to be cranked at 330 feet per minute to get half the water to the top. There was no propulsion device capable of this rapid power.

Meshach had the privilege of helping Bezalel build many of these prototypes to scale. They tested and tested and tested some more. Bezalel spent a good portion of his time out on the three-hundred-by-three-hundred-foot site, correcting, instructing, and verifying blueprints. Then he would go back to the laboratory, as he called it, and join forces with Meshach for as long as he could.

They were running into many architectural snags now that the monstrosity was beginning to rise from the ground. The pitch they had planned on using was seeping when they tested it with water and dirt and was already causing foundation deterioration. The bricks on some of the inner columns had to be torn down because they had not been baked properly. The level was off on the north side, and Bezalel hadn't yet figured out why. They had to effectively solve the seepage problems, or the office spaces under the would-be gardens would always be wet once the water started flowing. Problems, problems, and more problems!

Historical Observations
Bezalel was of a noble line. His father, Hur, was a son of Caleb from his union with Miriam, Moses' sister. Hur gave his life to

restrain Israel from the worship of the golden calf. As a reward for his martyrdom, his son Bezalel was to build the tabernacle, and one of his later descendants, King Solomon, was to build the temple at Jerusalem. Bezalel was not only of a distinguished family but also was himself a man of distinction possessed of wisdom, insight, and understanding.

—Jewish Tradition

"The Lord said to Moses, "I have chosen Bezalel son of Uri, the son of Hur, of the tribe of Judah. I have filled him with the Spirit of God, with skill, ability and knowledge in all kinds of crafts. He is skilled in artistic designs of gold, silver and bronze, and is able to cut and set stones, to work in wood, and to complete all kinds of craftsmanship."

Difficult as his work was, Bezalel thoroughly enjoyed it. Meshach soon learned that Bezalel had another, much larger set of problems.

One of the astrologers entered and addressed Bezalel, "The king wants to know your progress and also wants to know what the stars are saying concerning your success."

"We're making good progress."

"You need materials, don't you?"

"No, I have all that I have requested."

"I happen to know that you do need materials, and you need them delivered to the south side at 8 p.m. tomorrow."

Bezalel stared at him and stated, "Again?"

"Here is the list. See to it that they get delivered—*if* you want the gods to favor you."

Bezalel stared at him warily. As the man left, Bezalel called a servant and gave him the list and the order to carry it out.

When they were alone again, Meshach said, "You know, this could backfire on you. Next they'll be blackmailing you for squandering the king's resources."

"Do you think I haven't thought about that? Do you think I like this? I hate it. I just want to do my job. They all know that the king will give me anything I ask for in the construction of these hanging gardens. I don't have any choice."

"Maybe you do."

"Believe me, Meshach, I don't!"

The city of Babylon was protected by a double wall, with the great wall being 324 feet high and 86 feet wide. Chariot races could be held on the wall, and in times of danger, troops could be swiftly moved to points of attack. The city was so expansive that twenty-five bronze gates were in the walls on each side. It was ironic that Bezalel had designed parts of the great Babylonian fortress for the protection of Nebuchadnezzar's father and now Nebuchadnezzar, but he could not protect *himself* against the likes of the king's councilmen.

Bezalel continued, "I am important enough to be indispensable at this present time. Did you ever think about that, Meshach? The king really does need me, or he thinks he does. That sounds like a wonderful position to be in, doesn't it? Well, it's not! One of Marduk's more powerful priests took my wife to be his. Actually, she left me for him. I could have divorced her easily, but they denied my request. I have two young boys with this wife. The priest requires half my wages to 'look after' my children."

Meshach asked, "Why don't you just hire someone to look after them yourself for a lot less money?"

"When he says 'look after' them, he means not turning them over to the priests of Moloch for child sacrifice."

"Oh."

"They took my mother to another town. I hear from her on occasion, when they want me to; she is also part of their leverage. Anyone I like is in danger of being kidnapped for ransom. That may someday even include you, Meshach. If it does, I'm sorry. That's just how it is."

"If you went to the king, don't you think he'd give you justice, if he sees you as indispensable?"

"I'm afraid of Nebuchadnezzar, but yes, I think he would give me justice if I could prove something. But in the midst of the process, my kids could be tortured and killed. So would my mother. It is not worth it."

"What are you going to do?"

"Meshach, now what do you *think* I'm going to do? I'm going to build the hanging gardens, and they will become one of the marvels of the world. After that I am going to retire into obscurity and become as unimportant as possible. Then maybe I'll have a little peace. If the king forgets about me, so will everyone else."

Meshach didn't talk for a long time, except for the few comments that needed to be made concerning the model they were developing. At last Meshach said, "Bezalel, don't worry about me. My God will look after me."

Without looking up, Bezalel muttered, "Dreamer."

Historical Observations

[12]*Babylonian society, like most societies at that time, was governed by an absolute monarch who was over all areas of life. He was legislator, judge, administrator, and warrior. He was directly in charge of governing the system below him. He usually chose his closest friends as co-workers and governors. Local administration was performed by mayors and councils.*

The courts of Babylonia were central for justice. Each court maintained between one and four judges. Appeals could be directed only toward the king, who might or might not hear them. When he did hear the complaint, the judge was required to justify his verdict. Punishment varied from financial penalties, to death or mutilation, to flogging, to reduction to slavery, or to banishment.

Many of the rulings recorded in clay tablets involved indemnities. The fine varied from three to thirty times the value of the object to be restored. The wealthier individuals generally received the larger indemnities.

Abednego and Daniel were assigned duties working in the king's monitoring and control of the caravans. They rarely saw each other during the day because of their different responsibilities. They worked the same system, but at opposite ends.

Abednego was in the field and accompanied the soldiers who inspected the caravans. The tax collectors worked alongside Abednego and the inspection soldiers. Unlike Shadrach, Abednego had the upper hand in the area for which he was responsible. He quickly became a favorite with the merchants. He would estimate the taxes according to the royal collection tables and give the estimates to the tax collectors. He would also give these same estimates to the merchants, who would then have good reason to argue when the tax collectors wanted more. Extortion was cut in half within six months of Abednego's arrival on the job. He would have probably lost his job or life because of jealous critics except for the fact that the merchants bragged on him so much that it reached the king's hearing and he was personally commended for the excellent job he was doing.

Abednego knew that some of the soldiers and tax collectors had previously had extortion mechanisms in place, and he avoided conflicts with them whenever possible. He did his best to pick his fights carefully, choosing only soldiers to go with him who he knew would stick to their jobs. He also had his favorite tax collectors, some of whom he had studied with, and although he did not really trust them, he knew they would think twice about double-crossing him.

Daniel was placed in the palace as one of the monitors who received the merchandise on which Abednego, among others, had estimated a tax. Daniel was among those who were responsible for forming contracts of payment, issuing receipts, verifying receipt of taxes paid, signing payment orders, and executing broken contracts through the three-judge legal system.

There were constant disputes in Daniel's sector. Merchants complained about not being paid, others complained about not receiving the goods they had paid for, and still others complained that the payment was not in kind or in exchangeable merchandise. And, of course, there were the lawyers in the middle, lying through their teeth and protesting whatever proofs the other side brought up.

The more serious cases were usually out of Daniel's hands and sent to the already overloaded and equally corrupt legal system.

Daniel worked hard to resolve differences between people and to bring compromise where possible. He protected the king's interest but did not overcharge to line his own pockets in the process. Like Abednego, Daniel soon became known as the person to go to if one really wanted justice. He would do what he could. Those involved in extortion schemes carefully avoided both Daniel and Abednego.

Historical Observations

Babylonian cities resembled, to some extent, the modern villages in the Middle East. Most houses were only one story high and were built of mud bricks. Most had no windows toward the street and consisted of several rooms arranged around and opening into an inner courtyard.

Inside the house, one of the rooms would be devoted to the gods. Deceased family members were often buried in the ground of the house, together with items intended to help them in the afterlife.

Closer to the palace and the central markets, there were many two and three-story houses. Babylon was enormous, boasting 196 square miles inside the walls (fourteen miles by fourteen miles). There were irrigated pastures and vineyards within the city walls. It is assumed that there was a wide spread in the value of real estate within the city walls, since buildings of multiple stories were nearer to the palace and central markets and single-story homes farther out.

In the wealthier households, glazed tile was common on the walls and floors, as well as marble and fine woods imported from far away. In the ruins of Babylonian dwellings, many sorts of cosmetics, perfumery, medicines, pharmacological products, and jewelry have been found. During the reigns of Nebuchadnezzar, Belshazzar, Darius the Mede, and Cyrus, there is evidence of much affluence among the population of Babylon

----

Since the four Hebrews had rented a house, they were able to exchange notes during their evenings together. One night they had an especially long talk about corruption and how to deal with it. Shadrach complained, "I am stuck in that stupid room every day with my hands tied. I know my boss is getting rich off the fertilizer that comes in as well as the fertilizer that goes out. I sign the false receipts because I have no proof that they are false. My superiors don't care. If I were a free man, I'd change jobs."

Meshach responded, "I know it's hard, but I know someone who would change jobs with you."

"You would change jobs with me?"

"No, I wouldn't, but Bezalel would if he could!"

"I know; I feel so sorry for that guy!"

"In Babylon, corruption is a way of life. If you need ten of something, you've got to ask for twenty so you can pay people off along the way and end up with what you need."

Abednego spoke up. "It wouldn't have to be that way. We have made a little difference in the tax-collection area. There is still a lot of stealing and extortion, but there is less than there was."

Meshach answered, "Hurrah for you and Daniel—you've dipped a bucket of water out of a sea of corruption! I'm sorry; I did not mean to belittle what you are doing. It is commendable. I'm just being realistic."

Shadrach defended them. "At least they are doing something! I'm just contributing to the problem against my will!"

Daniel entered the conversation. "Corruption is here to stay. We can't avoid it, and we can't change very much of it either. We have to live with it."

The others stared at him. It seemed out of character for Daniel to talk like that. Had he also lost hope? Daniel began a speech that had been going through his mind for a few days. "Remember those judgments we talked about? We were judged in a national judgment for the nation of Israel, and we have suffered greatly. However, God has brought us this far, and He will not abandon us. We will not be judged for the terrible things we see around us every day. But we will be personally judged for our actions and attitudes before God.

"Shadrach, you are doing all you can at this time. Keep dropping hints to superiors. Do what you can to encourage others to report what you suspect, but don't get yourself killed trying to right the wrongs your boss is doing.

"Meshach, you are at the top of the world there with Bezalel, but what if you were to just disappear one of these days and become another pawn in the extortion game? It probably won't happen, but it could. To you, I repeat the verse you know well in the second chronicles of the kings of Israel [28:20] *Be strong and courageous, and stay at your job. Don't be frightened by the size of the task, for the Lord your God is with you. He will not forsake you and will see to it that everything gets finished correctly.* Halfway through, the other boys had joined in and recited the verse with him; it was a memorized favorite.

Daniel went on. "Abednego, sometimes I worry about you. You are so self-confident and so much younger than most of the men you deal with. I'm not sure what gives you the courage to call it as it is when you are surrounded by merchants, tax collectors, soldiers of the king, and soldiers of the caravan, each with different interests. I fear some days that I may never see you again. Then my fear quickly subsides when I think of where we've come from and where we are now. If an angry soldier or merchant does end your life, I'll know that our God has had a purpose in it thus far and will continue to be faithful to us.

"None of us know the future, but I admonish you to trust in the Lord no matter what. We cannot change much of the world around us. The God in whom we trust is able to deliver us, but even if He does not, we will serve Him." The others nodded, and all bowed in a prayer of recommitment to Yahweh, the most high God, the God of Israel.

[9]*http://looklex.com/e.o/babylonia.htm*
[10]*[http://ancienthistory.about.com/library/bl/bl_text_jewslegends3a 8.htm]*
[11]*Bible, Exodus 31:1–5 paraphrase*
[12]*[http://looklex.com/e.o/babylonia.htm]*

CHAPTER 7

Arioch, Captain of the Guard

At times Daniel would have to leave the premises and be taken to another location to inspect merchandise or to verify some discrepancy. His escort was Arioch [air-e-ock], the captain of the royal guard, or someone assigned by him. Arioch was not a friendly person, but he had the reputation of being straightforward and offensively honest. The fact that the king trusted him said a lot, because Nebuchadnezzar trusted almost no one. Daniel liked Arioch but always treated him with professional courtesy and the distance he seemed to desire. Daniel did not know it at the time, but Arioch had quite a story of his own.

Of Macedonian origin and the son of a farmer, he was just in the wrong place at the wrong time. Coming from a small village in a rural setting, Arioch had known the taste of hard work and sweat all of his young life. At the tender age of sixteen, he had experienced a similar fate as Daniel had faced a decade later.

The ruthless Assyrian army had been passing through the area when without warning a contingent of soldiers rode into Arioch's family's humble courtyard and began taking whatever they desired. At first Arioch's father had offered no resistance, knowing it was futile. However, when the soldiers began breaking their pottery and destroying their belongings, his father had politely objected. At first there was no reaction, but then the leader began to yell and swing his sword. A few short minutes later, Arioch's family lay dead or dying.

Arioch had escaped only because after a very narrow miss by a soldier's sword, he had run away. Two soldiers had followed for a short distance, but they were no match for sixteen-year-old Arioch's athletic abilities. The ones with horses in the group concluded the boy was not worth their time.

As soon as he determined that the soldiers had gone, Arioch returned to find that everyone in his family except for his mother was dead. He did what he could to stop her bleeding. It appeared that a sword had been run all the way through her lower abdomen, as there was a small protruding tear in the flesh on her back.

Arioch cried and cared for her intermittently the rest of the day, through the night, and into the next morning, when she died shortly after daybreak. Arioch never slept. His mother was weak and in and out of consciousness, but many of those hours, even through the night, they spent quietly talking with each other. His mother seemed to have an emotional strength in death that he felt he would never have.

At one point, Arioch had said, "Mama, I want to die with you."

As sternly as he had ever heard her talk, she answered, "Do you think that would make me proud? You'd be dying for no reason, just like I am. Make your life count. Do what you know to be right. Quit blaming yourself for running. If you had not run, you'd also be dead, and my sorrow would be much greater. I would be bleeding to death just the same, all by myself. You did the right thing, Arioch. Always do the right thing." Although they talked several times after that, it was that conversation that Arioch would carry with him in his memory and would be the overriding factor in difficult decisions throughout his life.

The next morning, when Arioch realized his mother was dead, he cried and then fell to sleep from sheer emotional and physical exhaustion. After what seemed to be a very brief slumber, Arioch was awakened by a neighbor poking him with a herding stick. Arioch woke with a start and began to get up, until he realized he was holding his dead mother.

The neighbor spoke, "I *thought* you were alive. Why didn't they kill you?"

In a surprisingly normal tone, he answered, "Because I ran."

The neighbor said nothing, but Arioch's own words cut him through to the core of his soul. The feeling was so horrendous that Arioch felt a change within his spirit. He knew at that moment, in spite of everything his mother had said, that he would *never* run again. Death would be better.

Yes, death would have been much better. Death would not have been bad at all. Death would have spared him from two more gruesome enemies: fear and remorse. It was quite clear now that he would never again allow fear to influence his decisions, nor would he ever again take a course of action that would cause him to suffer such remorse.

Other neighbors showed up, and Arioch numbly helped them bury his family. The remorse was so tight in his throat and head that he could not talk, cry, or even think. After the shallow graves received their all too lifelike victims, Arioch went home with a neighbor and slept for a few hours; then, feeling slightly more human, he went to a quiet place on the nearby hill to think—and pray.

He could not actually remember ever praying to the gods. He didn't know which one to pray to for sure, as his family had not been particularly religious though they had believed in all the deities for good measure. There was a compulsion in his heart to pray to a caring and understanding god, but he didn't know if one of those existed. He also wanted to address a deity who could look after his family in the afterlife, but there was some confusion there too, as he wasn't sure which one had control of that part of the spiritual realm. He knew that he could try for the big gods like Re, the Egyptian sun god, or Marduk, the Babylonian god who seemed to be credited for having conquered the other gods in a cosmic battle of some sort. But those gods were likely too busy.

An idea came to him that he could pray to "the most high god," and if that god was a powerful god—truly the most high—he would hear the prayer because he wouldn't allow any of the other less powerful gods to intercept his praise. It seemed to be a reasonably logical angle for getting the deity's attention.

So Arioch prayed every prayer he could think of and addressed them all to the most high god. It made him feel better, and eventually he got up and walked around, absently throwing stones and breaking sticks. Later he would feel like the afternoon had been wasted and that praying had been silly, but by sundown he felt a little better. He fell asleep right there where he had prayed.

The next day, he determined to return home to run the farm or what there was left of it. They had never had very much, and the land was not even rightfully theirs, as his parents had been squatters—although it was theirs as much as it was anyone's. Arioch took inventory of the damage and began to make some decisions. The team of oxen and the oxcart were gone. All three dozen sheep were missing, and so were the goats. Inside the house, a small built-in grain box had been emptied. The wine was gone, the oil was gone, and almost all the household furnishings were either gone or broken. He found eight measures of flour that they had inadvertently missed. The bucket from the well was lying on the ground beside the well. Evidently they had used it then cut off the rope and taken it with them.

Arioch fought depression with anger. How could people do this to other people who had never done anything bad to deserve it? He longed to get even. The rest of the day he spent cleaning up the house and taking the broken items to an area near the grave sites. Somehow it just seemed appropriate to pile the broken household items near his deceased family. There seemed to be many parallels as to why this was appropriate, but he did not really want to spell them out in his mind—it was all too fresh and painful.

At sundown he went to the creek to see if any of the sheep would return. When one sheep and four goats came for water, Arioch was overjoyed. He led them back to the sheep pen and went inside the house to sleep. Alone and frightened, he couldn't settle down for the night. An hour after dark, he went to the neighbor's house and spent the night with him and his family.

The next morning, Arioch awoke to the sounds of sheepherding and animals being tended. Instinctively he went out to help the neighbor with his chores, although the neighbor did not seem to want him around. He stayed and helped anyway.

Arioch soon realized that the neighbor had more livestock than before. Upon closer observation, Arioch counted at least six sheep that been his father's! Arioch flushed with anger then regained composure and said nothing. How could the neighbor steal his sheep? Just because they had gotten away from the Assyrians didn't mean they were fair game for anyone who found them!

Arioch politely asked the neighbor if he could borrow a rope for his well since the Assyrians had taken his. The neighbor gladly supplied this need. Arioch ate a cheese-and-biscuit breakfast, thanked his neighbor for his kindness, and left, never to return.

A week went by. Arioch killed a goat and dried the meat. He traded some of the meat for oil to make corncakes. Life was not worth living. If it had not been for his mother's words, death would have been an escape. He couldn't stay where memories of his family haunted him day and night. He guessed now that the most high god had not heard his prayers. Oh well, he hadn't known the right words to say—what could one expect? Perhaps the whole "gods" thing was just a figment of his imagination.

Then, out of nowhere seemed to çome a golden opportunity! A caravan was approaching, or was it a caravan? From a distance, he saw several oxcarts and perhaps thirty people on foot driving almost that many horses and mules. As they approached, at those times when the breeze cleared the air, Arioch began to see armed men, both mounted and on foot. His heart sank.

Then, out of the depths of his soul, he felt strength. If they attacked him, he would fight to the death and welcome it with great luster. As the caravan entered the courtyard, Arioch stood his ground, his fist gripping tightly to his herding stick. The leader motioned for the procession to stop, looked around sadly, slowly got off his horse, and took a few steps to the well. Then, sitting down on the side of the well, he said, "Did they kill your family? How many of them were there?" Bewildered, Arioch did not answer.

The man continued, "We are following the path of destruction those bandits left behind. When we catch them, they will pay for what they've done."

Arioch spoke, "The men who came through here were Assyrian soldiers."

"No, those renegades were *dressed* like Assyrian soldiers. They were mere bandits. The Assyrian army has a price out on their heads. If you were older, I'd let you come with us and take your revenge."

"I'm old enough," Arioch replied coldly.

The man looked away as if to ponder this statement then said, "May I have your permission to draw water for our men and animals?"

"What if I say no?" replied Arioch.

"If you say no, we will move on; this is obviously your well."

"Help yourself to the water."

For several minutes, Arioch sat on a log, watching the newcomers. The men were drawing water and were topping off their already plentiful water supply. The animals were drinking but were not particularly thirsty. Arioch realized that they would have had access to water three miles back when they crossed the creek.

The leader come over and sat down beside him. Though dressed in civilian clothes, he was accompanied by Assyrian soldiers. Finally Arioch asked, "Who are you?"

"Now that's a good question, because I've done just about everything one can do."

Arioch got specific. "What are you doing right now, with this caravan?"

"I am bounty-hunting those bandits. Everyone here will share in the reward, once we catch them."

Arioch's interest was heightened. "I will go with you!"

The leader calmly stated, "Let me see your weapons."

Arioch looked down and said, "I have no weapons."

"Have you ever fought with a sword?"

"No."

Irritated, the man objected, "Now, how do you expect me to take you with me? You've never fought, and you don't own any weapons!" Arioch did not answer.

"I'll tell you what. I will pick out a guy about your size and have you wrestle him. If you give up first, you stay behind. If you make him give in, you go. No weapons—I don't want to lose any men."

Arioch eyed him closely then said, "Let's do it!"

The leader of the caravan picked out a stout man of about the same height. Arioch guessed him to be in his midtwenties. Unsure of himself yet quite determined to win, Arioch threw himself into the fight. The next thing he knew he was on the ground, looking up at the sky, with a wiry mass of muscle straddling him.

Gripped with fear, embarrassment, and determination, Arioch bucked and thrashed and lunged until he was free; both were on their feet again. They locked arms and vied for positions. In a flurry of motion, they were on the ground again, but this time Arioch was on top. They rolled, and Arioch managed to get the opponent's arm behind his back with his face pressed into the dirt. The other man yelled; Arioch had won.

Both men stood up, the loser congratulating Arioch with a pat on the shoulder. The leader of the caravan approached Arioch and said, "My name is Gilmar. Welcome to the posse." Arioch thanked him, still trying to catch his breath.

"Okay, let's take care of business and get on our way."

"What business?" Arioch panted.

"How do you intend to pay for your food or buy your weapons or get others to teach you the skills of war?"

"I didn't know I had to do that."

"Of course you do. We are all in this together; you'll share in the bounty money also."

"How much do you charge for all that?"

"It is all separate. Let's see which weapons would be good for you."

Hardly knowing what to think, Arioch followed Gilmar to the large first cart. The canvas was drawn back, exposing an assortment of weapons. The man who had wrestled Arioch came along but said nothing. "Choose your sword," coaxed Gilmar.

Arioch picked up two or three, not really knowing what he was looking for in a sword, then turned to his wrestling partner and said, "Which one would you choose?"

The man picked out five swords and carried them away from the cart. He swung them, one at a time, and had Arioch do the same. "I think this one has the best feel."

Arioch swung it again and had to agree, for some unknown reason, that this was the right sword for him. He presented it to Gilmar.

"You've got expensive tastes, my boy! You got the best one." Fifteen minutes later, Arioch was dressed with leather upper-body armor, a spear, a sword, a leather utility belt with a fig-cakes pocket, and a knife and sheath. Gilmar calculated the cost and said he'd exchange the gear for five sheep.

"Five sheep!" objected Arioch. Gilmar ignored the objection and added in three months' rations, which was worth another five sheep.

"Ten sheep!" exclaimed Arioch.

With this, Gilmar sadly looked at him and exclaimed, "I don't know what I was thinking. I should have asked if you could pay your way before we started into this. I'm sorry. You can put the weapons back, and we'll be on our way."

"No!" exclaimed Arioch. "We can work out a deal. I'll give you one sheep and three goats."

Gilmar laughed but came back with, "Four goats and two sheep. That is my absolute bottom price."

"I have only one sheep and three goats."

Gilmar calmly replied, "I will accept that—and you will owe me one more sheep out of your bounty money when we catch the bandits." Arioch agreed.

Gilmar told the men to get Arioch's livestock and take them to the back of the caravan with the other animals. Arioch was shown to his position in the back with the new soldier recruits; he could now see that the caravan was much larger than he had previously realized. The company began moving again.

Arioch was following, now walking through his own courtyard again for the very last time. He looked over at his family's graves. He wanted to yank off his soldier gear and run to the decaying bodies, but common sense got the best of his emotions so he kept walking. He felt the sword sheath tapping his leg as he walked. A surge of pride and resolution mounted within. He was doing this for his family. He would get even.

They marched the rest of the afternoon and made camp just before dark. A series of thoughts had been going through Arioch's head. He examined his newly acquired armor. It was all used. It had belonged to others before him.

He and other new recruits began exchanging stories. Some had joined just by walking into the group. Others had stories of friends who had gotten them in. Still others had been conscripted against their will. A couple of recruits had stories similar to Arioch's. Arioch pondered all the information. He realized he had been tricked.

Arioch found the man who had wrestled him and abruptly stated, "You let me win, didn't you?"

"Yes."

"Why?"

"Because that is part of the recruitment technique. Gilmar knows how to talk to grieving farm boys."

"You're a bunch of lying thieves!"

"Take it easy, boy! Gilmar did you a favor. We could have killed you and taken your animals. But we were pretty far ahead of the herds and were ready for a break. By handling it like he did, he saved your life, got your animals, and made you into a willing recruit. By the time the herds caught up, we were ready to go again, and you were too."

"Humph!"

"And besides that, you got to choose your armor. Most have to use whatever they are given."

"And what about my armor? You were teasing me by trying out all those swords, weren't you?"

"Now you've gone too far. If you knew anything, you'd know that I picked out the best of everything on that wagon."

"Where did my weapons and uniform come from?"

"From dead soldiers on battlefields."

"That's what I thought. Anyway, I don't know how to use any of it."

"If you change your attitude a little, I'll teach you. It's my job. Let's go."

With that, he stood up and headed toward the outer circle where the new recruits were milling near a campfire. For the next two hours, the newcomers, both men and boys, learned the skills of war from various instructors. Arioch stayed back at first but then realized that the teachers were highly skilled and he could benefit from their instruction.

That night was to be the first of three months of training. Gilmar would occasionally appear and assure them that they were gaining on the bandits and that it wouldn't be long before the awaited confrontation. Arioch put his whole heart into every practice. His natural abilities did not go unnoticed by the instructors. He was soon regarded among most of the soldiers as a formidable opponent. In sword battles, they would spar right up to the point where one could have killed the other. Generally, it was Arioch who held the last position. He wondered what it would be like to actually kill another man. He and the others felt they had trained enough. They were ready for revenge.

It was about 11 a.m. in the first week of the fourth month; word spread quickly back through the caravan that the renegades dressed as Assyrian soldiers had been sighted. Adrenaline rushed, but after walking another thousand yards, the caravan stopped. What was going on?

Word came back that Gilmar had gone to talk to the "soldiers."

Word came back that they had captured him.

Word came back that they hadn't—he had been seen walking around. Three hours passed. This business of obeying orders was not sitting well with Arioch, but he held his peace and his place in rank.

At long last, Gilmar came riding along the lines of the caravan with six finely dressed Assyrian officers. They rode up one side and down the other. More time passed, and more questions arose in Arioch's mind. As the six rode off, Gilmar gathered all his soldier recruits together, numbering almost two hundred.

"Soldiers of the posse!" he shouted, "the Assyrian army has already captured the bandits we were after. Unfortunately, there will be no bounty money for any of us. However, since you are such fine soldiers, the Assyrian army has offered to let you join their ranks. As you know, the gods are on their side; they are conquering the entire world. Glory and fame can be yours, if you desire. Your other choice is to stay with me, clean up after the Assyrian armies, and train new recruits. Those of you who wish to stay with me, stay here. Those interested in joining with the Assyrians, follow me." With that, the charlatan turned his horse toward the Assyrian camp.

Arioch fumed inside. So that was it. His family really had been killed by the Assyrian army. Gilmar just followed them up, gleaning what he could from the spoils of war. He was being recruited to join the very army that had slaughtered his family. Arioch clinched his sword. To join the Assyrians was unthinkable, but to stay with Gilmar was worse. He thought of running away, but that was quickly dismissed, given the situation in which he found himself. He realized that if he joined the army, he could move around with them until it was time to break away, if he chose to do so.

Most of the men had formed a line leading to a table to get conscripted into the Assyrian ranks. As Arioch joined near the end of the line, he was able to observe the men as they were being divided up. Most of his friends had gone to the left and were gathered around an Assyrian official of some kind.

Arioch stood at the table. Gilmar, who had been sitting behind the table along with the official who was conscripting the men, suddenly stood up. "This lad stays with me—he owes me a sheep."

Arioch, filled with rage, answered, "I don't owe you anything. *You* owe *me*, you liar!"

"Shut your mouth, boy! Don't you know I could have you killed?"

"Try it!"

"If you knew what was good for you, you'd fear me!" shouted Gilmar.

Arioch answered with a cold stare, "I am not the one to fear you; *you* need to fear *me!*"

Guards stepped forward, hands resting on swords; both men calmed down. Gilmar muttered to the official, "This is the best new recruit I've got. I want double for him."

The man protested, "We only pay double for tested warriors."

"Have one of your guards attack him, and we'll see who is the tested warrior."

"He can't be trusted; he just blew up at you."

"Oh yes he can; he is very trustworthy! That is the whole problem: he will do exactly what he says."

The official eyed Arioch closely then eyed one of the guards; the guard nodded. Double it was. Arioch turned and abruptly marched toward his friends. The Assyrian clerk who was going to talk to him about his skills and services said nothing. He did not dare.

Arioch was a natural-born leader. The official in charge had the rank, but fellow soldiers looked to Arioch for their cue. The captain in charge of Arioch's division was a wise man and used Arioch's leadership to an advantage instead of trying to fight it.

For the first twelve months, they were in charge of raids on smaller towns. Typically, their division would be sent in to draw out the fighting men or even to go in after them. Once the enemy was softened, the regular army, or the destruction army, as Arioch called it, would move in. Many of Arioch's friends died, but a few managed to learn the skills of hand-to-hand combat and were "smiled upon by the gods," as the captain put it.

On several occasions, Arioch spoke to the captain about his dislike for the killing of innocent women and children. The captain assured him that this would not happen in their division, only in the destruction army that followed. Arioch knew it was a lie. He had already seen it, and it turned his stomach.

The captain knew that his success lay in keeping Arioch motivated and appeased, because the men loved him. They said among themselves that Arioch would go to hell and back again for those fighting next to him. He would never leave a comrade behind. The more dire the situation, the harder and smarter he fought. He seemed born to this calling. The men who battled alongside Arioch fought harder and more bravely because of his presence.

It was just after Arioch's nineteenth birthday when they came upon a small farming community. It was futile for the farmers, only 150 in number, to try to resist the Assyrian onslaught, but they did. When the captain told them to lay down their weapons and pledge allegiance to Assyria, they remained silent. The order to attack was given, and within fifteen minutes, Arioch and his men had killed half of the farmers. The other half ran away, and the captain beckoned the soldiers to let them go, as they would give no more trouble.

Arioch caught the order to stop fighting, but others did not and were still engaged. Arioch quickly approached a new recruit getting ready to kill a younger peasant. A female ran to the aid of the young farmer on the ground. The soldier thrust his sword through the man and with one mighty swing spun around and sliced the woman in the middle. She crumpled over, dying. Arioch yelled at the man, "We don't kill defenseless women!" With that, Arioch ran his sword through the young soldier and twisted it. The soldier collapsed in wide-eyed horror.

The captain was on the scene in a moment with drawn sword. The two stared intently at each other, Arioch waiting for the captain to make the first move. Many of the men ran to join Arioch. There was a tense moment, and then Arioch repeated, "We don't kill defenseless women!"

The captain disdainfully growled, "And killing a fellow soldier is treason. I'll see you in my tent. Alone!" The captain stomped to his horse and left.

Others milled around. Everyone wanted to talk; no one said anything. They walked back to the horses and rode to camp. There, a couple of friends spoke to him, "You shouldn't have done what you did."

"I know it. I acted foolishly by Assyrian standards."

"You know he is going to kill you."

"He can try. I am done with the murderous ways of the Assyrians. When he sliced that woman in half, I remembered my own mother. That's how she died. The last thing she said to me was to do what is right. She also said that I knew inside what is right, and I do."

"Yeah, well, what's right may be to stay alive, too."

"You are wrong. I am more afraid of fear and remorse over not doing the right thing than I am of death. I face my death with pride, even if it is tonight."

The men left Arioch, and he slowly headed for the captain's tent. He circled it at a distance once to see if there was any kind of ambush prepared, but all he could see was that there were several officials inside, most assuredly considering how to make a spectacle out of his treason. Arioch approached the tent, only to receive a sharp order to stay away until summoned. He went over to a campfire and sat down.

The servants cooking stew and roasting lamb didn't speak to him. Word of his atrocity had already spread through the camp. As Arioch sat by the fire, one by one his fellow comrades began to gather around. They, like he, had not taken off their battle gear. This worried Arioch; he could see trouble brewing, and he wanted to face it alone—not with everyone else also drawn into the fray. He was trying to think of what to say or do; then it was too late.

"Arioch, approach the captain's tent," shouted out a servant. As he went, he noticed out of the corner of his eye that many of the men had stood up and were following him at a distance. He wished they would not, yet he was comforted that they did.

Arioch entered the tent. As the flap closed behind him, Arioch noticed that all those present were of higher rank than his captain. The captain spoke, "Arioch, the gods smile upon you more than anyone I've ever known. When I returned to my tent, these officers were waiting with orders for me to supply them with fifty of my best men to work the trade routes. I will be getting in more recruits to fill the ranks, but they want seasoned warriors *whom they can trust!* They want *men of principle* who will not take bribes."

The captain coldly eyed Arioch and added, "The events of today's battle were not discussed because it was not expedient to waste these fine officers' time with such trivia."

The higher-ranking official then proceeded to explain that Babylon was attempting to take over the trade routes, even though they were not always doing so in the name of the king, but rather by means of covert operations. It was nearly impossible to tell who was on whose side. Both Assyrian and Babylonian troops dressed like bandits, and the bandits sometimes dressed like the troops. Trade with Babylon was still important to the Assyrian-based merchants, as it was their main supply of corn. Although Babylon had stopped paying tribute to Assyria, private trade between the countries was still of value to both. Assyria was expecting an all-out war with Babylon, but that had not come to pass yet. For now, the trade routes *must* remain open.

"The captain has suggested that you be named commander of this escort service. The men respect you. If you return with a full measure of success, you will be granted the rank of captain in the Assyrian army, with all the benefits and with full pay."

"That would be welcome," replied Arioch, "because so far I have not received *any* pay." The captain shot visual daggers at Arioch, but the other officers just laughed. They all knew the "don't pay the soldier; he dies and the money is yours" game—and they didn't care.

The ranking official looked at Arioch and said, "Will you do it? Can I count on you to escort a caravan?"

"Yes, sir."

"Then you may choose your men."

The ranking official pulled back the tent flap, and they all went out, finding they were surrounded by soldiers in arms. "These are my men," stated Arioch. The officials looked at the captain; the captain looked at the officials, then at Arioch.

Arioch smiled at the men, who looked even more bewildered than the officials. "These are my men. I am their commander. We'll guard the caravan."

The officials looked at the captain as if to ask how the men had known to be standing there, fully armed, to receive their orders. The captain, guessing what they were thinking yet knowing the real mutiny that had been avoided, simply stated, "Word travels fast, doesn't it?" With that, he returned to his tent, the officials departed to their tents, and Arioch proceeded to explain their new mission. The men were overjoyed!

Even before Arioch and his men joined their caravan, rumors abounded that the Babylonian army had defeated the Assyrians in several locations. Nebuchadnezzar was the name to ponder. Although he was the crown prince, he did not hide behind his title. He was a cunning and daring field general who had already struck fear into the hearts of the Assyrians. Arioch was glad for the smaller, more remote task of caravan escort.

Considering the time it took to drive the herds, it was three months to Babylon from their current location. As they traveled along, the caravan grew larger and larger. In these troubled times, many travelers sought the safety of the larger numbers and the soldiers. There was gold hidden in some of the idols; there were also precious stones, ointments, spices, and perfumes—all high-value targets. Hopefully, the enemy would not know these things, but it seemed that the information was always out there. Most had the capacity to become a traitor, if placed in the right circumstance.

Arioch now had three hundred men under his command, all on horseback, and he was protecting over a thousand people and a hundred oxcarts, not to mention the herds that accompanied them for food. He spoke often to the head of the caravan, but he did not like the man. He reminded him too much of Gilmar.

Two months into the journey, as they approached some hills, Arioch sent scouts ahead to make sure they were safe. It would be a perfect place for an ambush. By the time the caravan arrived at the pass, Arioch's men had assured him that there was no ambush lying in wait. By midafternoon they were through the pass and into safer terrain.

Then, mounted Assyrian soldiers lay ahead—seven hundred of them. They hailed the caravan. Arioch, five trusted warriors, and the caravan leader went out to meet them. The contingent claimed to have a letter from the king stating that the caravan should turn around, but they did not produce it. Even as they were talking, the seven hundred horsemen were surrounding the caravan.

The leader of the caravan quickly stated that the right thing to do was to pay for Arioch's services up until now and let him go, since the new military unit would now accompany them back from where they had come. Arioch smelled the stench of robbery and deception; he also sensed the impending danger to him and his men. He surprised those around him by responding, "Okay, settle up with us and we'll be on our way."

Gold pieces were counted out and weighed, and settlement was made. Arioch and his small army turned around and peacefully rode back through the pass. Once they were several miles away, they dismounted and gathered around, some expecting to receive their money and others knowing that Arioch was not one to run from a fight.

"Men," Arioch said, "we have been given charge of the caravan's safe delivery to Babylon, and that is exactly what we are going to do: deliver it to Babylon. If we had faced them back there, we would surely have suffered heavy losses. They may suspect that we will attack them on the pass tomorrow, so we are going back tonight to recover the caravan.

"Some of you have been with me for quite some time, and others are newcomers. This is a voluntary mission. We'll rest for about an hour; then we will return and kill about seven hundred bandits. Remember what the official said: we cannot trust the uniform. For us, they are the enemy. For all I know, the leader has planned all along to turn it over to them."

The soldiers had an hour to think about things and talk it over among themselves. All of Arioch's men opted to return with him.

By 10 p.m., most of the seven hundred Assyrian "soldiers" were either asleep or drunk or a little of both. Arioch's men quietly surrounded the camp, each man picking out two or three targets, and they attacked! It was swift and bloody. In no more than half an hour, most of the enemy was dead, the rest subdued. Arioch approached the leader of the caravan, who had been watching in dismay. The look on his face gave him away, and Arioch immediately put him in chains. The rest of the trip went smoothly.

Upon arriving in Babylon, although the former head of the caravan tried to lie about what had happened, there were so many witnesses to the contrary that he looked ridiculous. Arioch, on the other hand, was much admired for his bravery and cunning. He had done the unthinkable. He had received payment for his services and *still* returned to risk his life against more than double the number of troops—just to deliver a caravan to Babylon as he had said he would. This did not go unnoticed.

Once the truth was sorted out, the Babylonian official responsible ordered Arioch to execute the caravan leader. Arioch approached him and to everyone's amazement handed the man his sword. "Defend yourself!" Arioch retained his knife.

The man lunged toward Arioch. Arioch dodged the swing of the sword and struck him in the abdomen, causing him to lose his breath and fall to the ground. He then took his knife and slit the man's throat, to the cheers of Arioch's men. It was this kind of man that they followed, respected, and would fight for.

Arioch had no loyalty to Assyria. In fact, he hated the Assyrians. Gladly joining the Babylonians, Arioch grew in fame, which landed him positions guarding caravans for royalty, sometimes for Nebuchadnezzar himself. He was hard to fool, he was ruthless when he needed to be, he stuck up for his men and they for him, and he was loyal to his word under all circumstances. By 605 BC, at the age of twenty-five, he had become the captain of the palace guard.

CHAPTER 8

Daniel Builds a Reputation

Daniel had a way with people. Everyone liked him. He was smart, but not proud. He commanded respect without trying to do so. He knew exactly what he thought but was not offensive about it. In the face of a trap, he was hard to fool. He quickly read situations correctly. When he had the advantage, he was not selfish. When he had the upper hand, he was not vindictive. In widely varied circumstances, he was incredibly consistent. He was always faithful to his God.

On one occasion, Daniel had been called out to verify items that were supposed to be coming into the king's possession in the form of taxes. There were rugs, some tapestries, a cartload of precious lathed wood, and almost one talent of gold. As Daniel examined the receipt, he realized that the Assyrian merchant had been charged too much. Daniel figured the correct amount of the tax and told the merchant the new total. Without batting an eye, the merchant thanked him and proceeded to give Daniel half of the difference. Daniel knew what he was doing but let him count it out anyway.

When the merchant had finished, Daniel said, "I can't take that, because I already have a salary; it belongs to you. But since you've counted it out so nicely, why don't you take it down to slave station and buy food for all those who are hungry? It will make me happy to hear about that later. Maybe we can work together again sometime."

The merchant stared at Daniel in disbelief. Daniel added, "I'll appreciate your kindness, and so will God." Daniel and his company departed, leaving behind one slave.

The merchant, after recovering from his astonishment, approached the slave and said, "Now what was that all about?"

The slave replied, "It sounded to me like you were billed for the wrong amount. He returned the difference. You offered him money, and he asked you to share it with the outcasts down at slave station."

The merchant questioned, "What is slave station?"

"It's where the slaves go when their masters abandon them when they are too sick or injured to work. Follow me; I'll take you to the one in charge."

The perplexed merchant did what Daniel had asked. He reasoned that he might need a favor from Daniel in the future, so he'd better follow through this time.

On another occasion, Daniel was called out to inspect a large shipment of agricultural goods that the king was selling or trading for a long list of items in a caravan that had made camp. Arioch and twelve of the royal guard were summoned to go with Daniel because it was a large sum of money and there were some three-way trades involved with contracts and payments to be made to various individuals. As often occurred, the merchandise was not exactly as described in the contract. The merchant who actually had the advantage in the deal was, ironically, the one who was being the most stubborn.

Daniel eventually mediated understandings between the parties, and only one item remained: the taxes. This was obviously the most important item for Daniel, since this was his very purpose for being involved. Two of the parties were easy settlements, but the cantankerous merchant was hoping to wear Daniel down and eventually get his way.

After much unnecessary deliberation, Daniel divided the payments into three equal installments. The man argued that he did not have the money, but Daniel knew that was far from the truth. Arioch was just about to lose his patience when the man offered Daniel the first payment, in the form of a bribe, if he would drop the other two. Much to Arioch's surprise, Daniel said, "Alright, but I can't take it here. You'll have to deliver it to me in the main market square tomorrow at closing." Delighted, the merchant agreed.

As they rode away, Daniel asked Arioch if he would come to the market square at the appointed time tomorrow for Daniel's safety. Arioch agreed. The next morning, Daniel talked to a third party and asked him to meet them at the same time and place. When the time came, Arioch, six royal guardsmen, and Daniel arrived first; then came the merchant and his entourage with a sizable bag of gold coins. Subsequently, the third man arrived—who was a higher-court judge!

Historical Observations
Land Ownership and Influence

[13]*The upper class, or the "awilus," were king's officials, priests, wealthy landowners, and the more affluent merchants and traders. This group owned much of Babylonia's land; the other large land-owning group were the temples, which were controlled by the priests. Second to the monarch and his royal decrees, these classes wielded the most power and influence in Babylonian politics.*

The other group of free people, the "musheknus", were the craftsmen, clerks-lawyers, and farmers. It was not uncommon for selected slaves of important officials to give orders to free men and to hold respected positions. Sometimes, but not always, the slaves of greatest importance were castrated and made eunuchs.

Daniel produced the contract, which the judge glanced over; then Daniel introduced the wide-eyed merchant to the judge, saying, "Most excellent judge, this man has made a point of making his first payment in honor of the contract, and since it is a large sum, I thought it would be good to register it legally to make sure he gets full credit for payment. By doing this, he acknowledges the validity of the contract and agrees to make the other two payments."

Looking at the merchant, he continued, "Go ahead, sir, and count out the payment to the judge so he can validate the contract and the receipt for the first payment." The merchant had no choice but to pleasantly comply. The judge complained about doing this sort of thing after hours, but Daniel thanked him politely for making an exception this time.

With the contract duly signed by the merchant, stamped by the judge, and back into Daniel's hands, Daniel took the bag of gold coins and handed it to Arioch for safekeeping. Daniel smiled at the merchant. He faked a smile back, since they were in front of the judge. Daniel politely said, "These coins will be in the treasury tomorrow. You can come by for the official receipt."

As they walked away, Arioch declared to no one in particular, "That was interesting."

Arioch watched Daniel turn down bribes on several occasions; bring settlement to different disputes where it seemed that no settlement could be reached; and often influence, convince, or even trick people into doing what was right. Arioch grew to respect this young Hebrew as he respected few others.

Since they worked together often, Daniel was sensitive to Arioch's moods. One day Daniel noticed that Arioch was more aloof than usual. No, upon closer observation, Arioch was angry about something; he bristled at the slightest comment. Daniel asked, not necessarily expecting an answer, "What is it, Arioch? What are you upset about?"

"Nothing!"

"Arioch, just by the way you said 'nothing,' I can tell it is something!"

"All right, Daniel. I loaned over a year's wages to a general in the army, and he won't repay me. He has many possessions he could sell to pay me, and I think he has the cash too. I can't, or at least I shouldn't, press charges against another officer. It wouldn't look good. Besides that, we are not supposed to be too involved in civilian affairs. I should never have loaned him the money. No matter what I do now, it won't look good for me."

Daniel thought for a long while then asked, "Can you get to this man? Could you kill him or kidnap him if you wanted to?"

"I think so."

"A bill collection plan might work."

"And what might that be?"

"Does he have a partner or a wife who could pay this bill if they wanted to?"

"He has both."

"Okay, then, I've heard that this is how they do it . . ."

Three days later, Arioch and six royal guards rode to the general's quarters and invited him out for a ride. The general took three men with him. Arioch and the general visited about many things, including the debt, and the general simply said he was sorry, but he couldn't pay it at this time. After a while, they turned around and started back toward the city. Arioch asked the others to ride ahead so he could have a private word with the general. The others went on, and the two dismounted and talked.

When the others were over the hill and out of sight, Arioch overcame the general, bound him hand and foot, and gagged him. Throwing him over his horse, Arioch rode to the edge of a wooded area that grew along a creek. He crossed the creek and rode on for another half an hour; then he found a suitable tree and shackled the general with his hands around the tree. When he removed the gag, the furious general spent a minute or so swearing at Arioch. During the swearing tirade, Arioch calmly sat and waited.

When the general finished, Arioch stated, "General, I am leaving you here, and I am not coming back. When I am paid in full, I will tell your wife and your partner where they can find you or your body, but I myself will never return to this place. I am ready to hear how you are going to pay me. How will it be?"

"When I am released, I am going to kill you!"

"You won't kill me because I am the captain of the royal guard; you would be killed instantly by my people. You know the Babylonian soldiers are not particularly loyal; but the royal guard soldiers under my command are dependable, and you can be sure they will avenge my death by killing you. If you *did* kill me, Nebuchadnezzar would probably kill your whole family, and you know it!"

"What makes you think you can get away with killing me?"

"I'm *not* going to kill you. You are going to pay me. If you don't, you will die out here from 'natural causes.'"

"If I make the payment and you keep your word and I am let loose, then what's to keep me from telling the king what you did?"

"Think about it, General. You'll say, 'I owed Arioch a lot of money, so he tied me to a tree, and then I had to pay my debt to him, and then he let me go.' You will be the laughingstock of Babylon! That's why you won't tell what happened."

"If I die out here, you will hang for it!"

"Wrong again. If you die out here, you will be one of the hundreds of unsolved deaths in Babylon. There are no witnesses to any crime. Do you think your soldiers will risk their lives to tell that they suspect the *captain of the guard* shackled you to a tree? They won't open their mouths. If they were to testify, they would say they saw nothing except cordial conversation between us."

"This is *extortion!*"

"No, extortion is exacting money that does not belong to you. This is *bill collecting!* Let's start over from the beginning now. General, *I am never coming back to this place.* When I am paid in full, I will tell your wife and partner where they can find you—or your body—but I myself will never return to this place. I am ready to write down how you are going to pay me. This is your last chance to settle accounts with me. How will it be?"

The fuming general saw no other alternative. He had no doubt that Arioch would follow through. Through gritted teeth, the general instructed, "Tell my wife to dig up the gold north of the well. She will know what I mean. Tell my partner to cancel the olive oil transaction and to keep the funds in cash. These two sums together will more than cover the payment."

Arioch coldly replied, "It is really none of your concern, but I will have these sums delivered to Daniel, and he will officially cancel our contract, showing full payment. If it happens as you say, you can get the receipt from him, and we will officially remain friends; but don't ever ask me for another loan!"

The general said no more, and Arioch rode away, leading the general's horse behind him. In order to hide his tracks, when he reached the creek, he rode upstream almost a mile before cutting back to the road, where there were many other recent hoof marks.

Although it was very late when Arioch arrived back in Babylon, he went straight to the general's house and demanded to see his wife. When she came out, Arioch said, "Do you know who I am?"

"Yes, my lord, you are Arioch, captain of the royal guard."

"Are you aware that you husband owes me over a year's wages?"

"Yes . . . my lord."

"Your husband sent this message: 'Tell my wife to dig up the gold north of the well. She will know what I mean. Tell my partner to cancel the olive oil deal and to keep the funds in cash. These two sums together will more than cover the payment.'"

"Where *is* my husband?"

"He is at a location that only I know. When payment is made, I will tell you where to find him. If it is soon enough, he will probably still be alive."

"Sir Arioch, please come with me to talk to his partner in business."

Arioch dismounted and walked with her the short distance to the partner's house. He was startled at being awakened at such an hour and was confused at the sight of the general's wife accompanied by Arioch, the captain of the royal guard, leading the general's horse!

Quickly the woman explained what she had heard from Arioch. The partner, outraged, threatened, "I'll have you hanged for this!"

"You need to wake up and think more clearly. You can have me arrested, I'll go to jail, I will say nothing, days will pass, the general will die, I will be freed, and then, most likely, you will go to jail for accusing me without evidence."

"I will find the general, and that will be the evidence."

"How long do you think he will live without food and water? Do you really think I'd be here if I knew there was any chance you'd find him?"

"Exactly what did the general say to you?"

Arioch repeated the message one more time.

Looking at the wife, the partner said, "Do you know about this gold by the well?"

"Yes."

"We must do as the general has requested and save his life. What he does with Arioch after that will be up to him."

"I think so too."

Arioch went on to explain that they should make the payment to Daniel and where they could find him. It was almost dawn when Arioch mounted his horse and briskly rode away.

By midmorning full payment had been made, and by midafternoon the general was back home. At 5 p.m., he retrieved the receipt and the canceled contract from Daniel. As the general walked away, he turned and said, "Belteshazzar, do you know the story behind this payment?"

Daniel smiled and said, "Tell me about it."

The general stared; Daniel smiled. The general said, "Forget it," and walked away.

Daniel's fame for honesty and cunning spread slowly, like a smoldering fire. Because of his position, he often inadvertently became the middleman or self-appointed negotiator in deals that had gone sour. He could not help but learn which merchants were honest and which were not. Daniel began suggesting to some which merchants to avoid and which ones could be trusted. This did not go over well with the ones possessing fewer scruples.

On one occasion, a powerful merchant decided to take Daniel down. Daniel had thought that he could not be blackmailed if he did what was right. He soon learned that this was not so. One morning a court courier arrived at Daniel's work station with a summons to appear before the judge. When he appeared, he was read the accusation that he had been laundering money for this powerful merchant's archenemy. Three witnesses testified against him. He was given three days to prepare his defense; he would then be judged and sentenced.

At first Daniel was somewhat dismayed, but after talking with Abednego and the others and after considering the story of Joseph's cup hidden in the sack of grain, he considered exposing the merchant's travesty. Knowing that he would be inspecting this caravan, Abednego wrote out word for word in third person the sham that had been devised against Daniel. Abednego discussed the plan with Daniel.

"I don't know. It doesn't seem right to plant an incriminating document in the man's caravan."

"What's not right, Daniel, is for him to hire false witnesses against you and have you thrown in jail or worse, when you are totally innocent."

"I know; but two wrongs do not make a right."

"Sometimes they do. If you had the opportunity, would it be wrong for you to tell the judge exactly what is happening to you?"

"No."

"Well, what I have written is exactly what is being done to you. All we are doing is finding a creative way to get it into the judge's hands."

"I understand that, but it almost feels like a bribe. We are not paying anything to anyone. We are furnishing true information."

"A bribe is paying to avoid a punishment that is due you. Every other payment is a payment for a service rendered. Let's say a person is fined for selling without a permit. But this person is not even a merchant and has never sold in the marketplace. The man issuing the fine says that he will cancel it for 25 percent of the value of the fine. The innocent man can either appeal to the legal system, or he can pay the 25 percent. That would not be a bribe, because he was not guilty in the first place. It would be a payment for a service rendered, even though the service is to drop the extortion."

"I understand that, but . . ."

"Daniel, it is never wrong to expose the truth. Exposing the truth is what I do for a living when I inspect caravans every day. Now give me that parchment, and we will see to it that the judge hears the truth as well as the lies. It is not wrong for us to figure out a way to tell the judge the facts."

Abednego called to Arioch, "I need your help, Arioch. I'd like for you to go with me to inspect a caravan tomorrow. Whatever we find there, please deliver to the judge who is judging Daniel's case. You know he is innocent, and this will help us prove it."

"Consider it done."

The next day, Abednego's servant placed the description in some documents in the caravan. A few moments later, Abednego "discovered" it in the presence of several who were watching. He read a portion of it aloud then called Arioch, giving him the order to take it to the authorities. The merchant was not present, but upon his return, the servants told him that Abednego had confiscated a document, although they did not know which one. After looking through everything, they could not tell what was missing.

On the day of Daniel's judgment, the judge summoned the accusers, who repeated their accusations. The judge then asked Daniel if these things were true, and he stated that they were not. At that point, the judge produced a document and announced, "This document has come to me by way of the captain of the guard and was confiscated from your caravan by the officials. He then proceeded to read, "The best way to rid ourselves of Daniel is to accuse him of laundering money for our chief competitor. With testimonies, he will lose his job, and it will also hurt business for our opponent. Choose testimonies of confidence, and pay them handsomely; this must not be discovered."

The judge stared angrily at the merchant. He objected, "That was planted in my caravan! I would never do something like that, and if I did, I would not write it down!"

"Now you want me to believe two lies? There are legitimate witnesses who establish that the parchment came from your caravan."

"There are also legitimate witnesses who accuse Daniel!"

The judge calmly called forth the witnesses against Daniel and said, "In light of the possible attempt to blackmail Daniel, which has just been read, and knowing the serious consequences of perjury, ranging from a flogging to punishment by death, do you maintain your witness against Daniel?"

The first witness quickly stated, "I thought it was Daniel, but I cannot really be sure. Someone in his department was doing this, but I didn't really get a good look at him."

The second witness also folded. "No, sir, I am not positive beyond a shadow of a doubt that it was Daniel, I just thought it was, but I may be wrong."

The third simply said, "No, sir."

"The case against Daniel is dismissed! Daniel, do you wish to press charges against this man?"

Daniel acted like he needed to think about it, although he already knew his position. He squinted out the corner of his eye at the merchant and answered the judge, "No, sir, I do not wish to press charges at this time."

"Case dismissed."

Daniel's fame grew, but the more it grew, the more he, Shadrach, Meshach, and Abednego became isolated from the king's councilmen.

[13]*[http://thetigris.blog.over-blog.com/archive-11-17-2008.html]*

CHAPTER 9

Daniel Reveals the King's Dream

Nebuchadnezzar had grown up a prince but had earned his own fame by excelling in nearly everything he did. He was a connoisseur of learning as well as a successful field general. He had either conquered or made peace with his more formidable enemies, and he was attempting to successfully rule the 127 provinces that were now under Babylonian control.

Nebuchadnezzar was no fool. He had reached these heights because he could read people and use them to his advantage. At the slightest hint of disloyalty, he had put many to death. He was ruthless, but never without reason in his own mind. His objective was to create the greatest kingdom that had ever existed, and it was not a pipe dream. He knew not only that he could do it, but that, in fact, he was well on his way to doing so.

Historical Observations

The second year of Nebuchadnezzar's reign would have been sometime between April 603 and March 602 BC. At this date, Daniel and his friends would not likely have had time to finish college and become part of the wise men in the council.

In 600 BC, Jehoiakim rebelled against Nebuchadnezzar, who laid siege to Jerusalem. In 598 BC, Jehoiakim died, and his son

Jehoiachin became king for three months and ten days, then surrendered to Babylon. Nebuchadnezzar appointed Zedekiah to be his vassal king and took away eleven thousand captives, including the Israeli prophet Ezekiel.

The consolidation of the Babylonian kingdom could be counted from this date. If so, then the second year of Nebuchadnezzar's reign (over the consolidated kingdom) would be 595 BC, when Daniel would have been twenty-four, if he was fourteen in 605 BC when led away captive.

It was now the second year of Nebuchadnezzar's consolidation of the kingdom and nine years after his father's death. Daniel was almost twenty-four years old. Nebuchadnezzar had been used to dealing with soldiers and the military decision-making processes, and it had been quite an adjustment for him to take his father's place on the throne and work with the council of wise men, astrologers, magicians, enchanters, and sorcerers. Their elite air, their sophistication, their schemes, their treachery—it was all gnawing away at him. The only claim to power that many of them had was of a religious nature. They claimed to know how to win the favor of the gods, how to communicate with them, how to read future events in the stars, how to cast spells on his enemies, and, in general, how to guide the kingdom successfully through the perils of the spiritual world.

Nebuchadnezzar suspected that most of them had no such powers. He could quickly judge whether he thought a person was genuine. That's why he had promoted Arioch so quickly. He knew that Arioch was the real thing.

These wise men appeared to be living off of his fear of the gods and their imagined wrath. At different times, Nebuchadnezzar had fancied playing tricks on them to see if they really did communicate with the gods. He was also intrigued by the thought that now that he was on the throne, he was perhaps elevated to the status of a minor god, so why couldn't he make some of the rules?

Recently there had been several small ways in which Nebuchadnezzar had suspected that the wise men were not communicating with the gods at all, but rather were manipulating his decisions for their own personal and monetary benefits. It infuriated him that these men who could not stand for a minute in battle, who did not know the sacrifice it took in the field to consolidate the kingdom, who thought almost exclusively of themselves "advised," "counseled," and otherwise manipulated *him*, the great Nebuchadnezzar.

It came to a head around three o'clock one morning when he awoke with a start. He awoke from a dream, a significant dream about a statue made of different metals and its subsequent destruction. As he lay there in bed, he became more and more convinced that the gods had revealed something to him. It was an omen; he must find out what it meant.

He would call the wise men, astrologers, magicians, enchanters, and sorcerers. No! If he called them in and told them the dream, they would just make up some meaning for the dream. Any man off the street could do that. He needed a real prophet, and he needed assurance that the man was legitimate. Upon further deliberation, he had a brilliant idea: he would not reveal his dream to them; he would tell them to reveal the dream to him! If they did, they would prove that they could, in fact, communicate with the gods; if they could not, it was just as he expected—they were a brood of lying vipers.

An hour later, Nebuchadnezzar stalked into the throne room and announced to the sleep-weary guards, "Get me the wise men, astrologers, magicians, enchanters, and sorcerers." As they hesitated, dazed by the suddenness of it all, the king shouted, *"Now!"*

They hurried to awaken Arioch with the message. He was on his feet quickly and made haste to unlock the cabinet that contained emergency contingency plans of various sorts. He chose the container with the predetermined list of councilmen and their residential locations and distributed the names among royal guard couriers. The soldiers dashed off, each with his predetermined destination and order to bring the councilman with great haste.

Soon the wise men stood before Nebuchadnezzar. He had had almost an hour to sit on the throne, stewing about everything he didn't like about these men. The questions loomed ever greater in his mind: Could they make good on all their claims? Could they read the stars? Would the gods tell them his dream? He would soon know.

Without even a "good morning, gentlemen," Nebuchadnezzar stood up from his throne in the torch-lit hall and began to speak; the words were rehearsed and forceful. "I have had a dream this night that deeply troubles me, and I must know what it means."

The wise men, relieved that the problem was only a dream, responded, "Long live the king. Tell us the dream, and we will tell you what it means."

The king was ready and delivered his terrifying response: "You will tell *me* the dream; then I will know that the interpretation is true!"

The councilmen could hardly believe their ears. They muttered among themselves, milling around, searching out their friends and grasping for mental clues. After a few minutes, the head of the council addressed the king, "Oh king, live forever. Tell us the dream, and we will tell you the interpretation."

Nebuchadnezzar raised his voice. "I have firmly decided that *you* will tell *me* the dream and what it means, or else you will be torn limb from limb and your houses will be turned into heaps of rubble!"

They consulted among themselves and again said, "Your Majesty, tell us the dream, and we will tell you the interpretation."

Nebuchadnezzar raised his voice even more. "I know what you are doing. You are stalling for time because you know I am serious when I say that if you don't tell me the dream, you are doomed. You conspire to tell me lies, hoping I will change my mind; but tell me the dream, and *then* I will know that you can tell me what it means!"

The astrologers replied, "No one on earth can tell the king his dream! And no king, however great and powerful, has ever asked such a thing of any wise men, astrologers, magicians, enchanters, or sorcerers. The king's demand is unreasonable and impossible. No one except the gods can tell you your dream, and they do not live here among men!"

Nebuchadnezzar was furious and ordered that all the wise men of Babylon be executed. It was as he thought. They were all liars, and he could do better without them! How dare they talk to him like that, after all they'd claimed in the past! They couldn't talk to the gods any more than he could. What a bunch of filthy deceivers!

The command was given to gather all the wise men in the outer courtyard of the palace. Daniel and his friends were awakened with a loud knock on their door. The guard stated coldly, "I have come to arrest Belteshazzar, Shadrach, Meshach, and Abednego." When Daniel questioned why, the guard drew his breath and said, "The king has ordered that all the wise men of Babylon be executed."

Now the others were at the door, pulling on their robes and asking questions. As the guard handed them over to his accompanying soldiers, he replied, "It has to do with the wise men not being able to tell the king his dream."

When the four Hebrews reached the courtyard, they began to assimilate the gravity of the situation. They were placed inside a large circle of soldiers, along with the other wise men. Some of the men were sitting, and some were standing; some were praying, and some were despondent. Others were desperately talking about some kind of a plan.

Shadrach muttered, "So this is what we get for being the smartest kids in the class."

Meshach observed, "But we were never really even part of this group. We have not been called to the council meetings after those first few times."

Shadrach mused, "When it is time to call us before the king for counsel, they don't remember us; when it is time to get killed, they don't forget about us."

Just then Arioch, captain of the guard, entered the courtyard and walked toward the circle of soldiers. Daniel spotted him and started toward him. Arioch stepped past the soldiers and met Daniel just inside the circle. He was nearly white with dread, and Daniel saw immediately that it was going to be harder for Arioch to have him killed than it was going to be for Daniel to die. Daniel spoke to Arioch, "Why has the king issued such a harsh decree?"

Arioch quickly explained what he knew, and Daniel replied, "The king's decree is unjust. He didn't give a chance to all his wise men to interpret his dream. Meshach, Abednego, Shadrach, and I were never called. You know how the councilmen leave us out of everything. Let me speak to the king myself, and we'll see if my God will reveal the dream and the interpretation to me." That was all it took to convince Arioch of what he already wanted to do. He turned on his heel to arrange a meeting between Daniel and the king.

Soon Daniel was ushered into the king's presence. By now Nebuchadnezzar was having some second thoughts about killing all of his wise men, although he hated them so much that he didn't really care. When he saw Daniel, however, he thought he remembered him as being one of those exceptionally bright students he had interviewed a few years ago.

Nebuchadnezzar held out his hand as if to say, "Speak." Daniel stated, "I serve Yahweh, the most high God, maker of heaven and earth. My God knows what His Majesty has dreamed and the meaning of the dream. I request one day to pray to my God and ask Him to reveal the dream to me. It may be that He will heed my prayers and grant the king's wish."

Nebuchadnezzar looked intently at Daniel, who stared back at him totally unafraid. The king knew he was looking at a young man who fully believed what he had just said. Although he had not given the other wise men extra time to come up with the dream, the king thought Daniel seemed different. Most Babylonians considered Marduk to be the most high god, maker of heaven and earth. Daniel seemed as interested in proving his God than he did in avoiding death. Drawing quickly upon these thoughts, Nebuchadnezzar said, "You have one day."

Daniel was led back to the wise men, and a crier announced the king's delay of execution orders, stating the chance that had been given to Daniel to tell the dream. Daniel and his three friends were escorted back to their quarters and remained there under guard.

Placing all the wise men under house arrest closed down Babylon during that day. Speculation abounded wherever people gathered. Many stayed home for fear of the king's unscrupulous wrath. At least half of the population was hoping the wise men would meet their deaths. Others thought it was regrettable that the good ones had to die along with the bad.

There were rumors that a young man named Daniel held everyone's fate in his hands. Could he conjure up a dream? The general consensus was that it was considerably more likely to be struck by lightning than it was to guess what someone else had dreamed. There were many who knew that Daniel was a Hebrew and would be praying to the God of the Hebrews—whichever one that was. Was there even a temple to that god in Babylon? Most didn't think so.

The Jews were different. Many had not been following Yahweh or His commands, yet they knew the old stories of deliverance. Many of them fasted and prayed for Daniel, Hananiah, Mishael, and Azariah, pleading to God to spare their lives. Some prayed who had not prayed for a very long time.

Daniel and his friends fasted and prayed. At first the prayers were fervent and passionate. As the day wore on, they became resolute and even logical. Into the afternoon, they began reminding God of all His miracles of the past. Around sundown the four had drifted into more of a talking mode. They would alternately pray to themselves then talk to one another. By nighttime they began to think of the countdown: "Ten more hours to live, unless God reveals the dream to us." . . . "Nine more hours here on this earth . . ."

Finally, Daniel announced he was going to sleep. "We've done all we can do. If we perish, we perish. Our only purpose on earth is to serve the Lord our God. If He is through with us here, we should welcome death. If not, He will deliver us. Let's go to bed."

Daniel slept soundly, and as he slept, God gave him the same dream He had given to Nebuchadnezzar. Daniel awoke at sunrise, rested—and exhilarated!

"Wake up, men. God gave me the dream!" He yanked the covers off Abednego, then Shadrach. By now Meshach was already sitting up. Daniel talked quickly as he related the details of the dream; then, almost with the same clarity, he gave the interpretation. They hugged, they slapped one another on their backs, they lifted their hands in praise. They all joined in as Abednego led out in the one hundredth psalm of David.

There was no doubt that this was a supernatural revelation. God, the great Yahweh of the Scriptures, was with them right there in the room. One by one, they fell to their knees, almost weak. The four were now nearly speechless, although a soft partial prayer could be heard every now and then. This blessed scene lasted a full five minutes.

Daniel stood, raising his hands toward heaven and praised God. "Praise the name of God forever, for He has all wisdom and power. He controls the course of world events; He removes kings and sets them up as He wills. He gives wisdom to the wise and knowledge to the scholars. He reveals deep and mysterious things and knows what lies in darkness, even though He is surrounded by light. I thank and praise You, God of my ancestors, for You have given me wisdom and strength. You have told me what we asked of You and revealed to us what the king demanded."

The other three added prayerful comments of their own:

"Our God, *is* the most high God, maker of heaven and earth."

"Wisdom and power are *His*—not Marduk's!"

"He sets up and removes kings! Even Nebuchadnezzar is subservient to our God!"

"He knows what lies in darkness! He's over the evil demon gods."

"He reveals mysteries! Only *Yahweh* knew the dream."

"Light dwells in Him: physical, spiritual, wonderful *light*."

"Not even Babylon's depressing spiritual darkness hinders our God."

"I go to the king," Daniel declared as he strode to the door, eager to deliver the divine message. When he opened it, he found Arioch already waiting outside. He and the other soldiers had heard the exuberant noises earlier, then the silence, then the prayers. They were expectantly waiting.

Now it was Daniel giving the orders. "Do not execute the wise men. Take me to the king; I will interpret the dream!" Arioch complied at once.

When they arrived at the throne room, Nebuchadnezzar was just sitting down; the time was up. Wishing to appear in a favorable light with the king, Arioch declared, "The one I found among the captives from Judah is able to tell the dream to the king."

The king eyed Daniel skeptically and said, "Are you able to tell me my dream?" Although the king was hopeful, he realized that revealing the dream was humanly impossible.

Daniel answered, "No. There is no man alive who could tell the dream to the king." Arioch looked at Daniel in shock! Daniel continued, "There is no wise man, astrologer, magician, enchanter, or sorcerer on earth who could reveal this to the king. But there is a God in heaven who reveals secrets. He has shown the king what will happen in the future. Now I will tell you your dream and the visions you saw on your bed.

"While Your Majesty was sleeping, you dreamed about coming events. He who reveals secrets has shown you what is going to happen in the future. It is not that I am wiser than anyone else that I know the secret of your dream, but rather, because God wants you to understand what He put into your heart.

"In your vision, Your Majesty, you saw a great statue. This image was both very large and very bright. It stood before you and it was a frightening sight! Its head was of fine gold; its chest and its arms, of silver; its belly and its thighs, of bronze; its legs, of iron; its feet were of part iron and part clay."

Arioch noticed that the king had sat forward on his throne, his chin resting tightly on his hand. He had never before seen the king so intent. He could tell that this was, in fact, the dream!

"You observed a rock which was cut out of a mountain, but not with human hands. This rock struck the feet of the image and broke them into many pieces. Then all of the iron, clay, brass, silver, and gold were broken into little pieces and became like the chaff of the threshing floors and the wind carried them away. Then the rock that had knocked the statue down became a great mountain and then went on to fill the whole earth."

Nebuchadnezzar was numb with amazement. That was the dream—right down to every exact detail!

Without even giving the king a chance to confirm that, in fact, this was the dream, Daniel continued, "That was the dream; now I will tell the king what it means. You, oh king, are the king to whom the God of heaven has given great power, strength and glory; and wherever the children of men dwell, the beasts of the field and the birds of the heavens have been given into your hands. The God of heaven has made you ruler over them all: *you* are the head of gold.

"After your kingdom comes to an end, another kingdom, inferior to yours, the silver kingdom, will rise and take your place. When that kingdom has fallen, a third kingdom, represented by bronze, will rule the world. Following the bronze kingdom, there will be a fourth kingdom, which will be as strong as iron. That kingdom will smash and crush all these previous kingdoms, just as iron crushes these other metals.

"The feet and the toes you saw were a combination of iron and baked clay, showing that this kingdom will be divided. Like iron mixed with clay, it will have some parts that are strong and others that are weak. As the toes of the feet were part iron and part clay, so the kingdom will be both strong and brittle. This mixture of iron and clay also shows that these kingdoms will try to strengthen themselves by forming alliances with each other; but they will not hold together, just as iron does not mix with clay.

"During the reigns of these kings represented by the clay and iron, the God of heaven will set up a kingdom that will never be destroyed or conquered. It will crush all these kingdoms into nothingness but it will stand forever. That is the meaning of the rock cut from the mountain by divine hands. The most high God is showing the king what will happen in the future. The dream is true, and its meaning is certain."

Arioch expected Daniel to follow up with some kind of a confirmation statement, like "Is this what the king dreamed?" Daniel, bold as a lion, stared at the king and said no more. Nebuchadnezzar seemed to be recovering from a state of shock. All at once, the king of Babylon, the ruler of the world, fell on his face and began worshiping Daniel, a Hebrew slave. Arioch and the others in the court knew they were perhaps witnessing a sight unprecedented on planet earth.

After bowing repeatedly to Daniel, the king stood up and began giving orders. "Perform sacrifices and burn incense! We will worship the God of Daniel, the revealer of mysteries! All will pay homage to the Lord of Lords, the God of Daniel!"

Then the king said to Daniel, "Truly your God is the God of all gods, the Lord over kings, the revealer of mysteries, for He has revealed this secret through you."

Suddenly Nebuchadnezzar realized that his plan *had* worked. By requiring the revelation of the dream, he had discovered who had the real power and wisdom. He felt even smarter than he already thought he was. "Daniel" said the king, "what shall I do with the wise men?"

Daniel's quickly responded, "Set them free." Nebuchadnezzar gestured to Arioch, who promptly turned to carry out this order. Daniel had saved the day.

As Arioch walked away, he said to himself, "Babylon will never be the same."

The king appointed Daniel as prime minister over the province of Babylon and lavished many valuable gifts on him. He also named Daniel as the head of the wise men, chief councilman over all the astrologers, magicians, enchanters, and sorcerers. At Daniel's request, the king appointed Shadrach, Meshach, and Abednego to be in charge of all the outer affairs of the province of Babylon, while Daniel remained in charge of the king's court. Babylon would indeed be different!

CHAPTER 10

Changes in Babylon

Nebuchadnezzar was a conceited, egocentrical tyrant, but he did have some redeeming qualities. Although it was very difficult for him to realize when he was wrong, when he did, he admitted it. He realized now that he had been serving the wrong gods and was willing to correct that mistake. He also realized that he had put his trust in the wrong people, and he corrected that error also.

Even though Arioch was ten years Daniel's senior, he was quite happy to be working under Daniel. Truthfully, most of the people in the palace were glad for Daniel's appointment. Even though he was only twenty-four, he had proven that he was capable and wise. Unlike Nebuchadnezzar, he was approachable; he and his friends still ate at the servants' table. Many of his former professors bragged about how they had taught Daniel and his friends and what a wonderful job they were doing. The marketplace was filled with chatter about the young slaves who had been promoted to the highest positions in the land. The common people loved it, the Jews couldn't help but draw constant parallels to Joseph, and all those who had a propensity to do what was right were at ease with Daniel at the helm.

As Daniel had requested, Shadrach was put in charge of agriculture and food supply; Meshach was placed over infrastructure and development; and Abednego was now responsible for trade and commerce. These were huge tasks for young men to tackle, but the king trusted them. As far as Nebuchadnezzar was concerned, trust was everything. Besides that, Daniel had proven that he had spiritual access to the most high God.

The first year in the new offices was a difficult year by all measures except the king's. His life was now much easier. He concentrated on the smaller military campaigns, loyalty issues, and the squelching of rebellions. He called Zedekiah and some other vassal kings to Babylon to ensure their loyalties, and he concentrated on his pet projects, especially the hanging gardens.

The four Hebrews spent much time talking and analyzing changes that should be made in the administrative machine. Innovative ideas blossomed as they worked with others they trusted and with some of the wiser professors who had never had the desire to fight the political system. They listened to the councilmen also but soon realized that most of what went on there revolved around vying for position and making business deals. Little by little, Daniel sorted out the councilmen with whom he could work and those with whom he could not.

Shadrach's first order of business was to remove the fertilizer curator. He replaced him with a servant who had run the outer yard for three years, but who Shadrach knew loathed the stealing that had always gone on. Shadrach tripled his wages and told him to run the yard like he had always wanted to, being fair to all involved. "Furthermore," said Shadrach, "if there are ever threats of blackmail or other schemes in which you find yourself entangled, find a way to let me know. I will investigate it independently, and you will not appear in the process. Your family will be safe." Shadrach never knew how much that last statement meant to the new yard foreman; he would have given his life for Shadrach in exchange for this security for his family.

Shadrach developed a system for the farmers to sell to the king directly, cutting out greedy middlemen and even greedier tax collectors. He issued preset receipts for the farmers to produce under a quota system. These were their taxes, prepaid and pre-receipted; all other production was theirs to sell in the marketplace with no restriction. Once the farmer delivered his predetermined payment to the government, validating his pre-issued receipt, he was then given a voucher for tax-free vendor status in the marketplace. Because the farmers were motivated to produce and motivated to pay their taxes in order to get free market access, there was no need for the traditional tax collectors.

Shadrach threatened to remove these privileges after one year if there were those who did not participate in the system. Since the peasant farmers had never had such advantages, they policed themselves, turning in the ones who tried to beat the system. Food abounded, peasants prospered, and the former movers, shakers, and money launderers of the Babylonian elite were not amused.

Meshach had loved working with Bezalel and regretted giving that up. Daniel insisted that someone trustworthy *had* to be in charge of infrastructure and development. Meshach was the man. For the first two months, he floundered, mostly adopting a hands-off policy as he grew to understand the intricacies of the situation. How did one organize the 225,000 slaves that belonged to Nebuchadnezzar and were dedicated to his building projects? What could he do about the injustice, partiality, and stealing of building materials? Meshach knew that it would not be smart to start putting out fires one at a time. He must establish policies that addressed overall issues. He needed to treat the forest, not the individual trees, but how?

By the third month, Meshach was familiar with the active royal building projects, the maintenance projects, and most of the mismanagement concerns. One day to clear his mind, he visited Bezalel in the lab. Meshach asked if he was still being blackmailed.

"I'm still paying that priest, but I have not been asked to reroute building materials for a few weeks. Everyone is wondering what you are going to do. They see what is happening in agriculture and food supply, and they are running scared."

"Well, Bezalel, I'm here because I don't know what to do. Daniel has given different ideas, but I don't know how to implement them or even if they would be effective. I don't know how to tackle the problem."

Bezalel continued to fiddle with a water-screw prototype and said nothing for a long time. Meshach knew him well and knew that he was deep in thought, so he remained quiet as well. Eventually Bezalel walked over and scooped up a dozen or so small wooden blocks and laid them in front of Meshach, who gave him a questioning look.

"Build me a pyramid."

"All right . . . there it is."

"Now take out a couple of the bottom blocks."

"Now I've knocked it down; are you happy?"

"Meshach, I think you have to approach your problem from the bottom up. Otherwise, no matter what you do, it will come crashing down, if the bottom is not secure."

"Go on, Bezalel."

"Slaves are a nasty bunch to work with. Everyone knows that if there is not constant supervision, nothing will get done. Beating them is generally counterproductive, because it makes all the slaves upset.

"On the north side of the hanging gardens, there is a very capable slave who is working for his freedom. He's got three years to go. I have often wondered if there would be a way to motivate him and the others to be more productive. Food is going to be more plentiful this year and cheaper. What if we were to take a section of the base, calculate the time it should take to build it under normal circumstances, then offer the slaves extra days off or triple the rations if they meet the deadline?"

"I don't see how we could implement that on a larger scale."

"You can't do it on a large scale if it does not work on a small scale; that's what we've learned here in the lab. Why don't we talk to that slave I mentioned tomorrow and discuss the ideas?"

"All right, I guess it's worth a try."

Historical Observations

[14]*In Babylon a few slaves were lifetime slaves, but most were slaves for only a limited period of time. In those instances, they always maintained the rights of free people. Free citizens could become slaves, either as punishment for certain offenses or because of their inability to pay a debt. Wives and children could be sold*

as slaves by their husbands or parents, or children taken from the parents, as payment for debts.

Slaves, both temporary and lifetime, were not protected by many laws insofar as their relationship to their owners. It is believed, however, that they were treated relatively well, since a healthy slave could work harder and better. Slaves from foreign lands could usually buy their own freedom over time, they could indenture themselves for so many years in order to pay a debt, or they could get their freedom by marrying a free person. It is for these reasons that most slaves in Babylonia did not remain slaves their entire lives.

The average price for an adult male slave would correspond to about US$500 in today's values. Slavery was not in any way associated with race or color in Babylon. The lowest class of free, unskilled men sometimes found themselves in worse situations than slaves, because there was no one to care for them or feed them if they became injured or sick. It was also a common practice for a person to indenture himself to a tradesman for so many years in order to learn a trade.

By our standards today, these do not sound like fair social rules; but for Nebuchadnezzar's Babylon, it represented considerable advancement in social justice over the Assyrians. Nebuchadnezzar valued personal skills and abilities more than birthrights and this pervasive belief can be seen in the laws he sanctioned.

The next day, they talked to the slave and easily put together a thirty-day incentive plan, establishing triple rations for every day they finished early. This was a seventy-five-man unit with one task-master. They renamed the taskmaster "monitor" taking away his whip and his right to touch the slaves. This caused such an uproar that it was heard all the way to the palace.

Nebuchadnezzar called Meshach and Daniel before him. "Belteshazzar, what is this I hear about the slave driver having his authority removed from him?"

Daniel asked Meshach to explain his reasoning to the king. Quickly perceiving that the king was quite against the whole thing,

Meshach approached the issue from a different angle. "Oh king, the hanging gardens venture is a very delicate project. The base has to be constructed with great precision. On the north side, it is especially critical where the arches will support thousands of tons.

"There is a tendency, as you know, Your Majesty, for the slaves to do sloppy work. We have left the taskmaster there as an observer, and we can go back to the old system at any moment. These last two days, the slaves have worked well, and productivity has risen."

"Meshach, what makes you think that you, a twenty-something-year-old upstart, can change the way things have been done for centuries?"

"With all due respect, Your Majesty, I believe I have the same reasons that you have for thinking that the hanging gardens can be built."

"I have solid reasons why I believe the hanging gardens can be built. You are off on some whim of a notion that you got from who knows where."

"Your Majesty, the hanging gardens project has required the use of an extensive laboratory that has given us a lot of information. Research done there has given you the confidence to go ahead with the project. We have merely moved the lab experiment to the north-sector arches. That is all. It is no more than one more hanging-garden experiment."

Although he still had serious concerns about the loss of the taskmaster's authority, the slaves' unproductive thought processes, and even rebellions, Nebuchadnezzar decided to bide his time and see what happened.

No one was more interested in the slave incentive project than Bezalel. At first the taskmaster-turned-monitor had felt resentful and humiliated. Fifteen days into the experiment, he began to brag about how much work he was getting out of them. In three weeks, they had finished the project.

Bezalel outlined another thirty-day task, and they started into it; although, as agreed, for the following seven days, they received triple rations. The slaves involved in this pilot project sold some of the extra food or gave it to family members and friends.

One evening as things were winding down, a slave came up to Bezalel and gave him two raisin cakes, one for him and one for Meshach. Smiles were exchanged as the slave turned to leave. When Bezalel related this to Meshach, they both realized that the project was indeed destined for success.

News of the accomplishment spread like wildfire throughout the kingdom. The taskmaster became a self-proclaimed expert on how to get the slaves to produce more, although no one really paid attention to him. By the end of the first year, there were short motivation plans in place for almost half of the slaves in the king's service. When there were hints of rebellion, privileges were removed, but whips or other physical punishments were less and less necessary as the incentives proved to be more effective.

Abednego had been made responsible for trade and commerce, an area fraught with bribes and other illegal financial dealings. He was both cunning and fearless and proved to be a formidable enemy of the traditional Babylonian corruption schemes. When bids were let out on certain projects and Abednego knew that large amounts of moneys had exchanged hands to silence bidders or to agree on a higher price for each of the projects, he would cancel the project.

When this happened three times in a row, one of the main Babylonian subcontractors went bankrupt. This man had paid out all of his working capital to bribe the job and lost it all because the jobs were canceled. No one knew whether to participate in the schemes anymore. There was no security for swindlers, with Abednego at the top.

This, too, reached the king's attention, and he reprimanded Daniel for it. "Belteshazzar, the smaller building projects are getting cancelled, and people are complaining that Abednego is acting irresponsibly and has favorites."

"Oh king, Abednego is breaking a cycle of bribery and stealing that has long been part of the bid process in Babylon."

"I'm afraid that he will break it and won't be able to fix it. I want him removed."

"No, sir, I can't do that."

"Belteshazzar, have you forgotten who is king? You don't tell me no."

"I have not forgotten, Your Majesty, and I know my statement means that I will also be removed from my position. But, oh king, I must stake my position with his. We both stay or we both go."

Nebuchadnezzar would not have tolerated this coming from anyone else. However, there was no doubt about Daniel's loyalty, and there was not much doubt about his judgment. Nebuchadnezzar relented.

"You have three months to turn this around and reestablish confidence."

"Your Majesty, I need six months. Most of those on the hurting end of Abednego's plan are part of the council. Not that long ago, you had determined to kill them. They are not your favorite people."

The king contemplated this statement for a few moments then announced his decision. "All right, Belteshazzar, six months it is."

Historical Observations

[15]*The Euphrates, as it flowed beside Babylon, was lined with bricks laid in bitumen. The city canals were similarly constructed. Those canals connecting the two branches of the Euphrates and extending through the land between them are believed to have been dug originally by Hammurabi. Nebuchadnezzar reopened these canals and continued on to build an elaborate system of basins, dikes, and dams creating expansive irrigated fields. These works were so colossal that they stimulated the admiration of ancient historians, in particular the Greeks.*

It did not take that long after all. As soon as word got out that the king had upheld Abednego's decisions, everyone began adjusting to the new game rules. Projects were reinstated and were bid off for a fraction of what they had gone for the first time. All bids and projects were approved directly by Abednego, and he made sure the lowest bidder actually got the job.

The massive financial schemes that had been part of Babylonian construction for as long as anyone could remember were a thing of the past. Only a month after the talk with the king, Daniel was able to show seven different projects that had been let out originally for a total of 1,654 talents but now were going to be built for a mere 932 talents.

During the following months, the king watched his coffers grow and his work projects prosper. He was more than satisfied with Daniel as prime minister of the province of Babylon. However, not everyone was impressed.

After a year of successes, the world began to cave in around the four Hebrews. The military was not quite as congenial as before. Arioch was alert to changes and advised the Hebrews to be so also. The councilmen began meeting secretly. At one such meeting, a council member complained, "None of us have made money since the Hebrews have been put in charge of the province. The deals have dried up!"

"Things can't continue like this, or we'll all be ruined. I've had to sell slaves and cut down in almost every area."

"They won't accept bribes."

"Don't I know that! I still have a man in prison for trying to buy off Abednego. The man won't talk, because I'd kill his family; otherwise, I might be the one in jail. Imagine! A councilman in jail!"

"We have to kill them; there is no other way."

"They are favorites with the king; killing them is risky business. He will investigate, and people will talk to win his favor. It is too risky."

"Well, it has to be done one way or the other."

"It can't be done now. I say we try to make them miserable. There are priests of Marduk who would be delighted to do that. They have lost importance with the king, since he thinks Daniel's God is more powerful."

From that point on, there *was* a concerted effort to make the Hebrews' lives miserable in the hope that they would give up their jobs. The councilmen and those they employed were instructed to give the Hebrews the silent treatment whenever possible. If the king was not present, they ignored them if they could. The priest of Marduk began a campaign with the slaves to undermine progress on the work sites and paid cash money for their compliance. The Hebrews received threats on their lives almost daily. Sometimes they would find a dead black chicken and spilled wine on red cloth in the doorways of their homes, hexes placed on them by one the priests of a demon god. Notes were forged from friends, and the Hebrews sometimes became confused about who was on their side and who was lying.

Daniel discussed the problem with the king, who was not particularly sympathetic.

"You are too young for this job; I knew it all along. Still, I want you to stay. You and your friends are doing a good job. You just need to grow up and learn how to handle it. People in power are always at risk. Make a list of the people you want me to have killed, and we'll look it over together and take care of some or most of them. That should silence the others for a while."

Daniel did not comply with the king's suggestion. Instead, he made plans for his three friends and Arioch, along with a hundred of the royal guard, to escort him out of the city for a two-day retreat that weekend. Both Shadrach and Meshach sent word that they were too busy and would not be able to go, but Daniel sent word again: "You will go. This is an order."

Besides the soldiers, there were some fifty others who went along to cook, carry, and look after the physical needs of the group. Daniel, Hananiah, Mishael, and Azariah were glad to be together again. The burdens of life were truly heavy, and they needed one another's support.

The procession rode a half day out of the city of Babylon and camped under Arioch's watchful eye. The four friends removed themselves to the outskirts of the camp so they would not be heard by an enemy. With a twinkle in his eye, Daniel announced, "I'm ready to quit. Everyone that feels like quitting raise your hand." The young men lightheartedly gestured in accordance. "Do you agree that we can't quit?" Again, all nodded in accordance. Hananiah could not conceal a wide grin. "Everyone who realizes that we are all in this together, please signify." Hananiah chuckled; then so did Mishael. Then so did all four. It felt good to laugh.

They talked intermittently. "How much longer do you think we can take the kind of pressure we are under?"

"I don't feel like I can take it much longer. I'd rather make bricks with the slaves. I'm almost jealous of them."

"The councilmen are behind all the trouble."

"Daniel, you should have let the king kill them when he was in the mood to do so a year ago!"

Daniel spoke, "The king asked me for a list of the people we'd like for him to kill."

"Are you serious?" Meshach had a puzzled look on his face.

"Yes."

"You are not thinking we should make that list, are you?" Shadrach questioned.

"No, but it is a temptation. They don't deserve to live; they are worse than rats."

"David had opportunities to kill Saul, but he wouldn't do it," Meshach added.

"That's different. These men are not kings; they are not even our superiors. They certainly were not hand chosen by God," Abednego observed.

Daniel spoke up, "David killed many and then was not permitted to build the temple."

After a pause, Daniel spoke again, "So what will it be, men: kill the enemies or build a temple? Don't answer—I don't think I want to know." They laughed again.

Abednego spoke, "We are in a spiritual battle. I feel it all the time. The evil is nearly tangible; I can almost reach out and touch it. It is the same feeling I had back in college when that sorcerer was performing his magic. But now I sense it all the time. When I close my eyes, I see demons. I wake up with nightmares. I am worried about what I eat, wondering if it has been hexed. I even sometimes doubt God's ability to free me from this dreadful darkness."

Although Abednego had spoken the words, they were felt by all four. Daniel suggested they quote Scripture together. They began reciting verse after verse, especially the psalms. They felt rejuvenated as the Scripture drew them into the spiritual power and fortitude they had been missing. One or the other stumbled on the words, which made them realize that they had not repeated those sacred words together in a long time.

Abednego observed, "God has given us tremendous successes, but we have grown spiritually weak." The others nodded in agreement. They bowed their heads and took turns praying aloud.

Those in the camp called out that it was time for supper: meat roasted over the open fire, seasoned with rock salt. What a feast! For a couple of hours, there was lighthearted conversation, joking, and eating.

Different ones soon began to lie down; eventually so did the four Hebrews. When all was moderately quiet, Daniel said, not so softly, "Come on, men. Let's go make that list of names." Although his friends did not exactly know what they were doing, they followed Daniel's lead and left the campfire as Daniel took parchment, quill, and torch with him.

When they were far enough away, they sat down, and Daniel said, "I've been thinking about our earlier conversation, and I think it's time to make our hit list."

"You can't be serious!"

"I am serious that I want to make a list of people worthy of death, but I am not serious about killing them. We can surely be creative and influence these people without killing them. Of course, if God reads the list and kills them, that will be up to Him!"

The others chuckled, but Abednego questioned, "Why do you think we cannot have Nebuchadnezzar kill some of them? He kills enemies all the time."

Shadrach jumped in, saying, "To me, it is like not trusting God if we have to resort to murder to solve our problems." The three spoke intermittently.

"Vengeance is mine; I will repay, says the Lord."

"David outsmarted his enemies whenever he could."

"He also killed a lot of his enemies."

"David was an anointed king when he was living in the desert and was raiding the Philistine villages and killing God's enemies."

"So? I don't see where that has a bearing on the discussion."

"I do not think we should kill our adversaries, but we have to do something. We can't just roll over and play dead, or they will kill us and make fun of us as well.

Daniel interjected, "I like the idea of playing tricks on our enemies. It is certainly better than killing them."

"What kinds of tricks?"

"I'm thinking of ploys that do not physically harm them but are intimidating enough to cause them to want to leave us alone. King David acted crazy, and the Philistine king released him. It was a creative thing to do, and it worked. I'm not saying we need to act crazy; I'm saying that I think we can surely be creative enough to intimidate our enemies without actually harming them. At least we could try."

They considered several modes of actions against their black-listed politicians. Stress had been so high that the activity of solving these problems in a creative way became ever more stimulating. The very thought of men in their midtwenties devising schemes, threats, or even practical jokes that would intimidate older councilmen, politicians, sorcerers, astrologers, magicians, and other stuffy folks was invigorating and stimulating!

Daniel mused, "Arioch will be a great help with some of these."

The ideas flowed so well that the young men ran out of both parchment and torchlight. They would continue the next day. The next morning, Arioch came over to Daniel and said, "There is quite a chatter in the camp about your 'list' . . . whatever it is."

Daniel smiled. "If anyone wants to know what we are doing this morning, you just tell them that you suppose we are still working on our list." Arioch nodded.

The four spent about an hour finalizing their plans then committed their ideas to God in prayer and returned to the camp. After the noon meal, they taught Psalm 3:7 to *everyone* in the camp. They worked at it until the whole company, including the soldiers and the slaves, could say it aloud, perfectly in unison: "Arise, O Jehovah; save me, O my God: For thou hast smitten all mine enemies upon the cheek bone; Thou hast broken the teeth of the wicked." Arioch did not know what was coming but was smiling inside. The traitors in the camp would have some interesting news to report when they returned to Babylon.

The next week was the most enjoyable week they had had in a long time. It was business as usual, except for the mysterious preplanned activities. According to instructions, Arioch and twenty soldiers went to the house of one of the ringleaders of the councilmen.

"Sir, come with us." The man, having no choice and scared to death, mounted a horse they had brought for him. As they rode out of the city, Arioch began to talk, making a short, simple statement every ten or fifteen minutes: "Some things are more important than life. What would be more important than life?" . . . "Daniel would like to be your friend. It is really unfortunate that things haven't worked out." . . . "Daniel thinks people deserve a second chance, but I don't. You don't either, do you?" . . . "It is just too bad when things like this have to take my time." . . . "It's nothing personal, you know; soldiers have to do their duties."

Arioch rode out of town for about an hour; the whole time the councilman was sure he was going to meet his death. Then they all turned around and rode him right back to his house. Two hours later, Arioch ended the little excursion by repeating, "Daniel thinks people deserve a second chance, but I don't."

In the case of another councilman, Meshach hired a midget, dressed him in red, and gave him a very small bottle filled with cheap perfume. Meshach gave these instructions: "Just follow the councilman around everywhere he goes for however many days you can. Eventually he will have someone come up to you and ask what you are doing. At that point, you just say, 'Meshach wanted me to get the councilman to drink this.' They will take it from you, and you come and report to me." It all happened just as expected in the middle of the second day. The small bottle of cheap perfume was discarded, considered to be poison.

In the case of a councilman who was also a leading but corrupt merchant in town, Daniel asked for three members of the royal guard and one scribe with parchment and quill to follow him around everywhere he went, writing down all the places and times. They followed him for a week, severely hampering his business. The second week, he sought audience with the king, but Daniel interfered and he was not granted audience. After two weeks, he left town for a period of time then sneaked back in undercover—or so he thought. When Daniel learned of it, he had a crier go through the streets announcing that the man was back in town.

For the head priest of Marduk, Shadrach asked an assistant to take a square yard of red material and paint some unintelligible black lines on it. He was then to lay it on the ground by the front gate of the priest's house and have a load of fresh manure dumped over the cloth, totally covering it. Shadrach then placed four royal guardsmen to guard the manure and gave them the following instructions: "If the priest tells someone to move the pile, you tell him, 'No, Shadrach says it takes three days to work.'"

The priest was furious with the manure in front of his house. But the guards reiterated Shadrach's words. The priest said, "Yes, it will take three days for the smell to kill me and all my neighbors."

On the afternoon of the third day, Shadrach dismissed the guards. The priest promptly arranged for someone to clean up the mess, but when they got down to the red cloth, they ran away. Now it was the priest's turn to be frightened. He gently scraped off the cloth and tried to make meaning out of the meaningless lines. He moved it off his property to the middle of the street; everyone went around it and even avoided the street entirely.

Other priests were called. A great discussion ensued about how to dispose of it. No one could agree; every option was considered too dangerous. They could not decipher the meaning of the lines. The chief sorcerer of Babylon was called in, took one look at it, and said he was not equipped to deal with it. The priests of Babylon formally petitioned the king that Daniel or one of the Hebrews remove the curse. When the news reached the king, he asked Daniel what it was all about. Daniel answered, "It's nothing. I'll take care of it."

Daniel sent for Shadrach, and they decided to take their prank one step further. They had an oxcart carrying a clay jar accompany them. Reaching the site and in the presence of priests of different temples, they carefully removed the clay jar from the oxcart and set it down near the putrid red cloth. They loudly quoted Psalm 3:7, "Arise, O Jehovah; save me, O my God: For thou hast smitten all mine enemies upon the cheek bone; Thou hast broken the teeth of the wicked." With a couple of little sticks they placed the cloth in the jar. Once that was done, they carefully carried the jar to the cart, loaded it, and left. Once out of earshot of the priest, they laughed so hard they cried. The priests, meanwhile, discussed the Hebrews' ceremony in detail for hours. It did not escape their attention that this was the same verse that had been taught to everyone on the campout!

One councilman who was particularly conniving and dangerous, Daniel decided to handle with gifts. He had a servant go to the marketplace and buy some little thing every day and have different messengers present the item and say, "Daniel said to give you this." A woman gave him a single sock and said, "Daniel asked me to give you this." A beggar gave him a loaf of bread and said, "Daniel asked me to give you this." A slave offered him a drink and said, "Daniel asked me to give you this." A shepherd gave him a small trinket and said, "Daniel asked me to give you this." A tailor gave him a colorful cloth ball and said, "Daniel asked me to give you this." A soldier gave him a leather strap and said, "Daniel asked me to give you this."

After several days of this, the man was nearly numb with fear. What did these items mean? Why was this happening? Why didn't Daniel just kill him and be done with it?

There were other small schemes, and Arioch took a total of four-teen people for two-hour rides in the following months. The councilmen held another secret meeting amid quite heated debate.

"We are all doomed, I tell you, unless we back off and leave them alone."

"Nonsense! These are just scare tactics."

"You think so? Well, they are working on me. I had a slave die today, and I'm sure it is a result of that red cloth."

"You are so suspicious that you are scared of your own shadow."

"Well, we are in the shadow of Daniel's God, and I'm scared of that shadow too!"

"Arioch doesn't mess around. I know he didn't kill me because Daniel told him not to. Daniel told him to give me another chance. If it were up to Arioch, I wouldn't be alive today."

"That was a scare tactic too!"

"Shut up! You didn't even get a ride with the guardsmen."

The discussion went on and on into the night with no end in sight. A few left, then more. The last ones to leave were the ones most convinced that their days were numbered. That was the end of the concerted effort to make the Hebrews' lives miserable—at least for a while.

[14]*http://looklex.com/e.o/babylonia.htm*
[15]*[http://www.kellscraft.com/HistoryofBabylonians/HistoryOfBabyloniansCh05.html]*

CHAPTER 11

Kingdom Issues

Nebuchadnezzar was an intelligent and resourceful ruler. Nevertheless, ruling his vast kingdom required constant vigilance. There were always rebellions and uprisings to be quelled. Both Media and Persia had been allies in past battles, when it was to their best interest. Nebuchadnezzar had married a Persian princess to help ensure peace. Although the Persian armies were part of the Babylonian armies, there was always some question as to the loyalty of the Persian generals, especially the younger ones.

- -

Historical Observations

[16]*The Chaldeans, who inhabited the coastal area near the Persian Gulf, had never been entirely dominated by the Assyrians. Around 630 BC, Nabopolassar became king of the loosely organized Chaldeans. In 626 BC, he consolidated his powers among the Chaldeans and forced the Assyrians out of their regional headquarters of Uruk, crowning himself king of Babylonia. He subsequently took part in various wars aimed at the destruction of the ruthless and overbearing Assyrian Empire. Simultaneously, he began to restore the dilapidated network of canals in the cities of Babylonia, believing that agriculture was the future strength of the region. He fought the Assyrian king Ashur-uballit II and also Egypt, experi-*

encing both successes and misfortunes. In 605 BC, Nabopolassar died suddenly in Babylon.

Nabopolassar had named his oldest son Nabu-kudurri-usur II (Nebuchadnezzar) after the famous king of the second dynasty of Isin around a thousand years earlier. He trained him carefully for his prospective kingship and shared responsibilities with him. When the father died, Nebuchadnezzar was with his army in Syria and had just conquered the Egyptians at Carchemish, which is considered by some to be the bloodiest battle ever fought.

Upon receiving the news of his father's death, Nebuchadnezzar immediately returned to Babylon. In his many building inscriptions, he rarely told of his wars; he preferred bragging about his building projects. Most of the inscriptions end with prayers to one of the gods. The Babylonian Chronicle only covers the years 605–594 BC; very little is known about the later years of this famous king. This eleven-year period is well documented. The other three decades of Nebuchadnezzar's reign are also likely to have been well documented, but so far these records remain undiscovered.

Nebuchadnezzar went often to do battle in Syria and Palestine, either to drive out the Egyptians or to squelch a rebellion. In 604 BC, he took the Philistine city of Ashkelon. In 601 BC, he tried to push forward into Egypt but was forced to pull back after a bloody, indecisive battle.

After smaller victorious incursions against the Arabs of Syria, he attacked Palestine again at the end of 598 BC. King Jehoiakim of Judah had rebelled, counting on help from Egypt, which did not materialize. According to the Chronicle, Jerusalem was taken for the second time on March 16, 597 BC. Jehoiakim died during this siege, and his son, King Jehoiachin, together with at least three thousand Jews, was led into exile in Babylon. From all accounts, they seemed to be treated well there. Zedekiah was appointed by Nebuchadnezzar as the new vassal king.

- -

Egypt had been laid at bay and was no longer a military threat, but it was impossible to collect taxes from so far away without maintaining a strong military presence in Egypt. This was not economically expedient over long periods of time, so Egypt had entered into a cordial, non-tribute-paying submission to Nebuchadnezzar. On the other hand, Israel, the gateway to Egypt, was small enough to suppress. It *had* to be seen as totally subservient, or else the Egyptian position might grow and eat away at the edges of the kingdom like a cancer.

Tyre was a thorn in the flesh for Nebuchadnezzar. Since he did not have a fleet at his disposal, he could not bring it down, even after a thirteen-year siege. However, after destroying the mainland city of Tyre and forcing the Phoenicians onto the island, Nebuchadnezzar managed to place strict limits on Tyre's trading abilities and indirectly exacted tributes through the limitation of its trade options.

Historical Observations

[17]*According to the Old Testament, Judah rebelled again in 589 BC, and Jerusalem was placed under siege. The city fell in 586 BC and was completely destroyed. Many thousands of Jews were forced into Babylonian exile, and their country was reduced to an unimportant province of the Babylonian Empire.*

The revolt was caused by an Egyptian invasion that pushed as far as Sidon. Israel was forced, once again, to choose between Egypt and another superpower. Nebuchadnezzar lived at peace with Media throughout his long reign and acted as a mediator after the Median-Lydian war of 590–585 BC.

The Arabs of Syria were a difficult horde to maintain in submission. They would pick opportune times to rebel when the main armies of Babylonia were far away. Their rebellions cost them many lives and were, in the end, to no avail.

Early in Nebuchadnezzar's reign, there had been bloody revolts within the province of Babylonia itself, but Nebuchadnezzar's military prowess and ruthlessness had always prevailed. After two decades, the consolidated kingdom was secure, at least as secure as a kingdom can be when most of its subjects are looking for the right moment to revolt, break free, and stop paying tribute.

Many times Daniel wrestled with the issues of working for someone who was bent on building and saving his kingdom at all costs. Human life meant nothing to Nebuchadnezzar unless that life served his purposes. He was egocentrical and arrogant. He was cunning, calculating, and intensely focused on his personal plans and projects. Generally, his focus was on his kingdom, his power, and his majesty. These thought processes worked themselves out in his grandiose building projects, his military conquests, and his personal sense of supremacy.

During Nebuchadnezzar's life, Daniel continued as the chief ruler over the province of Babylon. When the king was in Babylon, Daniel was in daily contact with him, and that was no easy matter. Daniel realized that at any time he could lose his life for contradicting Nebuchadnezzar's wishes, but this was not a particular concern for Daniel.

On one occasion, Hananiah had said, "Daniel, are you ever afraid that Nebuchadnezzar may just become angry with you and falsely accuse you or have you killed, as he has done to so many others?"

Daniel's answer had intrigued Hananiah. "I crossed the life-and-death bridge with you just after we left Jerusalem." Hananiah said nothing and waited for him to continue. "It is as if I made the decision to die that night when my father said, 'The most important thing in life is to always, always, stay true to God.' I know you remember that the scribe also repeated these words to me later as we stood in the chain line. I have been ready to die for Yahweh ever since then. My time has just not come yet."

Historical Observations

[18]*The Babylonian Empire under Nebuchadnezzar extended from Media-Persia all the way to the Egyptian border. It had a very well-functioning administrative system. Nebuchadnezzar collected*

extremely high taxes in order to maintain his armies and carry out his building projects. He made Babylonia the richest land in western Asia, which is all the more astonishing because it had been rather poor when it was ruled by the Assyrians. Babylon was by far the largest city of the civilized world, covering 196 square miles. Nebuchadnezzar maintained the existing canal systems and built many supplementary canals, continuing the vision of his father and making the land even more productive. Trade and commerce flourished during his reign, with agriculture as the key element.

Nebuchadnezzar's building projects surpassed those of the Assyrian kings and for that matter, all the kings before him. He fortified the old double walls of Babylon, adding another third wall outside the second in certain more vulnerable places. In addition, he erected another wall, the Median Wall, thirty miles north of the city between the Euphrates and the Tigris rivers, making Babylon nearly impenetrable. According to ancient Greek estimates, the Median Wall may have been about one hundred feet high.

He enlarged the old palace, adding many wings with abundantly spacious, elaborately decorated rooms. Hundreds of quarters with large inner courts were at the disposal of the central offices of the empire. Colorful glazed-tile bas-reliefs decorated many of the walls. The Hanging Gardens, one of the seven wonders of the ancient world, was built after the palace expansion was complete. Hundreds of thousands of workers would have been required for these projects.

Hananiah thought aloud, "Do you relish the idea of being out from under the thumb of our dear lunatic king?"

Daniel surprised him again. "Hananiah! I am believing for his repentance and salvation!"

Hananiah forced a smile and responded with a line he had used years earlier with Daniel. "Daniel, you have one big imagination!" Both laughed. Hananiah continued, "Nothing is impossible with our Lord. I actually believe this in my heart, but my reasoning tells me that Nebuchadnezzar is the exception."

Daniel smiled and answered, "If God used *your* reasoning, then all hope *would* be lost!" Hananiah nodded in agreement.

Daniel further reasoned, "Our God has helped me do a good job administering the kingdom of Babylon. You three have been God's instruments in this task, and you *know* it has not been easy. Just as Joseph ruled effectively for the pharaoh, increasing his wealth greatly, God has helped me rule effectively for Nebuchadnezzar, even though I do not approve of much of what he does. My task before God is to be effective in my position and in some small ways right the wrongs that I can.

"In Nebuchadnezzar's defense, the only reason I am still alive is that he is an excellent judge of character! Time and time again, he has chosen not to believe lies that have been told about me. I believe this is the hand of God. As you know, in the end, my accusers have always been embarrassed or slain or both. This is not by chance; God's mighty presence is being felt by Nebuchadnezzar, even though he may not realize it." One could see in Hananiah's eyes that he knew Daniel was right.

One morning before breakfast Daniel was summoned by a clerk to meet Nebuchadnezzar in the throne room at once. Daniel hurried to the meeting, wondering what was the matter. The king seemed upset with Daniel, although, as Daniel would soon learn, it was not personal.

"Belteshazzar!" Nebuchadnezzar exploded, "Zedekiah has gone back on his word and rebelled against me!" Daniel drew a deep breath and shook his head but said nothing. The king continued, "I should have destroyed the city back in the days of Jehoiachim. It was partly out of respect for you, Daniel, that I did not destroy it at that time. Do you remember?"

"Yes, oh king, I remember well."

Daniel remembered ever so well. He had been twenty-two years of age at the time, and he, along with some other Jews in the government, had officially petitioned the king to save the temple and the city. Nebuchadnezzar had agreed to do so, deeming that the goodwill generated through this act would be more valuable to him than a destroyed city.

Even though he did not level the city of Jerusalem, he had taken to Babylon over eleven thousand prisoners as slaves, including the prophet Ezekiel. At that time, Nebuchadnezzar had placed Zedekiah on the throne, since he had maintained contact with Babylon throughout the years and seemed to be dependable and trustworthy. Now this!

Nebuchadnezzar, still fuming, continued, "Daniel, this time I am going to wipe Israel from the map. I will kill its inhabitants, destroy the walls, and turn their houses into rubble! If I don't do this, Egypt will be right there collecting the taxes that are supposed to come to me! I'm sure Zedekiah has a secret treaty with Egypt. He probably thinks he could outlast a very long siege, or he would not have rebelled. What a *fool!* He will learn who the great Nebuchadnezzar is!"

Again, Daniel remained solemn and silent. The king ranted still more loudly. "Belteshazzar, I want you to prepare the schematics and logistics for a five-year siege, rotating between the first, second, and third field armies. If we have to put more slaves in the fields for crop production, then pull them off the mountain waterway project. Once you have those numbers in hand, get back with me; then I will meet with the generals, and we will elaborate the dynamics of the campaign.

"And, Daniel, don't treat this any differently than any other military campaign you've helped with in the past. Use the same councilmen and mathematicians. If you sabotage the information because this is your homeland, I will kill you, your friends, and all the other Jews I can find. Do you understand?"

Daniel answered firmly and clearly, "Yes, Your Majesty, I understand. I will not sabotage the information. Zedekiah should not have gone back on his word. This is very unfortunate for the nation of Israel."

Nebuchadnezzar was somewhat consoled by Daniel's words because he knew they were sincere, and so far this man had never let him down. Nebuchadnezzar's final statement in this exchange cut Daniel to the soul. "Unfortunate for the nation of Israel? I would say so! After this campaign, there will be no more nation of Israel. They will go the way of the 'ten tribes,' as you call them, and the

Assyrians! The Assyrians led the ten tribes into exile, I annihilated the Assyrian nation, and now I will finish off what they started and wipe out the rest of Israel. I can't believe that Zedekiah could be such an idiot!"

Daniel couldn't believe it either. He remembered that his father had said that Zedekiah was the kind of self-serving politician Israel could do without. This was proving to be true, to the detriment of the nation. Daniel called in the standard logistics teams and went about the everyday work of figuring out the problems and laying out the schematics that would be used by the military. Although Daniel's main job was only to oversee that this step was correctly completed, this time it was different. He was aiding in the destruction of his own country. How could he do it?

Daniel called upon his trusted friends to guide and counsel him. As they talked, it seemed as though he already had more light on the subject than they did. It was very difficult. In a court of law, he would be considered an accomplice, an accomplice in the destruction of the city of Jerusalem!

Many nights were spent praying over this heart-wrenching issue. One Sabbath eve, Daniel made his way to the synagogue, as they had begun to call it, since it was a meeting place for the Jews who could not go to the temple in Jerusalem. He arrived at sundown as customary and participated together with the customary patrons in the service. After the service was over, most went home, but Daniel stayed around to talk to the priest on duty that month. He was an older gentleman whom Daniel respected. The priest had raised godly children, four of them in total; and for this reason, if for none other, Daniel felt like he could offer some solid advice. Daniel poured out his heart to the old man of God.

After listening patiently, the priest counseled, "Daniel, son, we live in a fallen world. The end never justifies the means if a black-and-white morality issue is part of the equation. However, in Babylonia, many times the concerns are not black and white. You have two moral issues, don't you? You are obligated to serve the king; God has given you that position. And you are an Israelite, not desiring that harm come to our people or nation. These two interests are in conflict."

Daniel smiled at the old man in the candlelight and said, "Well, sir, you have correctly stated the problem; now state the solution."

The old man smiled slightly and continued, "If you don't obey the king, you will lose your job or, more likely, your head. Then someone else will do it, and the end will be the same."

Daniel objected, "That is a classic the-end-justifies-the-means situation, and I do not think one can use this reasoning."

The priest, almost interrupting Daniel, continued, "I agree. One cannot make a judgment on this basis alone, but hear me out. If you don't do your job, you are morally wrong. If you do your job, you feel that you are still wrong. God is judging Israel for her sins. If you try to get in the way of this judgment, He will overrule you anyway. Our Lord controls the hearts of kings like a river, pointing them wherever He wants. His prophecies will be fulfilled. Have you ever thought, Daniel, that a portion of them are being completed with your help? They are!"

Daniel waited awhile then softly spoke, "Please do not take offense, but I wonder if you are looking at me like I'm Joseph, ruler of the land, and that I should not give up my job because God has given it to me. Some would say I am currently the most important Jew in the world, and that taints their judgment. I don't want it to affect me or you. The prophet told David to build the temple because he thought it was a good idea, and then he had to renege almost immediately when God corrected him. Don't tell me what I want to hear because it makes sense to you."

The old man stared at Daniel. "What is it that makes sense to *you?*"

"I don't know. Your words sound reasonable, but are they right?"

"I'm not even sure what I would say to tickle your ears, if that was what I wanted to do. What is it that you want from me?"

"Sir, I want you to tell me what is on your heart—that's all. I won't second-guess it. I will simply consider your words and pray about them."

"All right, Daniel. My heart tells me that God doesn't need your help with Nebuchadnezzar; He is quite capable of dealing with the man."

Daniel's eyes widened at the simple yet profound truth of the statement. It was true. God was capable of handling Nebuchadnezzar without the help of Daniel. He had taken a step in the thought process. It would take Daniel many more days to completely work through all the issues, but now he was on his way. Zedekiah had sinned, Israel had sinned, God was using Nebuchadnezzar to judge the nation of Israel, and Daniel was unfortunately an innocent participant.

Daniel remembered the words of the old priest, "We live in a fallen world." Nothing seemed to be wholly right or straight. Everything was crooked and unlike God had originally intended it to be. As Daniel walked home with his bodyguards, he marveled at the irony of a holy God being able to use wicked Babylon in His plans.

He looked down a side street and saw prostitutes and opium traders. Perversity was beyond description; lying, cheating, and all sorts of dishonesty were expected and accepted if the offenders could get away with it. Sexual immorality was limited only by the imagination, and that was proving to be nearly limitless.

Every week the faithful Jews looked forward to the time they would spend together in the synagogue, a temporary haven from Babylonian darkness. It was a special pleasure for Daniel, Hananiah, Mishael, and Azariah to worship Yahweh on the Sabbath, along with many others. The four had been instrumental in building the synagogue and had helped the Jews organize themselves into effective groups by tribe and by calling. Many traditions were started during this time of captivity, traditions that would be continued later when they were to return from exile. Quite a few Jews enjoyed places of prominence in the Babylonian Empire, both as slaves and as former slaves who had bought their own freedom over time.

As the years passed, Daniel, Shadrach, Meshach, and Abednego met together less often, but their meetings were generally focused and profitable. Each gathered strength from being with the others. The three were key components to Daniel's administrative strategies and were the backbone of his success, and everyone knew it.

Everyone knew it, both friends and foes: the Jews, the councilmen, the priests of the temples of the various gods, the priests of Marduk, the merchants, the farmers, the military officials, the court officials, the royal guard, the palace personnel, the professors at the university, the astrologers, the soothsayers, the magicians, the sorcerers, the common folks, and Nebuchadnezzar. The king was well aware that he could be successful abroad because he was well cared for in the home province of Babylon. He trusted Daniel; therefore, he trusted Daniel's team. Corruption was down, food supplies were in surplus, building projects were well administered, and he was accomplishing his goals on the home front.

Not everyone was happy about the Hebrews' successes. Many, especially in the ruling council, longed for the old days when their schemes yielded them handsome profits and when they had the ability to influence the king directly without having to filter it through Daniel. The deals had dried up, and so had much of their influence. Daniel had the upper hand, and although they were aware that he was virtually untouchable, it was impossible for them to accept this reality without resentment.

The wise men, astrologers, magicians, enchanters, and sorcerers waited for the right moment; they waited for Daniel to fall from the graces of the king. They waited for Daniel to fall from the seemingly perfect life they perceived him to live. They waited for Daniel to fall into their traps. They waited and they waited and they waited.

[16] *[http://forums.catholic.com/showthread.php?t=110897]*
[17] *[http://www.angelfire.com/nt/Gilgamesh/neobabyl.html]*
[18] *[http://www.gnmagazine.org/issues/gn21/archaeologyexile.htm]*

CHAPTER 12

The Statue, Part 1

The year was 580 BC, and Daniel was thirty-nine years old. The king called him into his royal chamber and excitedly announced, "Daniel, I am going to glorify your God by building the statue of my dream. It will be an image of me made of gold from head to toe. I will have all the nations of the world worship it. It will be part of the consolidation efforts, the finale, if you will. The 127 provinces will be invited; the dedication ceremony will be the grandest the world has ever seen!"

Historical Observations

[19]*The Hanging Gardens were built by King Nebuchadnezzar, who ruled the city for forty-three years beginning in 605 BC. King Nebuchadnezzar constructed an astonishing array of temples, streets, palaces, and walls. The Hanging Gardens probably did not really "hang," in the sense of being suspended. The name comes from an inexact translation of the Greek word "kremastos," or the Latin word "pensilis," which means not just "hanging," but "over-hanging," or "jutting out," as in the case of a terrace or balcony or peninsula. The gardens were described as "vaulted terraces" in some accounts; therefore, the English word "overhanging" is a more accurate translation. The Hanging Gardens lasted long*

after Nebuchadnezzar and Amyitis died. They lasted all through the Persian kingdom, because they still existed during the time of Alexander the Great.

Years ago when Daniel had told the dream to the king, Nebuchadnezzar had vowed to follow Daniel's God, although he did not know what that entailed, nor did he bother to find out. His devotion had lasted for no more than a month.

The king had done some crazy things in the past, but this one topped the list. Daniel tried a couple of times to get a word in but couldn't. The king continued to expound. Daniel clearly saw that this was not to honor his God; this was open rebellion by Nebuchadnezzar *against* the most high God. The king intended to build the *entire* statue of gold, not just the head. He, the great king Nebuchadnezzar, *was* that statue, and *his* kingdom would last forever!

After many years of meticulous planning and building, the hanging gardens were finally finished. The lush green trees and plants, coupled with the sound of running water from the fountains, gave the illusion of a verdant paradise. One could easily forget the surrounding desert when wandering through this sumptuous layered paradise.

The gardens had occupied Nebuchadnezzar's mind and fed his drive for recognition for a good many years. Already they were being termed the greatest phenomenon ever made by man. Not only were they an engineering marvel, but also they were astoundingly colorful and beautiful to gaze upon.

Fourteen large rooms had been built into and under the base of the hanging gardens, and they were now the office spaces of the elite and royal, being the coolest spaces available in the hot desert afternoons. Opulence abounded at every turn. The magnificent stairways leading to the top were a labyrinth of open walkways and hidden cavelike entrances covered with greenery on every side. Small waterfalls cascaded at every turn.

Historical Observations

[20]*The Greek geographer Strabo described the gardens in the first century BC: "They consist of vaulted terraces raised one above another, and resting upon cube-shaped pillars. These are hollow and filled with earth to allow trees of the largest size to be planted. The pillars, the vaults, and terraces are constructed of baked brick and asphalt."*

[21]*Diodorus Siculus, a Greek historian, wrote the following: "The platforms on which the gardens stood consisted of huge slabs of stone [otherwise unheard of in Babylonia], covered with layers of reed, asphalt, and tiles. Over this was put a covering with sheets of lead, that the moisture which drenched through the earth might not rot the foundation. Upon all these was laid earth of a convenient depth, sufficient for the growth of the greatest trees. When the soil was laid even and smooth, it was planted with all sorts of trees, which both for greatness and beauty might delight the spectators."*

[22]*How big were the Hanging Gardens? Diodorus tells us, "They were about 400 feet wide by 400 feet long and more than 80 feet high."*

[23]*Some other accounts, however, indicate the height was slightly higher than the outer city walls and could be seen from a distance. The ancient historian Herodotus said they were 320 feet high. In any case, the Hanging Gardens were an amazing sight in the ancient world: a green, leafy artificial mountain in the desert.*

[24]*Beginning in 1899, Robert Koldewey dug on the Babel site for some fourteen years and unearthed many of its features, including the outer walls, inner walls, foundation of the Tower of Babel [temple of Marduk], Nebuchadnezzar's palaces, and the wide processional roadway that passed through the heart of the city. While excavating the Southern Citadel, Koldewey discovered a basement with fourteen large rooms with stone arch ceilings. Some ancient records record "fourteen large rooms with stone arch ceilings" under the Hanging Gardens. According to historians of antiquity, only two locations in the city had made use of large stones: the north wall of the Northern Citadel and the Hanging Gardens.*

Since the north wall of the Northern Citadel had already been found and had indeed contained large stones, it seemed likely, then, that Koldewey had found the cellar of the gardens. He continued exploring the area and discovered many of the features reported by Diodorus. Finally, a room was unearthed, with three large holes in the floor. Koldewey concluded this had been the location of the commonly accepted theory of the chain pumps that had raised the water to the garden's peak.

Bezalel's experiments had led him to discover that the only material that would adequately waterproof the lower office levels and the foundations for decades to come was lead. Hundreds of tons of lead had been melted and molded to line the bottom planter areas and the hollow columns that housed the taproots of the larger trees. Extensive archways on three sides provided daylight for all fourteen rooms and good ventilation if torches or oil lamps were used at night. All of this also provided a pleasant, cool working atmosphere.

Partly at Meshach's suggestion, Bezalel had decided on two water-hoisting mechanisms. The main one, the one they knew they could build and trust, was located exactly in the middle of the three-hundred-foot square base. Two carefully designed openings allowed the buckets to dip twenty feet under the floor, loop around, and emerge from the other side full of water to be hoisted to the top. A third hole provided maintenance access to descend into the well. The hoist mechanism consisted of double chains attached to larger rectangular buckets.

At the top, the chains ran over a large iron wheel twelve feet in diameter and four feet in width, with a two-foot eight-inch axle protruding from each end. This finely machined axle was fitted with bronze sleeves and cradled in thick bronze *U*'s on each end. Carefully fitted leather seals on each end of the *U*'s guaranteed that the axle could always turn in a bath of oil. Both sides of the wheel featured gravity-actuated wedges and notches that prevented the wheel from turning backwards.

After the prototype had been designed, Meshach had jokingly said to Bezalel, "The only mechanisms we need to power this are fat slaves with good knees."

"Meshach, you lost me."

"How many times can a slave climb to three hundred feet in a day if he has good knees? Fifteen? One good-sized slave will weigh more than two buckets of water. There will be around 230 buckets filled; that's 115 slaves riding down on the upside-down buckets!"

"Uh . . . Meshach . . . uh . . . an idea that simple can't work, for some reason, but I haven't yet figured out why. Oh, there is the friction to consider."

"There is also the weight of the down buckets, which would offset some or all of the friction."

"It wouldn't offset it that much."

"Yes it would. But, all right, put 150 slaves on the down buckets! Every slave will want that job. Walk up and then ride down in a cool dripping shaft. I guess if the chain broke, they probably would all die. That's why we'd have to use slaves and not let schoolboys do it."

"The chances of both chains breaking at once are extremely slim, remember?"

"Oh yeah, that's why we went with the double-chain idea."

Bezalel actually ended up devising a system of inside platforms where ten slaves to a group would pull the chains down, five at a time, until the marker bucket would come around; then they would switch groups. This was fine and proper in Bezalel's mind; but it was not long at all until there were a lot of riders, and Meshach's idea was the one that actually prevailed in the end. Meshach rode the buckets many times, and so did many others, including some of the older school-aged boys.

Bezalel went on to design a prototype of a water screw powered mostly by the current of the Euphrates, but that project would have taken a long time to perfect, and Nebuchadnezzar had other ideas for the use of Bezalel's skills.

Daniel wished Nebuchadnezzar could be content just squelching rebellions and basking in the success of the hanging gardens. He disagreed completely with the king's plans to build a statue in his own honor; yet in spite of his high position, Daniel knew his personal opinions made no difference to Nebuchadnezzar. He paid no attention to Daniel's suggestions to improve the living conditions of some poorer neighborhoods in Babylon. He had ignored Daniel's ideas for eliminating bribes in the court systems.

It was clear to Daniel that he was in the king's favor because Nebuchadnezzar trusted him, not because the king agreed with him in all things. Through the years, Daniel had grown to respect Nebuchadnezzar's genius, but he had never become comfortable with his short temper and impulsiveness. Once he latched onto an idea, no one could change his mind. In military campaigns, it had been that way. In the hanging gardens project, it had been that way. Now the plans to build this golden statue were going forward at full speed.

Nebuchadnezzar rambled on. He would build it, not in the city but on the plain of Dura, because the city wouldn't hold everyone. Daniel's eyes widened as the king continued. "I will require that all my officials from all the provinces attend the dedication ceremony." Daniel's eyes widened further. "Not only will they come to see this beautiful Babylon that I have built, but they will also be able to worship my image. It will be the largest single gathering to pay homage to a king that has ever taken place here on earth! Even the gods won't miss it!"

The king looked at Daniel. "Yes, Belteshazzar, it will be unsurpassed here on earth and maybe in the heavens!" Daniel, purposefully expressionless, nodded his head. He knew the king was unconcerned about his reaction. Nebuchadnezzar was rolling on.

The following weeks, Nebuchadnezzar dictated his ideas to his personal scribes. He talked to various officials about his intentions, and of course, everyone was outwardly as enthusiastic as he was. He took stock of the gold in the royal coffers and determined how many more tons might be needed. He called in Bezalel and went over his ideas with him. Bezalel was torn between being excited about a new project and being disappointed that he would continue to be so important.

Dozens of small models of the statue were molded over and over until Nebuchadnezzar was satisfied. The king even had Bezalel bring in his pottery tools and work on the prototype right there in the throne room. This little detail was so important to Nebuchadnezzar that it took a full three days. At one point, when Nebuchadnezzar was not in the room, Daniel came over to examine Bezalel's work. "Meshach speaks highly of you; he says your skills are unequaled."

"I like him too."

"That is not really how the statue looked."

"What do you mean?"

"I had the dream too, you'll remember, and that's not exactly what it looked like."

"It will be ninety feet in the air, so it will have to be out of iron overlaid with gold; that's why I have to make the legs and feet thicker."

"I mean the face."

"Oh, well, you know whose face this is!"

"I know. You do really good work, Bezalel."

"Thank you!"

Nebuchadnezzar had embarked upon the biggest ego trip of his life. The gardens were barely finished, and he had practically forgotten them. Following the king's orders, Abednego was to procure and direct all iron and iron ore to the site that had been chosen on the plain of Dura. A small town was already being constructed to house the workers and to safely stock supplies and tools.

Bezalel's next feat was to design iron-smelting furnaces that would have the capacity to smelt the ore and render pure enough iron to be structurally safe. After that, huge amounts of clay had to be hauled in from the river and holes dug for the formation of the molds. The clay had to be formed exactly so that the iron parts would fit together once they were cooled down. Quality control on the gardens had been a manageable task that could be delegated— but not this! Bezalel would have to oversee each detail himself. Even then, he knew he would have to verify multiple times.

Models of furnaces were made. Bezalel was not happy with the end result. The iron had bubbles and flux in it. This would never do on a structure that had to support many tons. He worked on other smelting techniques. The first iron out was somewhat impure, the middle flow was perhaps acceptable, and the end of the batch was too brittle when put under stress tests.

Bezalel finally settled on a three-stage system. The first furnace, measuring about forty feet wide by sixty feet long and eighteen feet high, looked somewhat like a very short three-story building. It was fired with coal and accelerated with six bellows, three on each side. The fuel was stoked from underneath; the bellows also came in from below. The second floor, which was about six feet off the ground, was a series of perforated bricks about one foot thick, which evened out the heat. Above that was the smelting floor, which was of vented clay with *V* troughs running out the end of the furnace into small clay caster molds in the ground. The second and third furnaces resembled the first from the outside, but the inside of each was differently designed, as each furnace further purified and strengthened the iron.

Although Bezalel and Meshach no longer worked together, Meshach decided to pay him a visit. It was after the groundwork was well underway and the first furnace had been modified to satisfaction.

"Bezalel, you are certainly earning your nickname!"

"If I get this statue up and stable and manage to cover it with gold from head to toe within my four-year deadline, then I will have earned it!"

"I'm sure you've done a world of calculations to draw up the plans for this statue."

"Not as much as you might think. Like Bezalel in the desert many centuries ago, this is as much an art project as it is an industrial feat. The gardens were much more of an engineering challenge; here I get to be an artist."

"Right! That's why it's taken nearly a year for you to organize the work and design the furnaces!"

"Well, anyway, I like to think of this as a big art project."

"I wish you were using your skills to make something for Yahweh, like the first Bezalel. You know how I feel about idols."

"I know. This is just a statue of the king. Everyone's got their own way of thinking about that. If you ask me, it's pretty silly for me to pray to something I make myself. But maybe some deity will come down and inhabit it, like they say."

"No, you were right the first time. It's pretty silly to pray to something we can make ourselves."

"Whatever you say."

"By the way, are you still paying half of your salary to the priest of Marduk to keep your boys out of the fiery hands of Moloch?"

"They are too old for Moloch; they are nineteen and twenty. But yes, I am still paying for their keep."

"Would you like me to help you with that?"

"If I knew you could do it without causing harm to me or someone I love, I'd say yes."

"Daniel is good at this kind of thing, and I'm sure he'd be glad to use his influence."

"I don't know. Maybe it's better to just leave things as they are."

As Meshach left, he felt good about having renewed his friendship with Bezalel.

The next time Meshach saw Daniel, he told him about his conversation with Bezalel and that he was still being blackmailed. Daniel said he would give it some thought. A few months later, Daniel and the king received formal invitations to the funeral of a wife of the head priest of Marduk. Daniel knew this was Bezalel's former wife, and his mind went into high speed; this might be the chance to set accounts straight for Meshach's friend.

Daniel missed the funeral, but not the opportunity. Calling in a lawyer and a clerk, Daniel talked through his plan, and the lawyer helped perfect the legal wording. Daniel paid a visit to the king just before suppertime.

"Oh king, it has come to my attention that Bezalel has two sons."

"Yes?"

Historical Observations

[25]*Marriages were usually arranged by parents, and it was expected that the groom present a gift to the father of the bride. "Marrying up" in social status was a common goal for all parents, but it is also presumed that many times parents heeded their children's wishes about the choosing of a mate. The marriage was concluded by a contract inscribed on a tablet and was intended to last until one of them died.*

The woman could have property and engage in business in her own name. What was in her name was hers alone, what was in the husband's name was his alone, and what was in both names was owned jointly. The woman had some rights in the marriage, but it was the man who enjoyed the most rights.

She could not be unfaithful to him, but his unfaithfulness was somewhat ignored. He could easily divorce his wife, and/or marry a second if the first did not give him children or was unfaithful. It was a difficult thing for the woman to divorce her husband but could be done if he was thought to be lost in battle but no death certificate could be issued, did not come home for a very long time, mutilated her or permanently injured her, or if he simply allowed her to divorce him. If the man divorced the woman, she was awarded some sort of indemnity. If she divorced him, no indemnity was required, although it could be awarded by a judge if the wife had been mistreated, subject to the judge's opinion.

"It is widely recognized that Bezalel is one of the greatest craftsmen on earth. He is getting up in years, and his sons are now of a proper age to apprentice their father. It could be that one or both of his sons have the same abilities, and I feel it would be wise use to the king's powers to require them to apprentice their father. You gave me a chance to prove myself, and I hope I have served you well up until now. These young men need the same chance."

"What do you want me to do?"

"Sign this custody document, and seal it with your ring."

Without another word and without even reading the document, Nebuchadnezzar signed it, sealed it, and handed it back to Daniel, stating, "Usually kids don't inherit all of their parents' abilities, but I guess it's worth a try."

Daniel called a scribe and had him make three authenticated copies. Three witnesses signed that the king had, in fact, sealed the original, and it would be archived for safekeeping. Daniel called for the royal escort service to deliver the custody document to the priest of Marduk and bring the youths back to the palace with their personal belongings.

Two hours later, the escort service returned with the two young men. Daniel looked at their frightened, tearstained faces. They were scared, and they were brokenhearted, having just lost their mother. They wondered why they were standing in the king's palace in front of the famous prime minister Belteshazzar.

Daniel's heart went out to them. The time did not seem so far removed when he had lost his mother and been plunged into a new life.

"Are you men hungry?" No answer.

"Would you like to eat some bread or raisin cakes while I tell you what you are doing here?" One nodded yes; the other, no.

Then the one who nodded no said, "Yes, I mean."

"Follow me, and don't call me Belteshazzar; call me Daniel. It's shorter, and it's what my friends call me." Daniel took them to his personal quarters, and they sat down on pillows as servants brought in some food to eat. It was now about 9 p.m.

"Do you remember your father?"

"Yes."

"What do you remember about him?"

"When he wasn't working, he would play with us. He designed the hanging gardens, you know."

"Yes, I do; he is a greatly skilled engineer and craftsman."

"Some say he is the best in the world. That's why the king took him away from us, so he could work on the king's projects and not be bothered by a wife or children."

"Who told you that?"

"Mother."

"Did you like living with your mother and the priest?

"It was all right."

"What did you like about it?"

"It was just all right, that's all. We were allowed to leave the temple only on rare occasions. We've . . . we've never been outside the city walls."

"Do you have jobs?"

"No . . . well, yes. We spend most days helping out in the temple of Marduk since we live there anyway. In a few years, we may be able to apply for priesthood training."

"Is that what you want to do?"

"Not really; it is just what we have to do. Both of us would rather work with our hands, like our father. We like to make things."

"Did your mother and the priest get along well?"

"No. He had a couple of other wives that came in after her. She always slept in our room."

"Are you sad that I brought you to the palace?"

"No, but we are wondering why. Have we done something wrong?"

"Do you want to go back home?"

"No!"

"Where do you want to go?"

"Anywhere but back home."

"Why?"

"Because without mother there, things might be really bad. Beltesha . . . ah . . . Daniel . . . if you would talk to the king, do you think he would allow us to see our father for just a little while and talk about some things?"

"I think he might. We'll work some more on that tomorrow. Let's go to bed now."

The next morning, Daniel left a servant tending to the young men sleeping in his quarters. Amid the other urgent and routine things that he needed to take care of, Daniel contacted the university and sent for the now elderly Ashpenaz. When he arrived, Daniel explained that the king wanted to pay for a private tutor for Bezalel's sons so that they could complete their education and also apprentice with their father on the plain of Dura. Ashpenaz agreed to hire a tutor and have him sent out there.

Daniel also sent couriers to summon Bezalel to the palace. In the middle of the afternoon, Bezalel arrived at the palace, worrying why he'd been summoned into Daniel's presence.

"Bezalel, it has come to the king's attention that you are not actively training an apprentice."

"I had requested not to, and my request was granted."

"Well, he has changed his mind, and now he wants you to have two apprentices."

"Two?"

"Yes, two, and it will be required of you to spend much time with them. The king understands that they may not develop your skills, but you must dedicate yourself to their training."

"Yes, sir."

Daniel sent for the apprentices to be brought from his quarters. The boys were being led by a servant down the hall to Daniel; then as they turned the corner, they saw their father—and stopped in stunned silence. The initial shock was short-lived, as the three flew into one another's arms, the father weeping even more than the sons.

Daniel looked on with a mixture of sympathy and jealousy. He would have gladly given up his position as prime minister to go back in time and be reunited with his father. Oh, how good that would have been! Oh, how good it would be even right now! This scene lasted longer than Daniel had thought it would. He wiped his eyes.

Daniel spoke, "Young men, the king requires that you become apprentices to your father and *also* that you receive a formal education. If you do not apply yourselves to the tasks and work hard, the decision could be reversed. As long as you show you are working diligently, even if you do not have the skills of your father, you will be allowed to stay with him.

"Bezalel, you are to divide your time from now on between working and teaching. I have arranged for your elderly mother to be brought to you; she is said to be in good health. She will be charged with looking after the boys and you too, of course."

Daniel smiled then patted Bezalel on the shoulder. Bezalel started crying again. He awkwardly, stiffly bowed, but Daniel came forward to embrace him; the sons joined in also.

Daniel spoke, "Take good care of these boys." As they stepped back and wiped their eyes again, Daniel pulled from beneath his robe a fancy sealed parchment and handed it to Bezalel. "These are the custody-apprentice papers, and they are straight from the king; there's no appealing them."

With bottom lip quivering and an arm around each son, Bezalel managed to get out, "Thank you."

[19] *[www.crystalinks.com/hanginggardensbabylon.html].*
[20] *[http://library.thinkquest.org/C0125521/_babylon.htm]*
[21] *[http://library.thinkquest.org/C0125521/_babylon.htm]*
[22] *[http://www.cleveleys.co.uk/wonders/gardensofbabylon.htm]*
[23] *[http://dooroodiran.blogspot.com/2004_04_01_archive.html]*
[24] *[http://www.unmuseum.org/hangg.htm]*
[25] *[http://www.bible-history.com/babylonia/BabyloniaFamily_and_Tribe.htm]*

CHAPTER 13

The Statue, Part 2

Nebuchadnezzar went often to the plain of Dura to inspect the work and to imagine his day of glory. The base of the statue would be forty-five feet high, and the statue would be another forty-five feet tall. The base as well as the statue would be of iron. The image would be overlaid with gold and polished until it reflected even the moonlight. It would be magnificent. For all those visiting on the day of the inauguration, it would become quite clear that Nebuchadnezzar did, in fact, rule the whole world.

Bezalel's sons were delighted beyond measure to be working with their father; they learned quickly and were soon assets to his work. Finally, Bezalel had all of the parts of the statue formed on the ground. Would they fit together? He had measured so precisely, and everything had to join perfectly. With elaborate hoists, he lifted, turned, and lowered the upper part of the leg to the lower part. A perfect match! As each piece was added, it was heat-welded together with molten iron.

The furnaces poured out more iron, and more statue pieces were made to precision. After two and a half years, Bezalel had built the image of iron in a framework on the ground on the plain of Dura. Now it was time to hoist it to the top of the platform. Winches were built onto the top of an elaborate framework. The image was hoisted a little at a time and tied off. Stress checks were taken on the framework, and reinforcement was applied where needed.

The hoisting of the image and its placement on the pedestal took a full three weeks. The king was elated when advised that it was finally secured. Nebuchadnezzar was like a child who had opened a birthday gift and wanted everyone to see it. "Belteshazzar, let's go look at my statue!"

Daniel unenthusiastically replied, "Let's go."

Upon arriving at the site, Nebuchadnezzar quickly stepped through the framework and stared up at the looming image of himself against the clear blue afternoon sky. Bezalel had seen him coming and was waiting nearby. The king did not address Bezalel or anyone else; he simply walked around the base, gazing upward and muttering, "This is the largest statue ever to have been erected by mankind." Squinting upward, his imagination was running wild, and his pleasure was fueling it on.

"Bezalel, it is all I was hoping it would be. You have done fine work."

"Thank you, Your Majesty."

"Will nine and a half tons of gold be enough to cover it?"

"I believe so, Your Majesty."

"Have you sufficient skilled labor to accomplish the task?"

"Yes, sir, but the truly master craftsmen number only eleven. If you want it done quickly, we will include some others who are skilled, but not quite to the same level."

"No! I want it to be perfect! How long will it take using only the eleven?"

"Probably nine months to one year, Your Majesty."

"That is fine; it will give us time to send word to the farthest reaches of the kingdom, and it will give people time to make the trip here for the dedication. Bezalel, I want you to personally cover the face of the statue; it must be faultless. The statue represents me and my kingdom! The glory of the image will surpass anything imagined by men."

"Yes, Your Majesty."

Somewhat oblivious that he was talking to no particular person, Nebuchadnezzar began walking away from Bezalel and toward Daniel, who had not moved from the original spot where they had stepped inside the framework. "Everyone will recognize the great

Nebuchadnezzar for who he really is—king of Babylon! ruler of the world!" Now he was speaking loudly, almost as if to show his anger at those who had rebelled in the past. "I, the great Nebuchadnezzar, will be shown to all as supreme! None will question my power and my majesty; the dedication of my image will seal my power for decades to come!" Turning back toward Bezalel, the king shouted out with raised hand, "Bezalel, cover it with gold!"

Nebuchadnezzar left the dream world into which he had been drawn by his ego as his eyes met Daniel's. He saw the subtle disapproval in Daniel's gaze but maintained an I-know-what-I'm-doing posture. Tapping Daniel's shoulder, he began walking back through the framework.

"Belteshazzar, do we have nine and a half tons of gold that can go to cover the statue?"

"Yes, Your Majesty."

"See to it that the transfer documents are in place and that every ounce of gold will be accounted for that comes from the treasury to the statue site. Also see to it that there are mechanisms in place to guarantee that *all* of the gold that comes out here ends up on the statue."

"Yes, sir."

"And begin devising a plan to execute the mandatory-presence invitations to all the officials in all the provinces. I want everyone here. *No one* will miss the dedication."

"Yes, sir."

"And see to it that Babylon is well supplied with foods of all kinds to feed a hundred thousand extra people for three months, beginning one year from now."

"Yes, sir."

"When the time is closer, send special invitations to all the priests and rulers of all the temples of Babylon. They need a special place of honor, and they need to know ahead of time that they will all bow down to the statue. There will be no one exempt from paying homage to the image—and to me."

"Yes, sir."

"I *will* be supreme! Did you get all that, Belteshazzar?"

"Yes, Your Majesty, I did."

Nebuchadnezzar waited for a few moments and turned back, staring contentedly at the monument. They entered the chariot again and headed back to the palace.

The countdown was on. Twelve months remained until the dedication ceremony. Daniel made master lists and secondary lists of everything that needed to be done. He formed committees and subcommittees to cover each aspect of the great event. After one week of organizing and strategizing, he wondered if a year would be enough time to see it all come together.

Nebuchadnezzar asked Daniel to write the invitation, which he did. However, the king was not happy with Daniel's choice of words and insisted on his own wording:

To the Subjects of Babylon:

I, the great King Nebuchadnezzar, have commanded to gather together the satraps, the deputies, the governors, the judges, the treasurers, the counselors, the military chiefs of staff, and all the rulers of the 127 provinces to come to the dedication of the image that I, Nebuchadnezzar, have set up.

It will be commanded of you and of all the peoples, nations, and languages that at what time you shall hear the sound of the cornet, flute, harp, psaltery, trumpets, dulcimer, and all kinds of musical instruments, you will fall down and worship the golden image that I, Nebuchadnezzar, have set up; and whosoever does not fall down and worship, the same shall be cast into the midst of a burning fiery furnace.

Registration will be under the hanging gardens and will begin one month prior to the ceremony. Any nation or people not duly represented will have their taxes doubled for the following year, and their rulers will be replaced with those who are deemed more worthy.

Signed,
The great King Nebuchadnezzar

One official copy of each invitation was sent to each of the 127 provinces. An additional 2,700 simple copies were reproduced so that within the provinces there would be adequate collateral notification. Couriers were organized and given advance funds for their trips. Some would be gone four months to deliver the messages and return.

The couriers were issued official forms stamped by the king that were to be filled out and duly signed by the recipients of the invitation. Certain couriers were assigned contingencies of soldiers to accompany them. Others who did not have as far to travel went alone or with a handful of slaves or servants.

Exactly one month after the king had told Bezalel, "Cover it with gold," the invitations were ready to be sent off. Daniel advised the king, who said, "I want the people of Babylon to hear about it now, not later. Gather all the rulers of Babylon together and also the wise men, astrologers, magicians, enchanters, and sorcerers. We will read to them the invitation, and they will participate in the send-off of the couriers."

The officials of the province of Babylon were summoned the next day. Regardless of prior commitments, by 3 p.m. all had arrived. The king spoke from the first tier of the ziggurat of Marduk, some fifty feet in the air. He spoke briefly of his grandiose works, of the magnificent statue, and of his far-reaching kingdom. Then he personally read the invitation that was about to go out. When he finished, the people cheered and cheered. He was flattered with the enthusiasm of his people.

The ceremony ended with trumpet sounds and the couriers galloping down the wide avenue that ran in front of the temple and out to the wall—and beyond that, the road to the world. Many couriers simply returned to town again after galloping out for the show of the ceremony, because they planned to leave early in the morning. That didn't matter to the king, however; his ego had been uplifted, and he was ready for a night of music and entertainment.

Historical Observations
The Royal Road

[26] *"As regards this road, the truth is as follows: Everywhere there are royal stations with excellent resting places, and the whole road runs through country which is inhabited and safe. The number of these stages amounts in all to one hundred and eleven.*

"This is the number of stages with resting places, as one goes up from Sardes to Susa. If the royal road has been rightly measured . . . the number of kilometers from Sardes to the palace of Susa is 2,500. So if without encumbrances one travels 30 kilometers each day, some ninety days are spent on the journey." —Herodotus, describing the road between Sardes and Susa

----

After the king's speech, Daniel made his way over to Hananiah, Mishael, and Azariah and asked if they could come to the palace that evening. They arranged to meet in his private quarters, which were plush with luxuries and servants. As prime minister, he was always on call for the king and could attain audience with him almost anytime he wanted, if he felt the matter was pressing enough to warrant the king's immediate attention.

Many would have given anything to be in Daniel's position, but Daniel saw it as a gift from God and did not hold tightly to it. His commitment to God was primary, so much so that it seemed to others that Daniel did not really appreciate the wealth and power at his disposal. These things simply did not motivate him. Knowing that he was pleasing Yahweh was the *only* thing that mattered to Daniel.

When his friends arrived at the palace, they went to Daniel's quarters then decided it would be more private if they went for a walk in the main palace gardens. From where they were seated on some marble benches, they could hear the music and the dancing from Nebuchadnezzar's celebration in the entertainment hall.

It was 579 BC. Daniel and his friends were forty years old. Abednego led the discussion. "We are about halfway through our normal lifespan here on earth, and we have never bowed to a statue of any kind. What are we going to do about the decree?" Abednego had hoped to get a discussion going, but no one said anything. He continued, "It seems pretty simple: bow and live, or stand and die." Again silence prevailed for a longer time than Abednego felt was warranted.

Finally, Shadrach said, "It is not that simple. The king has been very kind to us, and we have been given positions of high privilege. If we don't bow, we will not only spoil the celebration, but we will also appear ungrateful after all he's done for us."

Mishael chimed in, "We bow to the king every time we see him. Why not bow to his statue?"

Daniel answered, "Bowing to someone out of respect and worshiping a statue are two different things."

Mishael came back with, "If I were to bow before the statue, I would not be worshiping it or the king. God knows our hearts."

Abednego jumped into the conversation again. "Pretending to tie our sandals is also not worshiping the statue."

This discussion continued for a while before Daniel said, "I think we need two plans. Plan one is to get out of going to the dedication ceremony altogether. Plan two is to decide what we are going to do if we have to be at the ceremony.

"We'll concentrate on plan one for now, but just for the record, I could not personally bow down to an idol, especially when it would be perceived as worship by other people. We were willing to die over the food incident way back in college, and God worked that out. He can work this out for His glory somehow, just like he did that . . . and Hananiah, don't tell me I have a big imagination!"

Hananiah smiled and said, "Daniel, if you think we can stand out there when the time comes and not get thrown into the fiery furnace, then you still have a big imagination." They chuckled a bit in spite of the gravity of the subject.

Daniel said, "Let's come back to plan two later and talk about plan one right now. You know the king will be requiring *everyone* to attend. I am probably the one who could justify absence the easiest.

The king has always thought that either he or I need to remain at the palace at all times. Since he will be at the ceremony, I may be able to miss it just because I would be expected to stay at the palace. It will be you three who will be most conspicuously missed if you are absent."

Shadrach joined in with, "I agree. You can probably miss it. I could find something that has to be done in the fields, but it would get back to the king that I was not at his statue dedication, and he would not like it at all."

Meshach spoke up. "Well, that would not be as offensive as going but not bowing. After all he has done for us and after all the years of work he is putting into the statue and the ceremony, going and not bowing will be *terribly* offensive."

"'All right,' said Meshach, "that brings us back to the point that we *have* to try for plan one of nonattendance.'"

The foursome worked on a plan for months. After traveling down several more elaborate thought processes, they finally decided that the very best option was one in which they would tell no one of their intentions ahead of time and then simply miss the ceremony. Any rumor that spread around the idea that they might not attend would fall into the hands of their enemies, which would not be a good thing.

Six months remained until the ceremony. Bezalel was ahead of schedule and judged that he would finish the statue a couple of months early. The king focused all his energies on the event. He planned to leave no doubt in anyone's mind as to his power and glory. Men would fear and reverence him even more than before. Daniel could see the potential disaster looming but did not dwell on it, as there was little that could be done to mitigate the situation.

At the three-month mark, rumors went around that the statue was practically complete. Meshach had not seen Bezalel for almost a year, so he paid him a visit to renew the friendship and to see for himself. Bezalel was pleased to see him and to show off the masterpiece.

"Look at that, Meshach. Isn't it beautiful gleaming in the sun?" said Bezalel.

"Yes, it is!" Meshach replied as he admired the masterpiece.

Bezalel took in the moment then spoke again. "This is the biggest art project I have ever done, and it is the one that has given me the most pleasure, because it is the first one in which I've been able to include my sons. Thank you, Meshach, for all you did to make it possible for me to be reunited with my boys."

Bezalel suddenly became serious. "Meshach, I need to say something that you are not going to like to hear."

Meshach gave him an inquisitive look and said, "Say it anyway, Bezalel."

"I know how you feel about idols. I know you don't bow to them. I know you don't pray to them. But, Meshach, this is *not* an idol; this is just a statue of the king. When the time comes, you *must* bow down to it. The king will not spare you if you don't. He will be furious and will kill you. He won't have a choice; otherwise, he will seem weak. You have to get it into your head that you *must* bow down to it just this one time. Do it for my sake, if for no other reason."

Halfway through Bezalel's speech, one of his sons arrived. As Bezalel finished, his son chimed in, "Some are saying you won't bow down to the idol. There are even bets out on it. What are you going to do?"

Meshach was taken back; he had not known their religious beliefs were such common knowledge. As he thought about it, however, it made sense, because they had a twenty-year history of not going to the idol ceremonies and not bowing to any god but their own. If the common people were talking about it, he was sure the councilmen were also talking about it. Meshach answered, "Our God will show us what to do."

Bezalel quickly added, "Good! Think about what I said. This time I am right, and you know it."

They visited a little more, and then Meshach left. As he was riding away, Bezalel said, "Son, I fear they will not bow to the statue. Meshach is not one to change what he believes just because it means he will die." Bezalel continued, as if to answer his son's puzzled look. "Life is important to him, but his God is more important. I hope he and his friends are not at the ceremony."

Upon returning to the city, Meshach sent word to the others that he would like to meet. All were very busy, so they arranged a time to meet two days from then, at night. When the time came, Meshach started off the dialogue by relating the story of his conversation with Bezalel and his son.

Daniel lamented, "I was afraid this would happen. Now the councilmen will do everything in their power to see that we are at the ceremony—hoping we won't bow."

Abednego solemnly added, "I think we need to work on our second plan." The others agreed.

Meshach stated, "I cannot bow to the statue and ruin the witness we have had for the last twenty years."

"Nor I," said Abednego.

Shadrach coldly stated, "Nor I, sitting here secure three months from the date. What will it actually be like when the time comes and we ruin Nebuchadnezzar's grand celebration and are grabbed by the soldiers and thrown into the flames? It will seem different when the time comes."

There was a long period of silence, and then Shadrach continued, "I have crossed that bridge in my mind. It will be too hard to live with myself if I bow. The only thing Nebuchadnezzar can hold over us is death, and our God ultimately controls that—not the king."

Daniel stated, "That is how I see it too. All right, let's say we don't bow, and we are taken before the king. He will be furious! We may not even have a chance to say anything, but if we do, it needs to be brief and clear."

The four deliberated together for a while and came up with a brief statement, using legal terms and placing themselves ultimately under the authority of their God—not the king. Once they had the statement like they wanted it, Daniel contemplated, "This very statement will be almost as offensive as the act of not bowing. But I think it is best to give him the truth plainly and take whatever consequences may come." The others agreed, but they looked at the statement one last time in light of Daniel's comments:

Oh Nebuchadnezzar, we do not need to defend ourselves before you in this matter. If we are thrown into the blazing furnace, the God we serve is able to save us from it, and we believe He will rescue us from your hand, oh king. But, even if He does not, oh king, we want you to know that we will not serve your gods or worship the image of gold you have set up.

Shadrach observed, "It is clearly a legal statement. We claim a higher authority as our judge, removing ourselves, then, from under the king's jurisdiction. We plainly question the king's right and even his ability to throw us into the furnace. We affirm that our God is able to save us from the king's hand, and we trust that He will. Finally, we declare that we will not bow to his image, and it is plainly understood that this is because we honor our God in first place. I think the statement says all we want it to say. It is short, concise, and, unfortunately, also extremely insulting!"

After reading it a second time, someone mentioned the possibility of the king giving them a second chance. Abednego laughed, "Nebuchadnezzar give us a second chance? He would be seen as weak!"

Shadrach challenged, "Yes, but he likes us and knows how valuable we are to the kingdom."

"No one is more valuable than his ego. Besides that, a second chance would demonstrate that we got away with something. Nebuchadnezzar never lets anyone get away with anything when it comes to challenging his authority!" They all nodded in agreement.

One month before the ceremony, Babylon began filling with people. All the inns and paid lodging facilities were soon full. With two weeks remaining to the countdown, caravans began setting up tents outside Babylon. The city was as full and as busy as it had ever been in its millennial history. At one week to countdown, all the representatives of the 127 provinces were registered. Attendance was complete.

Nebuchadnezzar called Daniel in and talked to him very seriously. "Daniel, this is a magnificent event. I have received presents and pledged loyalties from all over the world. On the surface, it is all well and good. However, I also realize that I have provided a chance for many to visit together and talk and compare notes, who otherwise would not have had the chance to do so if it were not for this ceremony.

"The Assyrian delegation can talk to the Persian and Arab delegations. All the smaller countries can compare laws with the larger ones. We have military officers from all the armies here in Babylon to see its greatness, but they can also see its weaker points. It could be politically dangerous.

"I want to keep a tight guard on all sides. I want you to tell me any rumors that you hear about. See to it that on the day of the ceremony, the royal guardsmen personally escort all the councilmen to the plain of Dura. Also, have them check the temples and the administrative halls for all others who should be in attendance. No one will miss it.

"Place soldiers at all the important posts so that stealing is not a problem. The city will be quite vulnerable on that day. Arioch should assign the posts, but I want him personally to stay with me, along with my customary bodyguards. Daniel, I'm sorry, but you will have to stay in the palace to handle anything that comes up."

"Yes, Your Majesty."

Daniel thought of trying to intervene for his friends, explaining the whole thing to the King, but as he drew his breath to talk, he felt strongly checked in his spirit. There was a keen sense that he would be disobeying God if he tried to get them out of the ceremony. Almost against his better judgment, Daniel remained quiet about the issue, as had been determined by the four. They wanted it to remain in God's hands only. Besides that, the king had turned away from him and was dealing with other subjects.

There were all sorts of parties, meetings, business deals, and social events where people were trying to impress one another, but the four Hebrews managed to meet together late at night. Daniel related the orders he had been given by the king, and the following discussion ensued.

Shadrach led off. "I feel the same helpless feeling that I did when I was first introduced to the fertilizer business. It is like we are in a funnel being sucked down."

Meshach interjected, "What about plan one, missing the king's party?"

Abednego quickly responded, "That would be like us preferring our lives over Arioch's. He might be killed if he does not follow his orders."

"Maybe not," contested Meshach. "If Arioch simply says he cannot find us and reports this to the king ahead of time, then it might not be so bad for him."

Abednego came back with, "Why are we afraid to face the consequences of serving our God? We didn't used to be afraid of the consequences. We didn't used to think twice about them!"

That was all it took. All were in agreement. Daniel had kept quiet because it was not his life on the line, but now he summarized the statement that would be given to the king: "The God in whom we trust is able to deliver us, but even if He does not, we will serve Him."

[26]*History of Herodotus 5.52–53 [http://www.iranchamber.com/history /achaemenids/royal_road.php]*

CHAPTER 14

The Fiery Furnace

The day of the ceremony had finally arrived. Shortly after sunrise, Nebuchadnezzar held a breakfast for the heads of state of all the provinces. Daniel, Shadrach, Meshach, and Abednego were there at their usual places of honor. Arioch and the royal guard were on duty and quite vigilant in their service of protecting the king. The king stood and boasted of his greatness, to which all applauded loudly and wailed out sounds of accordance.

Daniel and his friends did not know it, but there was a secret conspiracy going on against them. The astrologers were leading the way as they talked to the other councilmen about how they *had* to make sure the four Hebrews attended the ceremony. Perhaps this was their chance to get rid of them and regain control of the province of Babylon. It would be perfect—if they didn't bow.

After the breakfast, one of the councilmen approached Arioch. "Make sure the Hebrews attend the ceremony." Arioch answered him with a look of disdain. Another councilman reminded Arioch, "Make sure the Hebrews are at the dedication service." Arioch looked at him with the same disdain, wondering what it was all about. A third councilman approached him and drew his breath to speak, but before he got one word out, Arioch barked out a sharp, "Shut up!" The councilman sheepishly turned and walked away. Arioch would make sure Shadrach, Meshach, and Abednego were there, but not because the councilman asked him to; he would be following his orders.

As Arioch thought about the councilmen's obsession that the Hebrews be in attendance, he began to put the pieces together. He realized now that they did not bow to idols, and it almost made him sick to his stomach. Surely they would not consider this the same as an idol to the gods. Surely the king would not kill Daniel's friends, the trusted administrators of the province of Babylon! Yet, he *would* kill them if they did not bow—and he would ask Arioch to give the orders to do so. Now he was really sick to his stomach. He had always had as his motto to never do anything that would later cause him remorse. Now this!

After breakfast Daniel, Shadrach, Meshach, and Abednego went to Daniel's quarters in the palace to talk one last time. Daniel was as somber as they had ever seen him. They stood around a type of marble bar that contained a colorfully decorated basket of fruit.

Daniel spoke. "Just before my father died, he said, 'I know that God *can* save us, I just don't know that He *will*.' That is where we find ourselves. I wish I were going with you, because if you die today, which you may, it will be extremely hard to me to continue. I will be jealous of you, just as I was jealous of my family after they died. Unless God miraculously intervenes, I am talking to you for the last time here on this earth."

Tears streamed down Daniel's cheeks. The other three were also teary-eyed, but mostly as a response to Daniel's emotions. They were prepared and quite resolute concerning the intentional action they were planning to take. The four moved to the center of the big room and stood in a circle as they had done in times past. Shadrach, Meshach, and Abednego said short prayers of dedication to Yahweh and asked God to deliver them somehow from the impending fate they would be calling down upon themselves. Daniel, overcome by emotion, didn't pray aloud, but he was praying in his heart. He would not stop praying until he knew the outcome. Each returned to his home and waited for the soldier escorts.

With great pomp and not a little noise, Nebuchadnezzar and his procession prepared to go to the plain of Dura. The appointed soldiers of the royal guard collected and accompanied the councilmen, including Shadrach, Meshach, and Abednego. As they fell into the procession, the wise men, astrologers, magicians, enchanters, and sorcerers noticed their presence and nodded to each other in delight. Now the big question: would they bow? They certainly hoped not, but by the same token, they could hardly imagine the dedication—no, the stupidity—it would take to cause them to continue standing!

Daniel and several others who were required to stay behind climbed the wall to watch the procession as it left the city. Daniel remembered another time when he had been on a city wall just before loved ones had been killed. While those around him were making comments about the glory of the event, the power that Nebuchadnezzar had over the known world, and the value of the gold on the statue, Daniel's mind was elsewhere. He knew that the ceremony would soon be ruined, and he wondered what the outcome would be. He earnestly prayed for God to spare his friends' lives and to bring honor to Himself in the process. Now, he was second-guessing their decisions and the fact that he had not spoken to the King.

Daniel returned to the palace and gave the soldiers on guard orders to call him if there was any need; he would be in his quarters. Daniel fell on his face before the Lord. He prayed without ceasing for the next five hours, except for the three interruptions that he had from the guards to take care of some issue or another. He would find out only later what was taking place.

There were many others also praying. This had split the Jewish community. There were many other Jews in service to the king who had decided to bow before the statue, believing it to be permissible since it was required by the king and since they did not believe it their hearts. Others, especially those not going to the ceremony, vehemently opposed, saying that no one serving Yahweh should ever bow to a statue of any kind.

Daniel, Shadrach, Meshach, and Abednego had had lengthy discussions with some who thought it was acceptable to bow, and had explained their viewpoints, but in the end it had not made a difference in the others' opinions. It was difficult not to judge them, but they left it in God's hands, knowing that His justice would be correct and final. No matter which side of the issue one was on, however, *all* were praying for Shadrach, Meshach, and Abednego.

When the king's procession arrived on the plain of Dura, most of the thousands of guests were already there. Nebuchadnezzar was carried on the pole throne, which was then placed on a six-foot platform so that he could see over the crowd and enjoy himself to the fullest. Every detail had been meticulously planned. As the three Hebrews watched all the pomp unfold, they could not help but think of the irony that Daniel had helped plan this.

There was Arioch, a close friend of Daniel's and a close acquaintance of theirs. He would soon give the order to cast them into the fire, unless God intervened. Bezalel, dear friend of Meshach, had built the statue. As they looked around, they saw people they worked with, many of whom respected them deeply. They were about to get the shock of their lives when the three would appear to be disloyal to the king they had served so well. Maybe they wouldn't be shocked. Many probably were wondering if they would bow or not. It was for these people and for their God that they were *not* going to bow. Their witness would be true.

Then there was the king. If he were not so headstrong and set in his prideful ways, this whole thing could have been avoided. Now he would *have* to kill them, even though he really wouldn't want to. The councilmen and the others who had wanted them out of power had never been able to make it happen. Now the Hebrews were going to help these wicked people and remove themselves! There was simply a lot of irony everywhere they looked.

The criers were taking their stands. The one beside the king called out, "This is what you are commanded to do." The other criers in the audience repeated the proclamation, as they would do after each short sentence, until the words were heard all the way to the back of the great throng.

The king's crier continued, "Oh peoples, nations, and men of every language, as soon as you hear the sound of the horn, flute, zither, lyre, harp, pipes, and all kinds of musical instruments, you must fall down and worship the image of gold that King Nebuchadnezzar has set up. Whoever does not fall down and worship the image will immediately be thrown into a blazing furnace."

The band readied itself for the command to play. The king looked over the multitude of subjects and imagined what it would be like to see them all bowing to the statue and to him. Nebuchadnezzar raised his scepter then lowered it, giving the command to start the music. There was a mighty sound of movement as thousands of people, all at once, bowed toward the statue.

Nebuchadnezzar swelled with pride as he looked over the crowd. This was indeed the greatest homage ever paid to a king. He was indeed mighty—yes, the mightiest king ever to live. He was delighted with the thought that the gods were jealous of him. The music continued for a full two minutes, and the crowd stayed prostrate before the statue. What a glorious day it was!

The three Hebrews remained standing. It was an awkward feeling, as they were toward the back and off to the side and had a good view of the massive throng. Could thousands be wrong and they be right? There was now no turning back. They had sealed their fate through this intentional act of disobedience. They were not directly in the line of vision of Nebuchadnezzar, but they knew it would not be long now before he would be informed.

Bezalel was bowing with his sons. He raised up just enough to look around and caught sight of them standing tall. He slouched down, limp and weak, and buried his head in his arms and wept. Arioch also caught sight of the three and felt heartsick at their folly. The sick feeling in his stomach returned. The feeling had been this strong only years ago after he had run from the Assyrians when they killed his family.

The astrologers were also watching, but their reaction was one of pleasure. As soon as the music stopped, they quickly made their way to the king and announced, "Oh king, you gave the order that as soon as one hears the sound of the horn, flute, zither, lyre, harp, pipes, and all kinds of musical instruments, one must fall down and worship the image of gold that you, the great king Nebuchadnezzar, have set up. Whoever does not fall down and worship would immediately be thrown into a blazing furnace. But there are some Jews whom you have set over the affairs of Babylon—Shadrach, Meshach, and Abednego—who pay no attention to you, oh king. They neither serve your gods nor worship the image of gold you have set up."

Furious, Nebuchadnezzar summoned Shadrach, Meshach, and Abednego. Arioch gave the order to seize them. The three waited where they were until the soldiers arrived and roughly grabbed them. They hadn't been treated like this since the trip to Babylon. They were going back in time. Shadrach said to the others in Hebrew, "The God in whom we trust is able to deliver us, but even if He does not, we will serve Him." The others heard and acknowledged as they were being led away.

The great dedication ceremony was ruined! Word spread through the crowd that there were some who had not bowed. Those not in the know could hardly believe their ears. Everyone was straining for a view of what was taking place.

The three were roughly lined up before Nebuchadnezzar's platform. The king could not believe what he was seeing! These men, of all people, were the last ones he would have suspected of disloyalty. He knew how valuable they were to the running of the province of Babylon and how important they were to Daniel and to him.

Nebuchadnezzar faced a very difficult decision. Should he show his strength and immediately kill them as he had said he would, or should he give them a second chance? A second chance? Unthinkable! Not for this kind of blatant disobedience! But what would he do without them? How could they do this to him? Maybe they had not really understood. He *needed* them for the smooth running of the province. He would do it. He would do the unthinkable at the risk of appearing weak and give them a second chance.

Nebuchadnezzar spoke, "Is it true, Shadrach, Meshach, and Abednego, that you neither serve my gods nor worship the image of gold I have set up?" Without waiting for a response, he continued, "Now when you hear the sound of the music, if you will fall down and worship the image that I have made, very good. But if you do not worship it, you will be thrown immediately into a blazing furnace! Then what god will be able to rescue you from my hand?"

Abednego had been selected as the spokesman, and ignoring the second chance they had been given, in immortalized words he replied, "Oh Nebuchadnezzar, we do not need to defend ourselves before you in this matter. *If* we are thrown into the blazing furnace, the God we serve is able to save us from it, and we believe He will rescue us from your hand, oh king. But, even if He does not, oh king, we want you to know that we will not serve your gods nor worship the image of gold you have set up."

This carefully prepared statement that placed them first under the authority of their God and secondly under the king was immediately understood. Nebuchadnezzar caught the inferences instantly. He was filled with rage! His attitude toward them changed. No one would disobey him like this. No one! He ordered the furnace to be heated seven times hotter than normal. He would make an example of them! The king could hardly contain his anger. He would have killed them himself, except that the furnace would be more fitting for such disobedience.

The furnace keepers rushed to make the furnace as hot as it could possibly be. The more pragmatic observers wondered why the extra heat, since a furnace designed to smelt iron ore is quite hot enough to kill anyone. That was beside the point, since the king had ordered it in his anger against the Hebrews.

Nebuchadnezzar shouted, "I want the strongest men in the royal guard to tie them up." Arioch gave the order. He couldn't look them in their faces. He was having trouble swallowing. As the Hebrews were being bound, they wondered if God's deliverance would come. It didn't.

The king couldn't look at them either. He was torn between feelings of anger and betrayal. How could they trust in some god instead of obeying his orders! How could they ruin the ceremony! He had bragged of their services to many. After all he had done for them, how could they make him look like a fool in front of the entire empire!

Shadrach, Meshach, and Abednego knew what the king was thinking, and it hurt them deeply. They prayed that God would somehow be glorified through these awful circumstances. They prayed for Daniel; things would be so hard for him now. Daniel knew the hour was advanced, and back in the palace, he prayed for Shadrach, Meshach, and Abednego.

One of Bezalel's sons had managed to weave through the crowd and get near enough to see what was going on. He clutched his fist against his mouth as he saw Meshach, his father's best friend, with his hands bound like a common criminal, awaiting the flames. This was surreal. How could the king execute some of his top people like this?

Nebuchadnezzar called out, "Throw them in the furnace!" Again, Arioch gave the order. As he watched, he could hardly control himself. Arioch knew there was nothing he could humanly do to save them. If he were to oppose this action, he would be killed and they would still die. As they were being pushed up the ramp, Arioch entertained fleeting thoughts of hanging himself after this was all over. For the second time in his life, although he thought it was futile, he prayed a prayer to the most high God: "Please spare their lives."

Twelve men on the six bellows heaved up and down, forcing oxygen into the already overpowering inferno. Every time there was a surge from the bellows, flames shot out the doorway at the end of the ramp that led to the mouth of the furnace and from its other openings. The fire was so hot that the soldiers took cover behind the bodies of the Hebrews.

Shadrach was the first one in line, followed by Meshach and then Abednego. He no longer worried about Daniel or thought of the king's wrath. Peace enveloped him as he turned his heart toward Elohim, the most high God. He'd been true to Him, and his heart rejoiced that he'd soon be with Him face-to-face.

Halfway up the ramp, Shadrach tried to turn and say something to the others, but the guard wouldn't let him. All Meshach saw was his smile; Abednego saw it too. Shadrach fell off the 3½-foot ledge into the furnace; then Meshach, then Abednego. Once the Hebrews' bodies no longer shielded the soldiers from the heat, they were overcome by the flames and died almost instantly. Their bodies were now on fire.

Inside the furnace, Shadrach was still smiling, and so were the others; they did not feel the heat. Halfway up the ramp, Shadrach had noticed that the fire was not hot! Their ropes had burned off even before they hit the floor, yet they had not felt the flames. They laughed and cried all at once. Yahweh was delivering them from the heat of the flames!

Suddenly they realized a fourth man was in the fire. "Your prayers have been heard. Your commitment has been honored. He will cover you with His feathers and under his wings you will find refuge; His faithfulness will be your shield and rampart. You will not fear the terror of night, nor the arrow that flies by day, nor the pestilence that stalks in darkness, nor the plague that destroys at midday, nor the fiery flames of the furnace."

The three immediately recognized many of the words as being from one of David's psalms. They were awestruck that this was a fulfillment of those promises and that they were in the presence of a heavenly being. There was a peace in their spirits like none they had ever experienced. Even though everything was actually happening quite quickly, time seemed to have slowed down.

Were they talking with an angel? Or with the Son of God? Was this really happening? Yes, it was. But how could it be? Each analyzed his own mental faculties and knew that this was indeed a true event. They walked together on the reddish white-hot furnace floor. They glanced at one another and at the fourth man. Meshach thought to himself, "May future generations know of this amazing story of God's deliverance."

Nebuchadnezzar leaped to his feet in amazement and said to his advisors, "Wasn't it three men who were bound up and thrown into the fire?"

The advisors answered nervously, "Certainly, oh king." They could offer no explanation for what they were seeing.

Nebuchadnezzar was not analyzing the situation; he was just calling it like he saw it, and he was seeing the top halves of four men! "Look! I see four men walking around in the fire, unbound and unharmed, and the fourth looks like a son of the gods!"

The three Hebrews were jolted back to the outside reality when Nebuchadnezzar, getting as close as he could to the furnace, called out, "Shadrach, Meshach, and Abednego, servants of the most high God, come out! Come here!" When they looked around, the fourth man was gone. Walking over to the doorway ramp, they climbed out of the furnace. Calmly they stepped over the charred bodies of the dead soldiers and descended toward the king.

The king and everyone else crowded around them, touching them and talking all at once. Shadrach, Meshach, and Abednego said very little; their God had done the talking. As they were examined, it was discovered that their hair was not singed, their clothes were not burned, nor did they have the smell of smoke on them.

Nebuchadnezzar shouted, "Praise be to the God of Shadrach, Meshach, and Abednego, who has sent His angel and rescued His servants! They trusted in Him and defied the king's command and were willing to give up their lives rather than serve or worship any god except their own. Therefore, I decree that the people of every nation and language who say anything against the God of Shadrach, Meshach, and Abednego be cut into pieces and their houses be turned into rubble, for no other god can save in this way." Once again, Nebuchadnezzar had encountered the most high God and responded correctly to Him. His party was over, the all-important statue was forgotten.

Arioch stood speechless, wondering if the most high God actually had heard the prayers of someone as unworthy as he. He reasoned that most likely it had been the prayers of Daniel that had made the difference. Regardless of whose prayers had worked, Arioch then saw that all this had been for a purpose: to prove beyond a doubt the power of the Israelite God. And what power it was!

CHAPTER 15

The Dream of the Tree

Following the fiery-furnace episode, Nebuchadnezzar gave promotions to Shadrach, Meshach, and Abednego. The sectors that had not previously been under their care were now further consolidated and placed under the administration of the three. Daniel continued as prime minister. The councilmen lost all hope of controlling Babylonian politics during Nebuchadnezzar's reign. The astrologers, magicians, enchanters, and sorcerers had been put in their place by the display of Yahweh's power during the fiery-furnace incident. They knew their gods were inferior to this power and that they could no longer effectively oppose the Hebrews.

Nebuchadnezzar asked Daniel many questions about his God. Daniel's explanation that Yahweh required a commitment of the heart and obedience to the Holy Scriptures had seemed quite extreme to Nebuchadnezzar. He decided to serve Yahweh in his own way. He listened to Daniel on some of the social issues, especially those that related to slave station and to the very poor in and around Babylon. Nebuchadnezzar performed some kind deeds, but his heart was not changed. He continued to be the proud king he had always been.

Nebuchadnezzar could not comprehend the rationale of giving his heart to the most high God. It seemed quite clear to him that if he did this, he would lose his kingdom; and he was certainly not willing to go that far. If it came down to choosing between God and the empire, he would choose the empire. As the years passed, the impression left on him from the fiery furnace gradually wore off. He had learned to respect the Hebrews' God, and he completely trusted Daniel and his friends; but selfish pride continued to control his every decision.

Not long after the fiery-furnace drama, Meshach received word that Bezalel was bedridden; he lost no time in paying a visit. Meshach walked into the room where Bezalel lay on a mat.

"I knew you'd come. Thank you. All my life I've built things and solved difficult problems for others. Now no one can solve my problem." Meshach sat on the floor beside him and took his feeble hand. Bezalel continued, "I always wanted to be unimportant . . . I finally got my wish."

"You *are* important to me and to my God."

Bezalel smiled. "Yeah, I suppose I'm important to all the gods. They probably all want my services in the afterlife. That's really unfortunate too, because I've made promises to all of them. I should have had the foresight to choose one and not try to satisfy them all."

Meshach, encouraged by what Bezalel had just said, explained, "You can choose the most high God, my God, the only God who knows the future and controls the heavens—and saves from the fiery furnace—and commit your soul to Him right now. My God sees your heart, and unlike the other gods, He knows your innermost thoughts. He will receive you to Himself, even right now, if you turn your eyes toward Him. Would you like to hear what the great king David said about this?"

"Yes, I would."

"'Have mercy upon me, O God, according to thy loving kindness. According to the multitude of thy tender mercies, blot out my transgressions. Wash me thoroughly from my iniquity and cleanse me from my sin. For I know my transgressions, and my sin is ever before me. Against thee only have I sinned and done that which is evil in thy sight. Purify me with hyssop, and I shall be clean: Wash me, oh Lord, and I shall be whiter than snow. Hide thy face from my sins and blot out all mine iniquities. Create in me a clean heart, O God; renew a right spirit within me. Cast me not away from thy presence and take not thy Holy Spirit from me. Restore unto me the joy of thy salvation, and uphold me with a willing spirit. Then will I teach transgressors thy ways, and sinners shall be converted unto thee." [Selected from Psalm 51 KJV]

Bezalel thought for a while and answered, "That is very beautiful; how much does this cost?"

Meshach chuckled and responded with a question. "Now how much do you think it costs?"

"I think you are going to tell me it is for free."

"Yes, it is free, so long as you have a humble and contrite heart before the Lord, the most high God."

"You see there, Meshach, that is the whole trouble with your God. One never knows where he stands with Him. With the other gods, I pay for a blessing and a guarantee in the afterlife, and I get the receipt for the service and then know I have things covered with that god. I have committed to all the gods except for Marduk, and his priests are coming today. Look over there in that basket; I call that my afterlife basket."

Meshach noticed the assortment of colorful receipts, tiny bottles, small cloths, and other unidentifiable objects. "Bezalel, you can't take those things with you!"

"Well, I can try. They will be buried with me."

"Yes, and if your grave is ever opened in the future, there will be your bones and whatever is left of those clay inscriptions. *My* God looks after your soul, which is the only part of you that will enter the afterlife. No other god can do that."

"You say your God looks after the soul, but you've never died, and all you know is what your Scriptures tell you. If I turn my back on all these promises I've made to the other gods, what will happen to me if your God doesn't appear in time or if I don't have any record or receipt of commitment? You are a good friend, but it's my afterlife and your notions are too risky!"

Their conversation was interrupted by the entrance of one of Bezalel's sons announcing the arrival of the priests of Marduk. He asked if he should go ahead and pay them, and Bezalel answered, "No, wait until after they have guaranteed my blessing in the afterlife; then pay them." Bezalel turned to Meshach and said, "Thank you so much for coming, Meshach. I really appreciate the visit. Pray for me to your God; I need all the help I can get."

With tears in his eyes, Meshach said earnestly, "Think about what I said. My God is the most high God, over Marduk and all the others. You can always send one of your sons after me, and I'll come right away."

Bezalel squeezed Meshach's hand affectionately. "Thank you. You've been my most loyal friend here in this life. I'll ask to work with you again in the next one."

Meshach was choking up; he sniffed a sob as he left but said no more.

Waiting outside were seven priests of Marduk. They knew Meshach and bowed out of obligation, but they offered no greeting; Yahweh and Marduk were enemies. Meshach felt despondent. He was depressed that he had not convinced Bezalel to commit his ways to the most high God. Bezalel would not go to paradise—and they would not work together again someday. He would go to the place of his gods, the place of outer darkness, away from the blessings and comforts of the most high God.

Two days later, one of Bezalel's sons approached. Meshach hoped that he was coming at his father's request to know more about the most high God. As the son approached, however, Meshach noticed the redness of his eyes. The young man, in his father's abrupt fashion, blurted out, "My father just died. Can you come and pray to your God for him?" Meshach went out of courtesy, but he knew that Bezalel's eternal fate was already sealed, and it cut him to the core of his spirit.

-------------- // --------------

In the year 573 BC, Nebuchadnezzar ended his thirteen-year siege against the Phoenicians in the city of Tyre and gave up further conquest. He called it a victory because he had conquered the main part of Tyre. However, many of the people escaped to the portion of the city that was on an island and remained free.

It was not economically feasible to build a fleet of ships in order to take over the Phoenicians. Nebuchadnezzar talked to Daniel about his desire to destroy the city completely and rule the Phoenicians with an iron fist. The prophet made a lighthearted remark that the king took seriously: "Maybe, oh king, that will be for the silver or the bronze kingdom to do." The king took comfort in these words and used them as his reason to end the costly campaign against Tyre.

He was older now and was content to rule over the 127 provinces, to collect tribute, and to concentrate on his massive building programs. One night in 571 BC, about 8½ years after the fiery-furnace incident, during Nebuchadnezzar's thirty-fifth year as ruler of Babylon, he awoke with a start. He had had another dream that he perceived as being another special revelation from God.

He called the magicians, enchanters, astrologers, and diviners as well as Daniel, chief of the magicians, but Daniel was not immediately available. The others came and he told them the dream, but they could not interpret it for the king. Among the group were actually several who had theories on the meaning of the dream, but they did not want to risk voicing their ideas for fear that Daniel would have another interpretation. They knew that the king would side with Daniel, and then they would look like fools. They also sensed the dream might not be positive news for the king and were reluctant to be the bearers of bad news.

Finally Daniel arrived, and the king addressed him. "Belteshazzar, chief of the magicians, I know that the spirit of the holy gods is in you and that no mystery is too difficult for you. Here is my dream; interpret it for me." Daniel gave a slight bow of the head in acknowledgment, indicating that the king should go on.

The king repeated the dream to Daniel. "I looked and there before me stood a tree in the middle of the land. Its height was enormous. The tree grew large and strong, and its top touched the sky; it was visible to the ends of the earth. Its leaves were beautiful, its fruit was abundant, and from it came food for everyone. Under it the beasts of the field found shelter, and the birds lived in its branches; from it every creature was fed.

"I looked and there before me was a messenger, a holy one coming down from heaven. He called out in a loud voice, 'Cut down the tree and trim off its branches; strip it of its leaves and scatter its fruit. Let the animals flee from under it and the birds from its branches. But let the stump and its roots, bound with iron and bronze, remain in the ground in the grass of the field. Let *him* be drenched with the dew of heaven, and let him live with the animals among the plants of the earth. Let his mind be changed from that of a man, and let him be given the mind of an animal until seven years go by. This decision is announced by the messengers; the holy ones declare the verdict so that the living may know that the Most High is sovereign over the kingdoms of men and gives them to whomever He wishes and sets over them the lowliest of men.'

"That was my dream, Belteshazzar; now tell me what it means. The others could not interpret it for me, but I know you can because the spirit of the holy gods is in you."

Even as the king was speaking, God revealed the dream to Daniel. But could it really be? Surely not! If its meaning was true, how could Daniel tell it to the king? This was no distant prophecy, but one that would happen soon—to Nebuchadnezzar himself!

Daniel drew a deep breath. He bowed down on one knee and was perplexed. Daniel then dropped down on both knees, his arms stiff and his hands pressing against his thighs, his head bowed. He prayed that God would confirm the interpretation if it was correct. The longer he prayed, the more it seemed that the interpretation was, in fact, that which he had thought from the beginning. He prayed for God's help concerning how to relate it to the king and how the king would take it.

Nebuchadnezzar had given Daniel almost ten minutes to pray or to do whatever it was he was doing, and he could stand the suspense no longer. He spoke, "Belteshazzar, do not let the dream or its meaning alarm you. Tell me its meaning."

Daniel stood. Reluctantly and yet resolutely, he began to speak, "Your Majesty, if only the dream applied to your enemies and its meaning to your adversaries! You, oh king, are that tree. You have become great and strong. Your greatness has grown until it reaches the sky, and your dominion extends to distant parts of the earth.

"The most high God has issued a decree against my lord, the king. You will be driven away from people and live with the wild animals. You will eat grass like cattle and be drenched with the dew of heaven. Seven years will pass before you acknowledge that the most high God is sovereign over the kingdoms of men and gives them to anyone He wishes.

"The commandment to leave the stump of the tree with its roots means that your kingdom will be restored to you when you acknowledge that heaven rules. Therefore, oh king, renounce your sins by doing what is right and your wickedness by being kind to the oppressed. It may be then that your prosperity will continue."

The king sat expressionless, almost as if he'd had a premonition that the interpretation might be something like this. He had hoped it would be different; he knew that Daniel was probably the only interpreter who would give him this kind of answer, and he sensed that the interpretation was correct. He was angry about it, but he was not angry at Daniel; he was upset at the most high God. Yet that didn't do him any good, because intellectually he knew that he was subordinate to this God and powerless before Him.

At length he looked at Daniel and thanked him. Daniel bowed then turned and quietly left. The wise men had heard this interpretation, as well as Arioch, a few guards, and servants. Two hours later, it was all over Babylon.

The next morning, Nebuchadnezzar called Daniel into the throne room and had a long private conversation with him. "Daniel, what can I do to get the most high God to change His mind about this heavenly decree?" Daniel repeated what he'd said the day before and gave some specific suggestions. The king gave Daniel the orders to carry these things out.

Daniel answered, "Your Majesty, I will do these things and God will be pleased, but Yahweh requires a change of heart. You must give up your pride and acknowledge that the most high God is sovereign over the kingdoms of men and gives them to anyone He wishes."

Nebuchadnezzar objected, "I built this mighty Babylon with my own hands, and I did it before I even knew of this God. I built it honoring Nebu and Marduk!"

Daniel countered, "Your Majesty, the most high God gave you the abilities, the health, and the opportunity. You owe your very life to Him, and this is what He is trying to prove to you." The king sat silently for a several moments. He would have dismissed this all so easily before, but now he was afraid of the fulfillment of the dream and was therefore compelled to think about Daniel's words.

The king met with Daniel several more times in the subsequent days to discuss this "obligated" relationship with the most high God. On one occasion, Daniel asked some probing questions. "Your Majesty, what should I do when this dream is fulfilled?"

Nebuchadnezzar responded, "Not when, Belteshazzar, *if*."

Daniel nodded, "All right, then what shall I do *if* the dream is fulfilled?"

The king looked at Daniel and pondered. "Well, you will have to run the kingdom. And I guess you'll have to look after me because the dream says I will return to power. Belteshazzar, it can't happen like this; there is no way in the world a Hebrew slave could hold the Babylonian Empire together. You are not ruthless enough to do it. Something about this revelation will happen differently. Anyway, I have made some changes, and it's not going to happen at all."

Daniel's response to the king made him raise his eyebrows and think twice about what he'd just said. "If my God wants me to hold the empire together for you, He will enable me to do it without changing my ways. My God can humble my enemies, just as He can humble you, my friend." These were powers and concepts familiar to Nebuchadnezzar only in theory, not in practice.

Daniel wished that the king were right, but he feared he was not. As the months went by, Nebuchadnezzar became more and more convinced that the prophecy would not come to fruition. On the other hand, Daniel became more and more convinced that it would. His heart ached as he watched the king's pride grow to new heights.

Daniel talked to Shadrach, Meshach, and Abednego about the matter. "You know, we have to prepare for Nebuchadnezzar's absence. I believe the prophecy will be fulfilled in a literal sense."

Meshach challenged, "How? Once he drops out, every one of the provinces will rebel, and Babylon will fall apart!"

Shadrach chimed in with, "The Assyrian remnant will be first; then the Medes and the Persians will follow. There is a lot of dissent among the younger generals of the Persian troops—at least that is what I hear."

"Well, we have to do what we can to hold the kingdom together, because it will be turned back over to Nebuchadnezzar after the seven years. Maybe God has other plans, but until we know for certain, we need to do our best to prepare. In the past when we have done all we can do, God has met us at that point and made up the difference."

All agreed with this statement, and they began devising a "takeover" plan. It would have seemed like treason, except that Daniel actually told Nebuchadnezzar one day, purposefully in the presence of Arioch, that he was formulating a plan for maintaining the kingdom, should the dream be fulfilled. Nebuchadnezzar smirked and said, "That's good Daniel. You just go ahead and do that."

Over the next weeks, they arranged a type of holding pen for Nebuchadnezzar in some of the irrigated pastures near Babylon, along with a little shelter to get in out of the dew and the weather. It was made with a walkway around two sides of the area to allow for observers who would want to see the king. His opponents and his friends would have to observe him in order to believe that he was crazy. It was also designed so as to have ample guard stations serving a hundred or more soldiers. Daniel had one of Bezalel's sons prepare a finely crafted bronze ankle cuff that would not be as rough or as prone to causing infections as would a common iron shackle. He had the chain to the cuff made out of iron, to fit the "bound with iron and bronze" wording of the prophecy.

It was a bizarre task. How do you count on someone going crazy? How do you prepare? Will it be gradual or all of a sudden? If it is gradual, how will you know for sure when it's happening? Will Nebuchadnezzar resist? Will he be wild? How will we subdue him if he is? Will the soldiers obey him even if he is wild?

Daniel talked to Arioch about all these things. It was very difficult, because they were walking the fine line between treason and preparedness. Arioch did not like talking about Nebuchadnezzar in this way because it was so awkward. He probably would not have participated in the conversation with anyone except Daniel.

One day when the king was thinking about the possibility of going crazy, he prepared a statement for Daniel. He addressed Daniel seriously, but somewhat sarcastically. "Belteshazzar, if I lose my mind, I want you to read this to all the councilmen and everyone else in the kingdom." Daniel silently read the statement: "If you are hearing this read, then I have been judged by the most high God. This same God who has given me the mind of an animal has said I will rule again.

If you rebel against me, when I return to power, I will annihilate you and your families and turn your houses into rubble."

"You trust me a lot to give me a written statement like this."

"Yes, I trust you; but if you try to use this and I am not yet crazy, I'll have you killed. It is really no risk to me if I am not crazy, but it may give me a little more security in holding the kingdom together if something does happen to me, although I don't believe that it will."

Three months after the statement was written and one year after the dream of the tree, Nebuchadnezzar received some guests from the outer provinces. He hosted them in a grandiose manner, showing off the city, the temples, and the lush greenery of the hanging gardens. When they returned to the palace at midafternoon, they were walking around on the roof overlooking the city. Servants were attending them with water, wine, and refreshments. Half a dozen guards stood at attention near the group. Nebuchadnezzar held out his hand and declared, "Is not this the great Babylon I have built as my royal residence by my mighty power and for the glory of my majesty?"

The words were still on his lips when a voice came from heaven: "This is what is decreed for you, King Nebuchadnezzar: Your royal authority has been taken away from you. You will be driven from people and will live with the wild animals; you will eat grass like cattle. Seven years will pass by until you acknowledge that the most high God is sovereign over the kingdoms of men and gives them to anyone He wishes."

All present heard the judgment from heaven and were terrified. Some took a few steps back, and everyone quietly waited for the appearance of some god or angel. Nothing appeared.

The king fell silent, got a glassy look in his eyes, and slumped to the floor. Those around him rushed to his assistance and asked how he was. He said nothing. When they tried to help him up, he growled, then moaned, then slowly began to crawl in circles, staring blankly at those around him. Someone said, "An evil spirit has befallen him. Call the sorcerers! Call the magicians!" Another one called out to a servant, "Get Daniel quickly!"

When Daniel came, he took one look at Nebuchadnezzar and asked, "How did this happen?" Those around related the occurrence.

Daniel calmly responded, "This is what was foretold a year ago in his dream about the tree. He will have the mind of an animal for seven years; then he will once again rule this kingdom. I have been planning for this, as my holy God, the revealer of mysteries, has decreed this event." Daniel continued, "Guards, take him into the west chamber and don't let him wander off. Treat him kindly, as he will once again be your ruler. Tell Arioch that I wish to speak to him immediately, and ask him to bring the bronze shackles that have been prepared. He will understand."

Daniel quietly and systematically took over the situation, putting into action his predetermined plans. He summoned the head of the royal couriers and told him that the king had lost his mind. When the courier demanded to see the king, Daniel glared at him and spoke in an authoritative tone. "You will see the king later. Right now you will summon those on the lists. I will meet with the captain of the guard, the generals and chief military personnel, the wise men, and all principal administrators at sundown in the throne room."

The courier, stunned, responded, "Yes, sir."

Arioch arrived and followed Daniel to the west chamber, a room especially prepared by Daniel for the king's safety. It had a minimum of plain wooden furniture and nothing with sharp edges or points. When they arrived, there were three guards outside the door. Daniel asked, "How did you get him down here?"

Trying not to smile, one guard answered, "We put a rope around him and dragged him; he didn't want to be touched."

Another guard added, "Or dragged!"

With that, the third guard let out a barely audible chuckle then put on a straight face again. Arioch looked at Daniel, and they went in.

The room stank. The king had already urinated and defecated on his robes, which were now about halfway off his body. Daniel spoke to him. "Can you hear me?" No answer. The king lay on his side, staring blankly at the wall. He looked at Daniel but did not seem to focus on him. As Daniel reached down to touch his forehead, the king jerked, trying to bite Daniel. Daniel stood up and commented,

"It looks like it's going to be a long seven years." They left, giving orders that no one be allowed to see the king that night.

Nebuchadnezzar's fate and rumors surrounding it spread quickly through Babylon. On all levels of government, people met together to discuss this unprecedented situation. On the street, one could hear comments like, "What about the generals? Arioch will side with Daniel. But most of the military will look out for their best interests. They are much more likely to follow a son of Nebuchadnezzar's than a Hebrew slave."

"The astrologers are appointing one of Nebuchadnezzar's sons to rule in his place. I hope they don't get away with that! They will kill Nebuchadnezzar; the boy will just be their puppet."

"I think Daniel is behind this. He actually knew it was going to happen!"

"I know it looks awfully suspicious, but I've known Daniel ever since college, and I tell you beyond any doubt that he wouldn't do this! I, for one, believe that his holy God *is* responsible for this. He predicted this, you know. The same God that saved Shadrach, Meshach, and Abednego from the furnace—remember that day?"

"I think that Daniel *will* be able to take over. It certainly is ironic that a Hebrew, of all people, would wind up usurping the throne."

"You're wrong if you think Daniel will do that. He won't. Daniel would never come right out and say he's the new king. I know this man, and he is one clever fellow. He will somehow manage to hide behind a crazy king and act in *his* name! Mark my words."

"Did you hear? The astrologers are planning a coronation ceremony for one of the king's sons at sunrise tomorrow. The key wise men and some of the generals are having a secret meeting about this after Daniel gives his speech tonight in the throne room!"

Daniel entered a completely packed, torch-lit throne room and stood on the steps in front of the throne where he had so many times stood facing Nebuchadnezzar. This time, however, his back was to the empty throne, and he was facing 230 wise men, sorcerers, administrators, priests, astrologers, and military personnel. As these Babylonian authorities looked toward Daniel, they saw confidence, and behind him they saw a chain looped through and locked around the arms of the throne.

Daniel spoke forcefully. "As you have probably heard, Nebuchadnezzar has gone insane. He will be kept under guard outside the city beginning tomorrow. Anyone who attempts to harm him will be put to death immediately. As you will remember, this was foretold by my God, the most high God, who is the only God able to accurately reveal the future. In the second year of Nebuchadnezzar's reign, He revealed a dream to me. Some of you may remember that your lives were spared because of that revelation. He saved Shadrach, Meshach, and Abednego from the fiery furnace. He predicted this mental condition, and He declares that Nebuchadnezzar will rule again in seven years—and He will. My God is never wrong.

"Things will continue *as they are*. Nebuchadnezzar is still the king, and I am still the prime minister. Since he is incapacitated, during the next seven years, it will be just as if he were out on a military campaign. I am the final authority. I am not acting of my own volition, but under the power given to me by the most high God and by our king Nebuchadnezzar. My only ambition is to honor my God and to be true to the charge I have received from the king. If you do not continue to serve Nebuchadnezzar as your emperor and honor me as his prime minister, you will be guilty of treason and dealt with accordingly! If you kill me and usurp the throne, may my God deal with you in the same manner He has dealt with the king. Be assured that if you attempt to alter what has been decreed by the most high God, you will suffer grave consequences.

"There will be no questions until after you have viewed the king. No one will be allowed to see him tonight; he is under lock and chain at a specific location. In the morning, all will be able to view him and to try to talk to him, if so inclined. Those who have ideas of appointing one of Nebuchadnezzar's sons to the throne, those who think he has been poisoned and will get over this condition in a few days, and those who think they have room to rebel should wait until after viewing the king and having audience with me. Otherwise, you will be removed from the position you now hold.

"We will continue to work together to maintain a strong Babylon. The annals will be recorded as usual, and when the king returns, he will acknowledge all those who helped to strengthen and maintain a powerful Babylon.

"Posted at the entrance of the hall is a decree issued by the king ahead of time, should this happen to him. It is there for all to read and respect. It reads: 'If you are hearing this read, then I have been judged by the most high God. This same God who has given me the mind of an animal has said I will rule again. If you rebel against me, when I return to power, I will annihilate you and your families and turn your houses into rubble.'"

Daniel waited for a moment then said, "You are dismissed." He turned to Arioch and said, "Arioch, clear the palace and the court-yard. No one will reenter the palace grounds until tomorrow after-noon after all have had a chance to duly observe the king."

With that, Daniel walked out of the room. Arioch and other guards stepped forward. People cleared the throne room slowly but with minimal talking as small groups read the king's decree that had been posted by Daniel. Those who had been scheming beforehand were left somewhat confused and uncertain as to the security of the courses of action they had previously planned.

On the way out, one of the administrators who had studied with Daniel years ago muttered to his friend, "What did I tell you? This Daniel is one clever fellow. I called it right. He will hide behind a crazy king and act in *his* name. Only *Daniel* could pull this off!"

The friend answered with a smirk, "He can pull this off inside Babylon, but he will never maintain control of the kingdom! Can you picture the Assyrians, the Medes and Persians, the Arabs, or the Egyptians falling in line? They won't! *Now* you can mark *my* words!"

Shadrach, Meshach, and Abednego gestured to one of the guards that they would like to follow Daniel, and the guard let them through. When they arrived at Daniel's quarters, the watchman allowed them to go in, stating, "He is expecting you." As they entered, they saw Daniel sitting at his writing table, elbows resting on the marble top and chin resting on his hands. He greeted them warmly then sat back down.

Abednego spoke first. "You gave a fine speech in the throne room tonight, Daniel. All those who were scheming are thinking twice. You also cancelled a lot of the all-night meetings that would have taken place by insisting they first visit the king tomorrow morning."

Meshach added, "Yes, by putting it like that, everyone felt compelled to verify the king's condition over the next few days before considering their next steps. You slowed down the momentum that had been building since he went crazy this afternoon."

Daniel kindly thanked them, but his mind was clearly elsewhere. He spoke, "Remember that part of the dream where the angel said 'the kingdoms of men He gives to whomever He wishes and sets over them the lowliest of men'? Who could be more lowly by worldly standards than a Hebrew slave! Perhaps that part referred to me!

"Have you ever prayed, 'Lord, I know Your *general* will, but how much do I make happen and how much do I leave in Your hands?' Do I attack or sit back? Talk or be quiet? Stop or go? Should I, in fact, *try* to preserve Babylon for Nebuchadnezzar? How far should I go in doing so? Which of the abominable practices of Nebuchadnezzar should I abolish, which should I allow to continue, and which should I discourage but ignore?

"How much should I rely on the military as Nebuchadnezzar has done, and how much should I just trust God? Should I go about righting the wrongs? Which ones? Should I attempt to *establish* justice or just be happy to somewhat increase it? How far can I push the wise men, who will be serving me out of fear and reverence for my God and my personal abilities but always looking for a chance to rebel? Should I curtail the building of the expansive waterways, the elaborate mountain dam system and the canals through the desert at the expense of slave labor? Should I stop it?

"Should I further modify the tax structure to be less lucrative for the tax collectors? How should I deal with the countless attempts at insurrections that I will encounter during these next seven years? Nebuchadnezzar's response was always the same: kill them, their families, and their friends, and turn their houses into rubble. Should I have myself appear to be strong, or should I let everyone know that I am not but that they must respect my God?"

Even though many of these things had been discussed beforehand, it all seemed different now that the weight of the decisions was actually on Daniel's shoulders. After a period of silence, Meshach stated, "Daniel, there aren't easy answers to the questions you just asked."

Abednego spoke up. "God has obviously put you in this position. It is also obvious to me that He has prepared you to do this job. I agree with Meshach, but I will also say that since God has placed you here and prepared you, He intends to see you through."

All nodded in agreement, but Daniel responded, "I don't feel prepared for this job. I have only seen it done Nebuchadnezzar's way, and I can't do it that way."

Shadrach now joined the discussion. "Before we were thrown into the fiery furnace, I thought we were going to die. God didn't show us His salvation until we were going into the flames. This pattern can also be seen in other stories of God's deliverance from the past. If you obey Him to the best of your ability, I believe God will somehow make up the difference and bring it to the outcome He desires. You are only responsible for giving it your best, one day at a time. You are not responsible for holding the kingdom together for Nebuchadnezzar; that's God's job."

"I know you are right," Daniel reasoned, "but it seems overwhelming right now. It would not be true to say that I fear the future, but I am certainly apprehensive. I will have a lot of decisions that are not black and white."

Abednego challenged Daniel with, "You have had that for over three decades, and God has always been faithful to see you through. I know that it was different when you were just carrying out orders, but God has not changed. It would be my advice to not change things very much in the first few weeks. The injustices that are out there cannot be made right quickly and maybe not ever. Make small changes, and pray about each one of them."

The others agreed, and Daniel knew Abednego had given him good, practical advice. He also knew that there would be a lot of decisions that this advice would not cover, but he purposed in his heart to take one day at a time and trust in God. The three gathered around Daniel, who was still seated at his writing table, laid their hands on him, and prayed for God to give him the strength of Job and the wisdom of Solomon.

As they were ending the prayer, Arioch knocked on the door, and Daniel beckoned him to enter. "Daniel, the palace and the palace grounds have been completely cleared and locked down."

"Thank you, Arioch; keep them locked up until tomorrow afternoon. Anyone who wants to leave may, but no one gets back in without my specific authorization."

"Yes, sir," said Arioch, as he turned and left. Shadrach, Meshach, and Abednego also left, and Daniel was alone for no more than ten minutes when Arioch returned and knocked on the door.

A servant answered, since Daniel had gone back to the bedroom. The servant came to Daniel, saying, "It is Sir Arioch, captain of the royal guard." Daniel told the servant to let him in.

Arioch, never one to mince words, got straight to the point. "Daniel, I am sixty years old. I know that I am still strong and in good health, but I had been thinking of asking the king for a release from my duties. I'm too old to be captain of the royal guard. But now things have changed.

"I never told you this, but when your friends were being thrown into the fiery furnace at my command, I prayed to the most high God, your God, for Him to save them. He did it. It probably wasn't much because of my prayer, but I think my prayer helped. Anyway, I owe Him and you.

"I know you are His representative here in Babylon. As long as this God wants you to stand in for Nebuchadnezzar, I will follow your command just as if you were the king. You can count on me and all of the royal guard, and I wanted to come and tell you that. We will give our lives to keep you safe."

Daniel patted Arioch on the shoulder and smiled. "Thank you, Arioch. I appreciate your words, and I believe my God heard your prayers also. We were both praying; we both owe my God. Keep praying to Him, Arioch." Arioch nodded but said nothing.

Daniel repeated again, "Thank you."

Arioch said, "May I go?"

Daniel answered, "Yes, you may go. Have the cage and the soldiers who will bear it at the west chamber at sunrise."

Continued in Volume 2

Issues Daniel Faced

CHAPTER 1
At Home in Jerusalem
Issues Daniel Faced:
- Will God save us?
- Trust God no matter what?
- Cultural relativity: Should morality be adjusted to fit modern, post-Josiah Jerusalem?
- Moral relativity as it relates to the siege
- Truth: Who is speaking it?
- Correlations between material problems and spiritual causes
- Take action? In what specific way?
- Obey God rather than man?
- Speak out and draw trouble, or keep quiet?
- Does the end justify the means?
- Spiritual values versus physical needs

CHAPTER 2
Captivity Begins
Issues Daniel Faced:
- Really bad things can happen to good people.
- Evil people can indeed prosper and maintain the upper hand.
- There is no justice!
- Where is God when you need Him?
- Can no one be trusted?
- Watch what people do, not what they say.
- Most do what is expedient, not necessarily what is right.

- When things get really bad, one can more easily observe those who have true spiritual values.
- Should one repay evil for evil?
- Those whose lives are ruled by spiritual values change little in times of crisis.
- Life goes on when loved ones (all of them) are lost.

CHAPTER 3
The Road to Babylon
Issues Daniel Faced:
- Risking one's own security by sticking up for a friend
- Idle time: He made use of it and learned Chaldean.
- Accepting a terrible new reality in his life
- Facing unexplainable contradictions to what he believed
- In the face of the unexplainable, he held to the undeniable.

CHAPTER 4
Arriving in Babylon
Issues Daniel Faced:
- Where to draw the line on personal moral issues
- From where to draw one's sense of identity
- How to get around authority without directly confronting it for the second time (went to an underling with the idea of the ten-day trial)
- How to honor God without being too legalistic
- How to handle people who are jealous of you
- What to put into one's body
- What to put into one's mind

CHAPTER 5
The Dilemma
Issues Daniel Faced:
- What to put into one's mind
- Can I memorize something I don't believe? Should I?
- How to succeed in a system one doesn't agree with or believe in
- How to work toward excellence in a corrupt worldly system
- How to be a good winner

- How and when to stand against the king
- Being strong without being offensive or getting fired
- How to establish credibility and respect without being stuck-up

CHAPTER 6
Into the Real World
Issues the Hebrews Faced:
- Doing a job of performing a service that is directly related to or participatory in corruption (Shadrach)
- Relating to a friend who is in an impossible dilemma (Meshach)
- Courageously doing the right thing with shrewdness and tact (Abednego)
- Learning how to live with corruption as best as one can
- Relying on one another for accountability
- Encouraging others to keep up the integrity

CHAPTER 7
Arioch, Captain of the Guard
Issues Arioch Faced:
In a black-and-white world, one could consider him to have acted wrongly on several occasions:
- He was a coward, running away as his family was being killed.
- He acted ignobly, seeking revenge for the deaths of his family.
- He acted immorally, joining the very army that had killed his loved ones.
- He disobeyed orders and killed a fellow soldier who took the life of an innocent woman.
- He switched sides once in Babylon, eventually becoming the captain of the royal guard.

And yet, Arioch's world was not black and white; it was made of many shades of gray. Whether right or wrong, he established certain absolutes that ruled his life:
- He would never do anything that would cause him remorse.
- He would not allow fear to influence his decisions.
- He would always do what was right, so much as he could determine.
- He would always stay true to his word, even if it meant death.

CHAPTER 8
Daniel Builds a Reputation
Issues Daniel Faced:
- Does the end justify the means when both are morally justifiable?
- Are absolute morals defined by actions or end-result intentions?
- Drawing the line between vengeance and justice
- Is deception always wrong?
- Is it okay to help others do things that perhaps one would not feel morally comfortable doing?
- Is omitting the truth or a portion of it the same as lying?

CHAPTER 9
Daniel Reveals the King's Dream
Issues Daniel Faced:
- Being falsely accused
- Facing terrible undeserved consequences with no way out
- To rely totally on God for deliverance: The issue was 100 percent out of their control.
- How to relax and sleep in the face of death if there is nothing more that can be done
- Trust totally and boldly in God's revelation and guidance.

CHAPTER 10
Changes in Babylon
Issues Daniel Faced:
- How to wield power yet leave justice in God's hands
- How to fight spiritual battles with memorized Scripture, prayer, and fellowship
- Reacting to extreme pressure, stress, or threats
- Strategizing differently for different opponents
- Maintaining high commitment to integrity (didn't have their enemies killed)
- Becoming outwardly successful and growing spiritually weak in the meantime

CHAPTER 11
Kingdom Issues
Issues Daniel Faced:
- Holding positions that others want
- Praying for his authority to turn to God instead of resenting or fearing the authority
- Working for someone who is doing things of which one does not approve
- Correctly handling the responsibilities that have been entrusted to him
- Receiving advice from friends that is not particularly helpful
- Looking for another source of advice (different from the past)
- Discerning God's judgment and not hindering His work
- Letting God work without attempting to change the course of events

CHAPTER 12
The Statue, Part 1
Issues Daniel Faced:
- Going out of his way to remember and help a friend's friend
- Manipulating circumstances to work for the good of others
- Dealing with his own past grief
- Tolerating his boss's bad ideas and dealing with them appropriately

CHAPTER 13
The Statue, Part 2
Issues Daniel Faced:
- Pragmatically thinking through drawing the lines on what to do and not to do
- What are the criteria to use in determining worship of the statue?
- How heavily to weigh their witness and testimony to others
- How heavily to weigh the consequences of following God
- Trusting God whether He delivers or not
- Being forced to make a statement one way or the other
- Deciding to stand together (They all did the same thing.)
- Not using maximum leverage with the king to get his friends out of trouble. (They left it in God's hands.)

CHAPTER 14
The Fiery Furnace
Issues Daniel and the Hebrews Faced:
- Losing friends to death
- Actions being misunderstood
- Purposefully playing into the hands of their enemies
- Facing imminent death
- Not understanding God's plan ahead of time
- Willingness to go against the vast majority
- Dealing with friends who did not agree with their position
- Leaving in God's hands those who are in disagreement Him
- Experiencing God's miraculous delivery and handling the eulogies

CHAPTER 15
The Dream of the Tree
Issues Daniel Faced:
- Overwhelming responsibility that he did not feel prepared for
- Anticipation of important decisions that would not be black and white
- The leadership he had depended on was suddenly gone.
- Doubts as to his own capacity to carry out the task before him
- Extremely high stakes
- Looming uncertainty as to how proactive he should be in directional decisions
- Wanting to trust God but knowing many important decisions were going to have to be made very quickly, whether he had direction from God or not

LaVergne, TN USA
11 February 2010
172809LV00004B/4/P